The Dragon's Egg

Book 1

The Chronicles of Leaf

The Dragon's Egg

H A May

A Gift of Leaf Revised Edition

Copyright © H A May 2024
All rights reserved.

All characters in this publication are fictitious and any resemblance to real persons, living or dead, is purely coincidental.

This book is sold subject to the condition that it shall not, by way of trade or otherwise, be hired out, lent or resold, or otherwise circulated without the author's/publisher's prior consent in any form of binding or cover other than that in which it is published and without a similar condition including this condition being imposed on the subsequent publisher.

The moral rights of the author have been asserted.

Contents

Chapter One 1
Chapter Two 11
Chapter Three 21
Chapter Four 29
Chapter Five 38
Chapter Six 50
Chapter Seven 56
Chapter Eight 66
Chapter Nine 77
Chapter Ten 85
Chapter Eleven 91
Chapter Twelve 97
Chapter Thirteen 101
Chapter Fourteen 113
Chapter Fifteen 121
Chapter Sixteen 132
Chapter Seventeen 136
Chapter Eighteen 141
Chapter Nineteen 157
Chapter Twenty 167
Chapter Twenty-One 175
Chapter Twenty-Two 184
Chapter Twenty-Three 192
Chapter Twenty-Four 201
About the Author 214

Dedication

For J H M.

Acknowledgements

I would like to offer my grateful thanks to these people who have had a huge part in making this book possible:

Michelle Emerson for her time and professional expertise in producing the copies of this book,: Akira of Fiverr for his fab covers and Jon for all his help and patience.

Chapter One

'Get up!'

My hand flies up to my throat, and a cold sweat engulfs me. I blink as light blinds me. With it comes his foul smell; Mabe.

'Get up, you!' he says again.

Wriggling away from his prodding foot, I roll the blanket around me tightly, but he tugs it off without effort, and I am shivering.

'Come on, Weirdo,' he shouts, kicking me in the back until I have to obey. If I don't, he'll get earache from Pounce, the only Junior Librarian left, and then I'll *really* get it.

Shadows shift even though the cavern is lit only by a swarm of fireworms parading around the uneven stone ceiling on the hunt for thin finger-fungus. Rising, I mouth a curse, and he flicks his whip, narrowly missing me. Then, yawning wretchedly, I stagger upright.

All fifty or so of us eat and sleep here, so this place is always filthy and unkempt. The chill doesn't figure as we work until we are almost too exhausted to eat, let alone stay awake. Some of us shovel compost or dig the drainage tunnels free of muck, but a favoured few, the literate, like me, work in the ancient records preserved in the deepest part of the Holtanbore.

All of us are foundlings or orphans with nowhere else to go except, possibly, me. When the new Master replaced the old Mayor, my world changed for the worse. I'd been happy with my foster family since I was a toddler until, aged six or so, I was dragged, kicking and howling, from Three Gems Cavern and Ma.

I don't know how long ago that was now, but the heartache stays fresh. I remember watching Ma's face change from astonishment to fright as the Master's man hit her and she fell. Thinking of it still makes me feel sick and numb, and my eyes sting as I roll up my pallet and retrieve the grimy blanket Mabe kicked into the dirt. But I'm not weeping. No way. Not me. I'm too tough for that.

There'll be nothing to eat for hours yet, so I drink my fill from the cold stone cistern to fill my belly. Taking up my bag and a lamp, I plod unhappily down to the lowest level of the labyrinth. Black shadows gather behind as I pass, but at least Mabe doesn't follow this time.

In the archive cavern, I begin sifting through one of the vast stacks of ancient documents. The chill is penetrating, and the shadows seem darker and thicker. In this vast cavern, it's heartbeat quiet, yet my strange inner voice doesn't bother me.

'Take care,' Mabe said when first he led me here. 'These stacks can shift, and one little snot was buried alive. He was lucky we got to him before he kicked it!'

He laughed happily, waiting to see the effect of his revelation, but I'd already heard that story. The thought of it makes me sick. Who would expect a Library to be dangerous, paper cuts aside? And there is always the threat of fire. Down here, that would bring a swift end as the way from the upper levels is twisting and narrow, and desiccated records burn easily. So I am extra careful with my lamp. It is a blessing that Ma taught me to read and write as soon as I was old enough. She said I learned easily, that word-smithing suited me. The illiterate and far less fortunate take nastier or more dangerous tasks.

A memory surfaces: Ma settling me firmly on her knee, as I had been wriggling and grabbing for the big ladle.

'Now Jinny,' she'd said, 'sit still. We must be careful because this waxen is very, very hot and will burn you. It will hurt if it does. So let me stir the pot, and you be a good girl and watch.'

The fire sent shadows and flames leaping and flickering over the shimmer of the fools-gold walls as the stuff boiled. Gloopy bubbles slowly formed and burst, the surface wrinkling like an elder's brow.

'See,' she said, gesturing with the ladle, 'we have to make sure it is well mixed. Soon it will be ready to dip.' Her hands, holding me, felt big, and safe, and warm.

Here there's no warmth, only chill shadows stiff with menacing silences. Rubbing my hands in a vain attempt to warm them, I look around. Some of the oldest documents have been dumped down here since record-keeping began, and my task is to fossick through them to find anything worth keeping. Unwanted rubbish is composted, making space for newer versions, yet all seems such a waste of time. Soon, despite the cold, the work becomes tedious and my eyes grow heavy. The world wavers like the bottom of a shallow pool, and I have to slap myself to stay awake. If they catch me sleeping, they'll beat me, but - and this is a big but - if I work hard, perhaps they'll allow me to visit Ma again. But my heart sinks even as the thought comes: this false hope is stupid. They'll never let me go.

I start, looking up. Someone begins whistling tunelessly, but they are moving away. As I hurriedly dig into a new stack, I jerk to a stop, wincing. My wrist is gripped painfully. I know this feeling: a worm's rasp mouth is stuck fast to my wrist. I pull back hard, and the worm, with a dry sucking sound, slips free. The creature has the grace to look abashed. However, for a rock worm, it is tiny, only about as long as my forearm, with threadbare white fur. My wrist stings and pulls as it writhes.

'Let go, you!' I growl, poking an old quill at it.

The worm blinks, wriggling. Then, fixing me with its huge round eyes, it spits me out.

<*Shorry,*> it mouths. <*Thought you wazza shnick.*>

Huh! Snicks are tiny, about the size of a thumbnail, but vicious. A snick my size would be lethal! My arm is showing a puffy, livid welt by now. However, something about this creature makes me look twice.

'You're that hungry?'

It looks up at me dolefully.

<*No shnicks. Big vorms ead 'm all,*> it says.

How is it doing that? Surely it is almost impossible to talk with that rubbery, circular mouth? But because my arm still stings, I snap, 'You hurt me!'

The worm has the grace to blink in embarrassment, and I feel sorry for it. Under its patchy fur, it is much too thin, mere skin and bone.

'If you hang on and let me alone, I'll take you back with me. Lots of snicks in the sleeping cave for you to eat, long as you keep out of the way.'

The worm corkscrews and, blinking gratefully, says <*Fank-oo.*>

'Stay and wait. There,' I tell it, pointing to one of the other stacks.

As it wriggles away, it dawns on me that the worm didn't actually speak aloud, although I heard it. Slithering up onto a nearby stack, it sits, quivering with anticipation, unwilling to be forgotten. So. rubbing at my sore wrist, I turn back to the records, but as I pick another from the top, the pile instantly collapses. Now open to the air, the fetid centre releases a vile odour. But, there is - yes - something in there.

Holding a rag over my mouth and nose, I hold the lamp as near as I dare. A solid shape inside - a half-buried, squarish wodge of stuff. I lift it gingerly, but it is heavy and unbalanced. It slips, thudding into the shadows by my feet. The concealing shadows …

A flash of memory takes me back to a time when, as Ma worked, she would relate exciting stories of things lost and found in unexplored darknesses of empty caverns. And one day, she told me about the waxen and how it was made.

'It is mined from a good fat seam of old beeswax, which, mixed with enth, makes good candles. Mages say it comes from a time when the whole world was covered with flowers and leaves. The big blue fur-bees that make the wax were so happy that they made more than enough of everything, and their wax leaked out onto the floor of the forests. That is why we can dig it out from under the layers of earth and rock that cover it now.'

Stirring the big pot, she glanced at me proudly.

'See, Jin? Three Gems Cavern makes the best candles and dips in the whole of Holtanbore. Our candles are ordered as far away as the Bole, and we barter them for food and other good things.'

She nodded, smiling to herself, her face fire-lit.

Comforted by this happy memory, I scrabble around and find the object I dropped. It is very strange, a block composed of many leaves, sewn together along one side, yet only holding dull lists of produce. I flick through it, wondering if this is a tome, a thing I'd never seen before that Ma said was incredibly rare. But the central leaves are unexpectedly thick, and there is a hard lump in the middle. I tease the leaves back gently at first, but then, when pulling harder, the top section tears away, revealing a cavity nestled inside, an object. Shivering a little, I hold the lamp dangerously close to see.

Tucked cosily inside the cavity is a broken, whitish-yellow disk. Although small, no longer than my two middle fingers, it is exquisitely carved in relief. A hole is pierced through the long, broken edge as though it may once have been a pendant once. The carving depicts a Tree which cradles a star in its branches. Rising from it is a faint tang of sweetness, dizzying me for a second or two. A tremor passes through me as though somehow the world has shifted. Yet, an instant later, normality resumes.

Entranced, I stare. A pity it is broken. *Like me*, I think, and as I glance at my left leg, the whole horrible episode inevitably plays itself out behind my eyes again.

It was a day when Da and the boys were working two levels away. Alone with Ma, I had dipped my first candle, utterly thrilled to have emulated her. Suddenly, there was a rough voice outside. Heavy footsteps echoed in the passage, and three men barrelled rudely into our cavern. Ma stopped, stared, then scowled, looking like an angry cottage loaf. She pushed me behind her, and I dropped my beautiful candle, which broke into pieces.

'Three Gems Cavern?' the first man growled.

Incensed by this rudeness, Ma stood as tall as she could.

'How dare you burst in!' she said with a scowl. 'Have you no manners? Who are you?'

The big man smirked as though finding this funny. He stepped close, his knuckles whitening.

'We have orders to take the foundling, Jinny Morai, to work in the labyrinth of the Library by order of the Master,' he said. 'It is said she can read?'

Ma, flustered, waved her hands at them as though shooing rocksnakes away.

'Of course she can. She can write too,' she said. 'She's a clever girl ... but you can't just break in like this! And you can't take her! She's mine. You have no right! Get out!'

Her voice rose to a screech of fear and rage, and she flapped her hands behind her in a shooing motion. After hesitating for a split second, I ducked sideways to run to the little warren of store caverns, but this was long enough for another man, smaller but immensely strong, to grab me by my arm. It hurt, and I screamed. Ma launched herself at him, but the bigger man hit her hard on the side of her head, yelling, 'You do as you're told, woman.' She fell down like a stone, eyes closed. I pulled frantically to get to her, but I couldn't budge.

The smaller man dragged me to him and, with a hand around my throat, choked me, forcing me to submit until I could hardly breathe. Frantically, I kicked out, but my left leg caught between the wall and a jutting stalagmite. As he dragged me away, something gave with an audible crack, and I screamed soundlessly in agony. He kept pulling, and it twisted. When he had to stop to release it, it was broken. I fell over screaming, and he picked me up anyhow. Writhing and howling, I tried to bite, and he hit me hard on the ear. Ma was still sleeping, but I yelled, 'Ma? Ma!' over and over.

'Stop that,' he said, and my head seemed to burst as he hit me again, and my neck felt funny …

But this won't do. Cursing my lack of a birthing record, I wipe my eyes, trying to resist rubbing the feel of his horny hand away again. When I turn again to it, the sight of the stone is strangely comforting, and the longer I look, the more I am sure that I was meant to find it - it has always been meant for me.

A scraping sounds further down-cavern, so I cover it quickly. No one must see it, touch it or try to take it. I look around. Mabe is coming, checking up on me, but with a glance, he disappears. So, discarding the loose leaves, I slip what remains into my pouch, the stone nestled inside. Although I'm always hungry, this is far too exciting to surrender to the Librarian, even for extra food. It is mine, and I'm keeping it.

The proximity and thought of the stone fizzles at the top of my mind. I glance at my bag frequently, gloating at my good luck, wondering why it was broken and where the other half is. Finishing my shift, I nod to the worm, which is still waiting. It humps itself down from its perch and slithers quickly into my pouch.

When we arrive, the sleeping cave is empty, and the worm slithers out and away. There are so many annoying snicks in here it'll get fat in no time.

'Good luck,' I call after it.

<*Fank-oo,*> a retreating rubbery voice says in my head. It feels different from my inner visitor, but by now, I am far too weary to wonder why.

Delving into my bag, I bring the broken stone to light. It is treasure. I have never owned anything so fine except a doll Da once made for me. Wrapping it tightly in a piece torn from my tunic, I thrust it deeply into the narrow crevice between my bed space and the great Tree root behind it, silently thanking the Tree for providing such a good hiding place. Surprisingly, the Tree comments thoughtfully, '*Do not worry - I will guard it.*' And I see the Tree's speech is similar to the way the worm spoke - directly into my head.

Later, when my leg is aching and keeping me from sleep, I distract myself with thoughts of my new treasure. As usual, my nightly visitor breaks into my thoughts, bringing its usual plea for help from someone I've never known. But there is nothing I can do - I can barely help myself.

' ... ease, help me ? ... please, please ... help me? ...' it continues relentlessly

I shake myself like a worm sneezing, hoping to dislodge it, but it never works. The voice becomes less obvious when I'm awake, like a heartbeat, but it makes sleeping difficult. I can't ignore it, so give in and touch the smooth skin of the Tree's root beside me. Soothed by its warm, inner pulse of life, I try again to sleep, but the voice continues, louder and louder, imploring my help. Even though I have asked it again and again what it wants, it won't explain and continues until I feel as though my head will explode. Tears of weariness and frustration drip down my chin. Every night, every day and every hour, it begs. Sometimes its babbling fills my mind so that I hardly know what to do, and even the beautiful Tree root cannot completely halt it these days, though it dulls it for a while. Unable to sleep and sometimes unable to eat, I am getting desperate.

~*~

Blotting out the crepuscular light, a stinking shape kicks me.

'Mabe,' I say, 'don't. Please? I'm ill. Please don't make me work today.'

Looking down at me, his mouth twists into its ubiquitous sneer.

'Ill? Lazy little bitch! You're not lying there all day. Get up!'

He aims another kick but misses as I roll away, so he grabs me by my hair, pulling me upright. Again I shrink to the size of a snick as he pummels me into obedience. When he stops, I stagger up, cowed and tearful, to trail him to an unexpectedly globular grotto half-choked with a vast mound of ancient debris. A fireworm swarm illuminates one edge of the ceiling, so there is just about enough light to work.

'Start digging,' he says, chuckling sadistically. 'I have orders to get this cleared out soon as possible. Someone'll be along to take these to the compost when you've filled 'em.'

He nods at the empty barrels squatting along the passage and gestures rudely with his short whip. Grinning, he turns and strolls away, whistling. My heart sinks. It will take weeks: the unseen floor is hidden beneath years of the deposited strata of wood pulp and skin. So. before I begin, I rest, sipping water until I can rouse myself enough to pretend this is a kind of treasure hunt, where I dig down and down to find hidden things. But I will not find anything better than my beautiful broken stone.

~*~

One day, when my inner voice is quiet for once, and I have eaten and slept well, something odd occurs in the globe cave. While I am digging through the deepest layers, I am suddenly overcome by dizziness and nausea. A vision of the half-stone erupts unbidden in my head, pressing me to do something - but what? Stop? No - dig, dig harder, deeper! As I reach this conclusion, the vision and sickness fall away to be replaced in the blink of an eye by a pleasurable buzz. And while I dutifully delve through disgusting layers, tough and dark with years, my relentless voice is dulled.

As I dig, small long-legged crawlies, pallid and eyeless, dangle above on filigree threads, swinging lightly in the draught from an air duct in the vault of the round roof. They drop and scuttle to be pursued by the horde of local snicks jumping and uttering falsetto cries. Then, as I unearth layer after layer, tiny nestlings emerge which can burrow through anything vaguely edible, sometimes even rock. These I avoid, but again the local snicks rush in to make short work of them.

Then, my hand spade strikes something hard, turning my wrist. Sitting back for a moment, I rub it, dumbfounded. Of course - I must have hit bottom. But when I thrust the shovel into one side, it slices through further strata of compacted gunk, revealing a thin, hard layer of ancient dirt.

So what was it? I push my spade deeper and there, in the midst of the pulverised rock and rubbish, is something hard and round. A rock? Is that all?

In the Holtanbore, stone-fashioning is an art, yet when I have roughly cleaned off the dirt, I have never seen anything so fine. Like the half-stone, it is carved, but this has tiny overlapping scales, like the vast plate armour of a rocksnake. One of these plates, beautifully etched with fine lines, sat proudly decorating our neighbours' cavern, and brings back thoughts of Three Gems and Ma. Instead of weeping, I unearth the rock completely, exposing a blunt end which tapers to a narrower, rounded point: it is a dull grey egg.

Hearing shuffling footsteps, I decide I'm not sharing it and, quickly covering it again, I cast my shadow over it.

'Hey, Weirdo? Heard any good voices today?' growls Mabe.

From the side of my eye, I watch him approach the lip of the globular cavern. Crouched in the circular depression, I feel snicksized. My neck begins to throb. I rub it. Every instinct screams 'run', but I stay put. He can do what he likes with me here. I must appear servile.

'You down to rock yet?' he asks.

'No.'

'Librarian thinks you oughta be finished in here by now. Wants you out. There's cleaning to be done.' He smirks, and I ache to clobber him. A beautiful vision in which I actually bash and bury him under all this crappy stuff flashes through my mind. But someone would eventually wonder where his big mouth was. Then they'd find him, and I, the ubiquitous scapegoat, would be implicated. Not worth the hassle.

Sniffing, he shambles away, and I throw a rude gesture at his back. He stops and looks back suspiciously, but I have my head down like a good little slave, and he goes away.

I work steadily until I'm certain he's gone and then uncover my prize again. It is beautiful and, in the hand, feels strangely perfect, its length, width, and scales exactly in proportion. Perhaps it was a carved toy or decoration.

A strong, unexpected possessiveness floods me. So, cleaning it as much as I can, I stash it in my pouch to be cached later with the half-stone. Now I have two treasures. I'm rich, yet I still long to be free. I would willingly give both to see Three Gems and Ma again. Shaking my head to dismiss these miserable thoughts, I work on. Later, when this second treasure is secreted with the first, I fall asleep, too exhausted to notice the other poor denizens of this abominable place.

Chapter Two

My work continues until the bottom of the round cave is visible, ready to house a new set of stacks. On a day when I am close to finishing, my nose twitches: that sewer smell again.

'You! Get up!' Mabe grunts. 'You're to see the Boss. Now, Weirdo. Get a move on!'

I scramble to my feet, utterly astonished. Us Unwanted are never addressed by bosses. A kindly old Mayor ruled the Holtanbore when I lived with Ma. Now I look down at myself, horror-struck. Long years of digging and sifting have left me in rags that Ma wouldn't have cleaned our privy with. No point in trying to look better so, stumbling, I anxiously ask my way up through the levels to the Head Librarian's Office and eventually stand timidly before the entrance.

Finding the courage, I knock. The door opens to reveal a tall woman with strangely bright hair and a pungent perfume, dusty and cold. She wrinkles her nose at me, sneering.

'What do *you* want?'

'I've been sent for … er, by the Librarian,' I say. 'I'm Jinny Morai.'

My left hand clamps tightly on my throat, and I am trembling. Heat flushes my skin in embarrassment as she looks me up and down, flapping her hands as though fanning away something disgusting.

'Come. Here. Wait. There.' She points at a spectral point on the floor, crosses to another door and goes through, speaks to someone and is answered by a deep bass voice. She returns and gestures me in.

'Go in,' she says, sneering, 'but don't touch anything. You're filthy, and you stink.'

Dirt is something I never bother about now because there is only one bowl and jug between all of us Unwanted on the lowest level, and seldom any water left to wash in. At home, Ma used to insist we wash every day and bathe at least once a month. I remember the voluptuous silkiness of the hot soapy water and, afterwards, the comfort of clean skin, Ma's kindly hands, and Da's rumbling voice …

'Now!' the Sneer growls, breaking my reverie. I limp through the doorway and stop, waiting. The new Head Librarian sits at a wide table. A heavy man, and, like me, he stands head and shoulders over the community of small, pale troglodytes.

He looks up from whatever he is reading and says, 'You are Jinny Morai?' My stench must go before me as his brow and nose furrow. I rub hard at my throat. 'You are a foundling?'

I jump a little and half-step back, trying not to scratch.

'Yes, Sir,' I say politely, as Ma taught me. She was always one for manners.

'Hmm.' He looks me up and down. 'You can read?' he asks.

'Yes, Sir!'

He pushes a document from a pile to me.

Picking it up, I begin, 'Five weights of crushed stone, twenty weights of ore and thirteen weights of …'

'Can you write?'

'Yes, Sir, a good clean hand.'

He pushes a pen and a small piece of clean paper across the table.

'Copy.'

I copy the text.

At length, he stops me and takes it up. My writing is shaky but legible.

'Well, good enough, so we'll see,' he says. 'I need extra help on the fourth level. I'm told you work quickly and well.'

I am so astonished that I forget to rub my neck.

'You want *me?*' I blurt out.

He gives me an old-fashioned look but calls, 'Nara?'

The Sneer comes in.

'Get her cleaned up. Then take her down to the fourth level and set her to work. We'll see if she will do. She can sleep where she is now until she proves herself useful.'

Nara gestures me to follow. She obviously thinks I'm lying about my abilities, her face disdainful. We cross a dark passage to a well-lit room with a steaming tub, a bucket of soap-weed, and towels.

'Get yourself clean,' she says but watches as, blushing, I undress. Again that strange smell of hers - cold and dusty. She turns me round to look at my duff leg and snorts, shaking her head.

'How did that happen?' She turns me roughly, peering at my back. 'And what are these?' she asks, slapping my shoulders. It stings, and I jerk away, bleating. Frowning, she waits for an answer.

'I broke my leg when I was small. But Mistress, what's wrong with my back?'

'You've two small lumps there, between your shoulder blades. Don't you know what they are?'

'No, Mistress.'

I wonder what in Leaf she means.

'Never mind. Get on. Wash yourself. I'll send in clothes.'

She doesn't come back, but her smell hangs in the air like a curse. I am trying to feel the swelling when a pretty girl enters, about my age, short, plump and smiling. She is clean and neatly gowned, with her fine white hair caught in a long net down her back and the enormous dark eyes of the cave-dweller.

'Jinny Morai?'

I try to cover up. Politely, she looks away.

'I'm Karel,' she continues, looking only at my face. 'Mistress Nara told me to see you are bathed and to bring you clean clothes.'

She begins to cluck over me like an old dame. 'My goodness, you are filthy! D'you want help with your hair?'

'Please,' I say rustily. 'Thank you.'

She doesn't ask how I ended up like this, and I'm grateful for her kindness. When I slip in, the hot water feels wonderful. Immediately Karel grabs soap-weed and a brush I hadn't noticed before and begins to scrub. This takes me back to bath night with Ma, but she is gentler. First, she tackles my hair. Its tangles are matted and full of dust, dead insects, and various unmentionables. I haven't had the opportunity or energy to worry about it for a long, long time. Now, as she works the tangles free, a new colour emerges, a red so dark it looks almost black.

She babbles away about her friends, her work, and her favourite foods as she scrubs, and I enjoy her chatter and easy laughter. So different from my nightly voice, which sobs and begs interminably. I like her kindly touch too. Hardly anyone has touched me since I was little unless to beat me.

'There now, all done. Isn't your skin lovely?' she says at length, chuckling as she holds her white arm next to my brown one. 'And what a good colour! Better than the usual pasty.'

She does not mention my many scars or my leg. The new clothes are stiff and fresh, my stink has vanished, and my twisted leg is decently hidden under long skirts.

'Now,' she says, pulling a comb through my hair. 'You'll need to put this up. It's so very long! And so curly! I'll go get you a net and pins.'

It is. I hadn't noticed. It sticks to my fingers silkily, floating upwards, like crawlies' webs in a draught, although the ends look chewed. I suspect rats have been at them.

She comes back. 'Here,' she says, 'see?' She twists my hair and slips it into the net behind my ears. 'Then we just put some pins in to hold it in place, and you're done!'

She turns me around, admiring the effect she's produced.

'It looks marvellous,' she says chattily. 'You look so different. Really pretty! And you have such a lovely slim figure.'

She flashes a tiny metal mirror far too fast to see anything.

'Thank you,' I murmur, surprised and embarrassed by my own voice. It's rusty and creaky, but it didn't matter until now. And being alone for so long, I have lost the trick of polite conversation.

We go out. Catching an indistinct glimpse in the polished metal of the door, I wonder, *is this me?* Pleased, I straighten, trying a smile out for size as we descend to the fourth level. If I could only show Ma now! I feel reborn.

My new work is much easier than all that digging, and the food is much better, but I'm still wading through smelly old records. Here the vast upper library caverns remind me of home, despite the massed scrolls and leaves stored in niches around the walls. The air is fresh, without the cold dead feel of the labyrinth, and there are lamps and candles aplenty. Other people are working nearby, so there is always someone to watch and possibly talk to. The only rub is that I have to sleep in my usual place four levels below and put up with the spite and jealousy of the others. Mabe, in particular, enjoys deriding my new clothes and beautifully clean state.

'Think you're better than us now, don't you?' he bellows one evening as I arrive back. He tries to swipe me on the ear, but I duck quickly. Picking up my new skirts and wobbling only a little, I manage to land a good hard kick bang on his knee. There is a sharp crack, and he howls in pain: beautiful. He limps off to flop onto his own pallet, cursing me while looking around for support and sympathy. But as he is universally hated, he is totally ignored. I expect fast retribution from him, but oddly, it doesn't come.

A few days later, when everyone is asleep, I draw out the half-stone, its light dimly illuminating my palm. Pulling a long thread out of the cover of my ancient pallet, I double it. Feeding it through the hole in the half-stone, I tie a knot and slip it over my head. The stone will be safer under my clothes. The egg-stone, being bigger, is harder to conceal in this nest of thieves, and when I am gone, it's certain the others search my bed for anything they can find. Now I carry both stones with me all the time.

And then, one night a few weeks later, when I take out the wrapped egg-stone, it is hot enough to burn my fingers. Gasping, I drop it onto my pallet, although that could catch fire. The wrappings fall open to reveal a flush coruscating over the egg's surface like embers burning on a hearth. It ripples with ruddy light, glowing with heat. Is this some sort of magic? Unnerved, I throw my blanket over it quickly, making a rancid red-lit tent, but outside, there is a grunt, and a sleeper turns, muttering, as though disturbed. I quickly wrap the egg again: I need a far safer hiding place than my pouch.

~*~

Reaching for my pen knife, I realise I've been up here for weeks now, and I am glad of it. With practice, my writing skills have returned, and my writing is clear and neat, my reading swift and accurate, and I have my own desk, stool and lamp. The work though dull, is easy, cataloguing and copying fading documents. The cavern I work in is large and bustling, so I'm never really alone, and that has taken a while to get used to. But it is clean, the air is fresh, and the whole cavern is well-lit, with no sign of rats, worms or snicks.

Existing on this level is a strange hierarchy now that most of the Junior Librarians have been discharged. The new Head Librarian and the Sneer seem to know almost nothing about how a Library should work, simply concentrating on keeping us busy. The last nervous and panic-stricken Junior Librarian left in charge of the records is continually dithering about what to keep and what to discard: a snick in charge of fireworms, in the pay of a steelworm. I don't envy him at all.

The rest of the staff are ignorant thugs, installed to make sure we work, except the lad, Dran, who supplies us copiers with paper and ink. He winks at me these days and yesterday showed me the paper store, a largish grotto off the main cavern. I half-expected some sort of trouble, but nothing untoward happened - he was simply being friendly. Karel still rushes about doing whatever the Sneer wants, so I don't see her very often.

From past experience, I don't tell anyone about my nightly visitor, my strange voice. Everyone thinks I'm normal, like them, and I like it this way. Dipping my nib into the thick brown ink, I peer down at the old document I'm about to copy. Karel's light voice suddenly breaks my concentration. The ink blots on the page, and she clucks, but ignores it and goes on.

'Hey! Jinny! Isn't it great you're here! Nara says you can sleep up on this level now, so come on and I'll show you where our sleeping room is and where you can put your …' her voice falters as she remembers I have nothing. 'And - and - I'll find you some new things and a change of clothes.'

'What about these?' I ask, looking down at my newish finery, now quite grubby.

'You'll want to have a change, won't you?' she says, with a slight frown. 'Those need washing.'

'Oh, of course,' I say, blushing and blotting my spill. 'Of course! You're right.'

I've forgotten how to keep clean, forgotten that clothes need washing; forgotten how to be normal.

'Well, come on then,' she invites, smiling again, 'now's a good time as long as we're quick.'

She takes my elbow as we rise, and, taking her lamp, steers me down an unknown passage. This is clean and well-lit, leading to a small, tidy cavern with beds with mattresses, pillows, sheets and blankets. There are even small presses by each one. And I'm staggered: I can't remember when I last slept on a proper bed. In a small adjoining cave is a row of jugs and basins and a small rill of clean water set in a carved channel in the floor. And, incredibly, a very private privy. Briefly, I wonder if my voice will still pester me when I sleep here …

'Well, what do you think?' she asks, moving her lamp around.

'It's absolutely lovely.' I feel like a lowly snick suddenly ballooning into a real girl. My delight could ignite a lamp.

'Here, the bed next to mine is empty,' she says generously, and I blush again, unaccustomed to such kindness. I manage a nod.

As we return to the main cavern, I begin to wonder if she's been told to keep an eye on me. But she turns to me with such a wide, happy grin, my snick persona dissolves completely. I grin back. Having a new friend is delightful, and I float along as we chat our way back to the copying cave. Shadows play along the walls, and long blue moulds sway to the beat of our footsteps. I stroke them gently as we pass. Pretty and soft, like worm fur.

'I'll go find you some extras and put them on your bed,' Karel says. 'You can put them away after work.'

'Won't someone take them?' I ask, slightly shocked.

'Steal them?' she says, face horror-struck. 'NO! No one would dare to steal here! Nothing will be touched.'

A far cry from the black labyrinth below.

'Oh.' I look down. 'Oh, that's great, isn't it? Thank you.'

Karel smiles rather tautly now as she says, 'I'd best dash. Nara will miss me. See you later.'

I smile back, but my face feels frayed. It seems the rules are different here, and it is up to me to find out what's what. I will need to be more careful.

~*~

The small, perfect press at the foot of my new, perfect bed has a lock, and I have the key. The half- and egg-stones are safe for now, although if I want to look at them, I'll have to smuggle them out to somewhere more private. No point in tempting the girls here. And there's a thing! The sleepers here are all girls: the boys sleep elsewhere, so different from what I'm used to and much easier in lots of ways.

But the egg-stone worries me. Heat still spirals over its surface, and it is slowly expanding. I don't understand why, and I can't check it as often as I would like to. I have to hope nothing terrible will go wrong because life is so much better. Karel is still friendly, and Dran chats if he has time. This new life is peaceful, almost pleasant, yet still full of work and words. However, my inner voice continues to pester me every night.

One day, this fragile peace is interrupted. We have an unexpected visitor. Midway through the afternoon, Karel, juggling a pile of papers, sidles up to me, beaming.

'Hey, Jinny, Salla says our visitor is a Mage - a novice, to be sure, but still - a real Mage! They say he's coming to inspect us!'

She rushes off again, leaving me wondering what a Mage looks like. I've never seen one. Maybe he will look strange; possibly exotic. Perhaps he keeps a familiar. But when he arrives, he is quite a disappointment, merely a tall young man who stands head and shoulders above everyone else. He has no familiar and is smoothskinned, although in tales, Mages reliably sport warts and other odd protuberances. He has a short, fine beard and clear brown skin and looks fresh and clean.

Karel stops by my desk again.

'What d'you think?' she whispers, watching furtively as he moves closer.

I shake my head. 'I don't think much of him, really. I thought he'd be more interesting.'

'Well, I think he's handsome - and *so* tall!' Then, pouting, she whispers, 'Shame, really.'

'Shame? Why?'

'Mages are not supposed to … you know? With girls *or* boys. Against the Code of the Order or something - thy shalt not drop thy drawers!'

She giggles, and I join in helplessly before looking him over again. 'They don't marry? Or - you know - ever?' I ask her in an undertone as he walks nearer, then stops to chat with another scribe.

'Or anything! They're prohibited,' she says, eyebrows wagging. 'See what I mean? A real shame. He's far too good-looking to waste. Salla says he's staying down here till tomorrow, and she's going for it!'

She giggles again and sighs.

Ah. I've watched the boys with the other girls since I was small. They always ignored me, and I'm grateful because I have never found one bit of all that appealing. Until now, it has never occurred to me to wonder why. Perhaps my twisted leg put them off, or, more likely, my stink. But this tall man - well, he looks well-made and reasonably attractive. *And yes,* I think, as something stirs inside me, it does seem a shame.

Karel stands straight, patting her hair into place as the Mage strides towards us. The Sneer trots alongside him, grimly explaining everyone's tasks, and the odd, cloying scent she wears wafts our way. As the Mage comes closer, his brown hair neatly braided, I can see in his face the boy he was. When he stops, he stands stiff, as though uncomfortable in his early dignity.

'… and this is our newest recruit from the lowest level,' Nara says, waving at and dismissing me in the same breath.

He stays still as a Tree root. Karel flutters her lashes and pats her hair again, but he ignores her. Instead, he fixes me with a puzzled gaze. A shiver passes up my spine, yet I cannot wrench my eyes away. He nods to me once, and I am sure that somehow he is probing me. It is far too intimate, but I cannot move or speak, like the immobility you sometimes find in dreams. Our mutual gaze goes on and on: ages could be passing. Great Tree seeds could germinate, mature under a new sun, and fruit, wither and die. And after, my head is dark and empty, with a strange fizzing warmth running through me. Our mutual scrutiny is only broken when Nara tugs hard at his sleeve, shooting me a look of pure loathing. Our rapport broken, he turns away sharply. Only Karel's urgent hiss and heavy hand restrain me as I half-rise to follow him.

'What are you doing? Sit down! You'll get into trouble!'

She pushes me back onto my stool as Nara glances back, a thunderous frown replacing her usual sneer. I pretend to retrieve my dropped pen, a hand shaking to my throat. Karel looks at me, perplexed.

'What's got into you?' she asks.

I shake my head dizzily, wondering what just happened.

'Nothing … I um, I dunno.'

She glances at the retreating backs, clucks at me in concern, and sets off in pursuit.

And I am left trembling all over, heart racing, and it is a while before I am calm enough to resume my work.

Chapter Three

Later, my voice excludes sleep, although the sleeping girls around me are emitting gentle, ladylike snores. I quietly take out the egg-stone and tiptoe along to Dran's paper alcove to examine it. But, even concealed under leaves, a thick rag, and my nightshift, its radiance lights my way, and I'm thankful no one is about. The empty work cavern echoes softly to my muffled footsteps, but I manage to reach the alcove with no one the wiser.

Pulling the heavy curtain across to conceal my presence, I put the stone on an unoccupied ledge to unwrap it. A dazzle of heat flickers over its surface, banishing the darkness, and I peer nervously through the heavy curtains looking for trouble.

Nothing. But now, when I glance back, the stone egg is rocking along its long axis, glowing with heat and too hot to touch. The rocking speeds up, pitching up and down in concentric circles, and the egg inches along the ledge until, with a sharp report, a deep, sizzling crack runs up and down its length. A flash of incredibly intense red light spears into my eyes, and a deep red glow, like the last crimson embers in the depths of a fire, emanates from within. The movement of the stone becomes frantic. I automatically reach out to steady it and, squealing softly, withdraw burned fingers.

And then – there it is! Something is moving within the stone. Something alive! It *is* an egg! I gasp in amazement and panic, wondering what in the Light is going to emerge. The crack grows wider as its inhabitant rotates, pushing the halves aside. Despite the heat and my stinging fingers, I step closer to see a tail, a wing, a tiny, armoured nose.

And staring up at me, dark liquid eyes are reflecting red as tiny jaws open to reveal the living fire within. The little creature, whatever it is, twists itself around, pushing and shoving until the halves part company with another sharp crack. And turning its face up to gaze at me is a tiny, perfect dragon! Only dragons were ever born in heat, and this matches a description I read once: wings and tail, scales, teeth and claws, born in fire.

We stare at each other.

Hey, you? I think.

Its eyes are darker than the deepest pools in the labyrinth. I sigh, feeling joy and wonder. Into this world, and here, with me, this beautiful little creature supposedly extinct has come. Its perfect scales shine with the same metallic sheen I've only seen on oil-streaked puddles. How long has its egg lain hidden: how ancient is this tiny new life?

It doesn't stir. Silently watching me, it rests within its open shell. And now I am flabbergasted: what do you do with a newly-hatched dragonet? I can hardly go back to the sleeping cave and gleefully announce its birth.

As I stare into its eyes, a feeling seeps into me, filling my mind. I know we will be friends for life, friends in the bone, and I will protect this small being with my life. But when I reach out to touch it, the dragonet takes fright, fluttering its tiny wings. My heart goes out to it as somehow its fear and uncertainty reverberate in my mind. So small, so new, so alone … Before I can form another sensible thought, it scoots out of the broken shell and darts around the alcove, wings humming too fast to follow. At last, panting, it flops onto a pile of parchment, which immediately begins to burn. My heart sinks. *However will I explain all this,* I wonder, and then I am mortified as the whole place might catch alight. And it is only now I remember - the old dragons were a species of salamanders, the fire lizards.

The parchment blackens and curls in the heat, although I try to beat it out. Beside it, an expensive pile of the finest paper ignites with a whumph.

Flaming flakes of paper float up and away on the draught, burning wildly, and spreading the fire all around. My nostrils tingle in the acrid smoke as one blazing shred shears a stray lock of my hair. I beat it out with a cry as multiple piles catch fire. Within minutes I am standing in the midst of a deafening inferno. Then something unseen under a ledge explodes with a deafening roar, hurling me bodily through the burning curtain into a smoke-filled darkness.

Shaking my head, I look around. The dark is opaque with sparks and smoke billowing and curling out of the alcove. Groaning, I pick myself up to hover near the entrance to the grotto, straining to look inside. Surely the little dragon is dead by now? Although the smoke stings my eyes and throat, it is this that brings my tears. Such a short, unfulfilled life. Such a mould-rotted shame.

I start as a scream shatters the smoke-filled darkness. Others waking, coughing, shouting, and running about like maddened snicks. Then someone yells 'Fire!' and a figure looms up out of the smoke.

'Come on! Move! Get away from there!' he mouths, waving.

I can't hear anything, and my eyes feel as though they've been pierced by shards of glass. Wet, wobbly prisms restrict my sight.

'There,' I croak, pointing at the blazing grotto between coughs. 'It's still there.'

'What is?' he bellows over the roar of the fire.

I dither, knowing I must answer. Telling the truth will surely see me back to the labyrinth and the horrible Mabe.

'D - dragon,' I say, twisting my scorched shift in my hands, then I drop it to cover my throat.

He looks at me as though I've two heads.

Around us, people in various night attire are carrying buckets of water, spilling most of it on each other in the dark and roiling smoke. Shadows flicker and race as lamps are waved and dropped. Others wail on the sidelines, shocked out of sleep.

He stares, eyes widening, ignoring the hullabaloo behind us, and bellows, 'A dragon?'

When I nod weakly, he pulls me away from the entrance to the grotto, sitting me down on the cold stone. The smoke is less here, and my breathing a little easier. I hadn't noticed how bad it was.

'Stay there,' he commands, going back to the grotto. I can just make him out in the murk. He stands unmoving, a figure isolated in an eerie green light, dispelling all smoke and noise in a penumbra around him. We could be entirely alone, except for a host of stunned faces gathering to watch. Then my throat clogs. It is hard to breathe, and a feeling of dizziness and nausea makes me retch. I rub and rub at my neck with scorched fingers as the young Mage stands like an island, like a stone god, murmuring nonsense.

He stops. Lifts a digit.

A green flame shoots out from the end of his finger to touch the raging furnace within the grotto. Instantly, the fire vanishes as though it never was. A stale, burned smell fills the air as a small figure shoots out, half-flapping, half-running. It stops once, sniffing, nose up, then rushes at me, springing into my lap like a hungry worm. I gasp, yet it doesn't burn me: the dragon's intense birth heat has already dissipated. Gingerly, I stroke it, and it licks my sore hand with a tiny, hot blue tongue, turning huge, melting eyes up to mine. And I'm lost, basking in a precious new love.

'Young woman?'

Again the words, sharper now.

'Young woman!'

Reluctantly I look up at the Mage, hand on throat, thinking *this is my dragon, and no one is going to take it from me …*

He is standing over me, lamp in hand, his attention riveted on the small, curled creature. Behind him, but not too closely, press all the folk on this level, staring intently.

'This is it?' he asks. I nod at the floor, unwilling to meet his eyes.

'I'm sorry, Sir,' I croak desperately, 'I didn't know any of this would happen.'

Then, the dragonet stirs as one of the crowd steps back a pace, but the Mage crouches down to see better.

'A little beauty,' he says, looking at it. 'How did he get here?'

I try to swallow, but my throat has rocks in it. Sweat, running, stings my burns.

'I found a stone on the lowest level, Sir,' I croak, 'but I didn't know it was an egg.'

'No, you wouldn't,' he says thoughtfully. 'You didn't tell anyone?'

'I didn't think it was important, really,' I say, a hot blush of shame rising under the soot.

'Well, there's no point sitting here now,' he says, 'so get up. I want to examine this little one and listen to your whole story. Go back to your bed cave, wash, and dress. Take him with you. Then I will see you in the Librarian's office as soon as you're done.' He turns. 'See to it we're not disturbed,' he orders the smoke-blackened Head Librarian, who, glaring a white-eyed, sour-faced protest, looks keen to punch me.

Cradling the baby dragon, I walk past the awful ranks of eyes. Nara stares, coldly intent, while Karel and the dormitory girls scurry away, round-eyed and weeping. Dran, standing with the other lads, looks puzzled and upset. I try to hurry. I've kept them all from their beds long enough, and there's nothing I can say now.

Back in our water cave, I try to wash the smoke stains from my sore skin, but one or two patches simply won't shift. My eyes hurt and water, my burns smart, and my breathing is laboured. The dragon, minute and perfect, sits in the centre of the water cave, gazing around. He stays well away from spills when I cough and retch but makes no attempt to escape or wander. Wincing, I make sure the half-stone is still around my neck in case I am ejected for my sins.

~*~

'Come in.'

This room sings with light. Lamps are burning everywhere, with hardly a shadow!

Eyes running, skin burning, and coughing, I almost fail to notice that the Mage has risen. No one has ever done me this courtesy before, and I am shocked almost to tears.

'Sit down, if you will,' he continues, eyeing the dragon in my sore hands. Making no attempt to touch the creature, he hands me a cup of cold water, waiting while I sip. 'Now, tell me exactly how you found this little one.'

Trying to juggle the dragonet into a more comfortable position, he insists on climbing onto my shoulder, fixing his eyes on the Mage.

'Um,' I croak, rubbing at my ear, wondering where I should begin. 'Um, er …'

'How did you find him?' the Mage repeats, still staring. 'You found his egg, didn't you?'

This somehow releases my tongue. Haltingly, with many sips, and much coughing, I tell him the whole of it: the digging through the strata in the globular cave; unearthing the stone; the glowing, and at last, the hatching. He stops me several times, asking about my origins and life on the lowest levels, but listens politely until I've finished.

'… so it was my fault that the paper caught fire, but I didn't know that would happen. I should have. I didn't know the stone was an egg or that it would get very hot. I am sorry.'

'It is no matter - you could not have known,' the Mage says, dismissing my misdemeanours shortly. Then, as if speaking to himself, he continues, 'No one could have. A dragon!' and then mutters, 'A form of suspended life, perhaps? What woke him to life and surely …?'

All I can hear is that I'm not in trouble, at least not yet, so I offer nothing further. I don't think this Mage knows much about dragons either. He sits silently, thinking for a while. I am afraid he'll decide to take the newborn away from me, so I stay silent, but eventually, writhing in pain, I have to ask.

'Sir? Am I to be punished? And I don't know how to look after him or what to do with him. Can you tell me? Please?'

My voice is plaintive, mirroring my wretched state. My skin is hot and sore, and I am bruised all over.

He looks at me quizzically.

'No one is about to be punished, and no, I know nothing of dragons, and nor does anyone else, so now I'll take you to the Mage Seat of the Bole. Once there, we will talk to the Three.'

'I? I am to come?' I mumble.

'He's obviously taken to you, so you will escort him, and there we will tend to your ills.'

The Mage extends a slow hand to the dragonet, but the little creature hisses, emitting a small tongue of flame.

'Stop that,' I say.

The dragonet whips his head around to look at me, then stops.

'There, you have already started training him,' the young Mage says with an oddly disappointed smile. 'So, you are a dragon mistress now!'

He opens the door before rising, a swift green glow stretching and buzzing from his upraised hand to the latch, which opens itself. A second glimpse of magic. He gestures for me to precede him.

Outside, Karel is waiting with a bag and behind her is Dran and a small gathering of onlookers.

'I was told to gather your things and bring them all here,' she says, eyeing the dragonet. The little creature coos at her.

'Oh, he's so sweet,' she says, putting out a hand. The dragonet immediately hisses and flares out a hot tiny flame which only just misses her.

'Sorry,' I say, 'he hasn't any manners yet. Thank you for my things, Karel.'

'You're welcome,' she says, keeping her distance, adding, 'You're going then?'

'Yes. I don't really know how long for,' I say, and can't help saying, 'but we're going up to the Bole!'

'Lucky you,' she says, a trifle sourly.

The Mage follows me through the door as Karel backs away respectfully.

'Come, we must hurry,' he says, walking away. 'Bring your bag and him.'

Someone mutters, 'Where's she off to? She's just a dirty little foundling!'

Ignoring them, I scramble after the Mage. You don't fail to obey, whether a Novice or a Master. It's said they can turn you into horrible things. But I can only move slowly, everything hurts, and my breathing is bad.

He looks back and, seeing my limp, checks his pace. I follow him like an aged crone until we are at a deserted stairwell. This must lead up to a further level, but he doesn't begin to climb. Only one guttering stone oil lamp pierces the musty darkness.

He glances at us.

'I am taking us up to the Mage Seat in the Bole. I am going to use magic. Be ready.'

My head's in a spin. First the fire, then the dragonet, and now magic? *No, I'm not ready*, I think. But the Mage has already turned away, already crossed his hands oddly. Cupping them, he starts to mutter, and we are enveloped in weird green light again. As I clutch the dragonet to me hard enough to make him squeak, the Mage's voice reverberates in my head, intoning strange words. My inner voice comes back now as, hand on throat, I begin to feel peculiar. In the midst of its usual babble, it asks, 'Where are you?' and a vision of Three Gems in the Holtanbore flickers through my mind. Then, gasping, I try hard to hold onto reality but fail miserably.

Chapter Four

Everything hurts. It is much too bright! I try to rise, but a gentle hand pushes me back down. My chest rattles, and I cough hard and long.

'Don't,' someone says. 'Wait.'

I screw my eyes shut against light and bodily irritation. Someone places something damp and dark over my eyes, and the light is gone.

'Th - thank you,' I croak.

A splash of liquid nearby. Something moist and cool moves gently over my burns, and it feels wonderful. I sigh in relief, cough again and again.

'You got much too close to that fire,' the voice says. 'This will ease the heat and clean the skin.'

It is a kind voice, gentle, like Ma's when I had the flux. So whose?

The careful swabbing takes away some of the discomfort, and I am beginning to feel a little better.

'Now, wait again, please,' the voice says. Another damp cloth is placed over my eyes, then I hear a swish of fabric; curtains, I imagine.

'Now then, that's done. You can open your eyes now.'

Tentatively, marvelling that I have a working hand, I pull the cloth away. Blink. Blink again. Feel surreptitiously for the half-stone, hand on throat. Still there. Nebulous shapes waver and flicker when I try to focus. Firelight and shadows. Someone is here to the left, yet a thin line of brilliance behind them occludes recognition. I'm in a sort of room, yet the walls look strange, made of a smooth, blonde material instead of rock.

'Where am I?' I ask, my voice barely more than a whisper. I cough weakly. My chest hurts. So tired.

Now there's a noise behind the speaker as someone else has entered.

'How is she?'

I know that voice: the young Mage.

'She's awake and coughing,' the unknown voice says, 'and any light bothers her. You should have given her a healing much sooner!'

There's a silence in which I can hardly believe someone has challenged the Mage about anything, let alone the health of a mere drudge.

'In that case, I will help her now,' he says. 'Please leave the room. You're not protected.'

There's a scraping as the unknown someone rises and leaves.

'Jinny?' the young Mage asks. 'How are you?'

'I'm alright,' I croak. And then it dawns, and I panic. Where's my dragon? How on Leaf have I forgotten? Has he been taken away?

'Where is he?' I choke, unforeseen grief rising.

'Your dragon's just down there, by the hearth,' the Mage says. 'You can see him if you lift up a bit.'

Relieved, I try to rise, but my arms are too weak, and I collapse with a sigh. His tall figure eclipses the thin shard of light as he comes near enough to slip an arm under my shoulders and frowns.

'What did they feed you on down there?' he asks. 'You're featherlight!'

I can't reply, coughing hard as he helps me to sit with my back braced against the odd wall. Now I can look down with an inner smile for the dragonet, who, curled with his back to the fire on the warm hearthstone, is snoring quietly. He's just a baby, isn't he, right out of the egg?

'Now, keep still. This won't hurt.'

'What?' I caw with my incredibly sore throat.

'I'm going to use magic to sort out your eyes and the rest of your ills. Stay still.'

Seeing his expression, I nod. He makes a strange gesture, saying something under his breath. A greenish light moves and pulses in his cupped hands, then he uncrosses them and places one over my eyes, one below my throat on my chest. An odd, heavy feeling envelops me, and as I grow torpid, something whispers to me in an unknown tongue. All is quiet. All is still. Then, when he takes his hands away, the world comes back, and I wake. It's dark.

'Why is it dark?' I ask with not a whisper of a croak. My breathing has eased, my throat feels better, and my eyes don't feel as though they're stuffed with splinters. 'What did you do?'

'I've healed you,' the young Mage says, looking at me strangely, then at the dragon. 'You're his keeper now, so you'll need to be well.'

He stands up, and there's a swish of fabric. A shaft of brilliant light falls across the bed, startling me to a thin scream.

'What …?' I begin, then falter, lost for words, hiding my eyes.

'Look,' he says.

'I can't.'

'Yes you can,' he orders. 'Come on. Now!'

Tentatively, I look and find that - Great Trees! - I can cope.

'That, Jinny, is daylight. With a little help from the Tree, I've adjusted your vision. Anyone from the labyrinth usually needs weeks before their eyes adjust properly. I've simply hastened the process for you.'

The light is incredible, illuminating the entire room. Colours zing and sparkle as my eyes adjust.

'I'm healed!' I say in awe. 'Thank you, Sir Mage. Thank you very much.'

'You must take it very slowly today, but you'll be up and about tomorrow, I expect.'

He smiles, a dimple settling in one cheek. Karel was right. When he relaxes, he really is quite handsome. I smile back.

'But … what do I do now?' I ask, mystified.

'Rest and try to feed your little friend there,' he says. 'Beala will bring food and look after you, and I'll see you both again tomorrow.'

'But I don't know how to look after a dragon! And what in the Light do I feed him on?'

'Dragons were always traditionally fed on coals or charred woods in the old histories and tales,' he says. 'But I think the best thing to do is simply see what he wants. And while you're at it, you could use a little more flesh on your bones, too.'

'Thank you, Sir,' I repeat as he strides out of the room, but I am at a complete loss to know what to do next. I have nothing - no work to do except wait for this Beala. However, she must be a good sort as she's left my half-stone alone. It lies warmly against my skin, and I feel that, in some peculiar way, it is alive.

As I lie thinking, a tall girl, all willowy legs and neck, strides in, tidies the curtains, and glances from me to the tiny sleeping dragon.

'How are you?' she says. 'I am Beala, a healer here. You look much improved, and I see your marvellous little friend is still asleep.'

That gentle voice has a name now.

'Thank you for looking after us,' I say. 'And … he's only a baby, so I expect he'll sleep a lot.'

'Well, that's so,' she says, 'but now, I think you could both do with something to eat. I'll go and fetch you something.'

She feels my forehead, smiles, and leaves, coming back after a few minutes with a tray bearing a large jug and cup and all kinds of unknown foods. I can't remember ever seeing so many before. It is a feast!

'I'll leave you alone while you eat,' she says, 'and come back in a little while. Will you be alright?'

'Thanks, we'll be fine,' I say.

Alone again, I push the bedclothes back to look at my lame leg to see if that has been healed too. But no, it looks just the same. The smell of the food must have aroused the little dragon, and he sits up, yawning, mouth glowing with heat, and stretches with a tiny grunt. Then, with a leap, he's up on the bed, trying to climb onto the tray.

'No!' I scold him. 'Settle down. Behave!'

As I gently push him away, he looks up at me in surprise, trying to melt me with his huge eyes.

'None of that,' I say, grinning as I decide what to give him. 'Wait.'

On the tray is a lump of strange, smelly food, possibly cheese. Breaking off a tiny piece, I offer it to him. He sniffs but turns his nose up. Then I see something familiar: the staple of the lower levels, bread-fungus, a dull food enlivened only by whatever we could get our hands on. I offer him a bit which he wolfs down. Next, he makes for a peculiar round thing, heavy and fragrant. A fruit? I offer it, and he takes it gently. Biting it, he hisses with pleasure and begins to eat in earnest, his small fangs flashing like knives. After this, he simply grabs whatever he fancies. He's a messy eater, but he'll get better - I hope.

And now I can take a good look at him. He's tiny, only as long as my forearm, but looks exactly as I imagined dragons should, with a mouthful of teeth and scales that flash with unexpected colours. Along his serpentine neck and armoured back, spines or barbs march to the end of a sinuous tail. His head is similarly protected with scales and thorny spines which he can rattle, and his feet boast sharp little claws. But by far, his best feature is his glorious eyes which can transfix me in an instant.

He belches a thread of fire, then satisfied, relaxes, and I look around the room. So much light! More than I'd ever thought possible. And the colours! I have never seen such amazing colours, vivid and ravishing. The bedspread is red, woven here and there with a pattern of pale blue. Beautiful! We doze until there's a step outside and a knock on the door.

'Hello?' I say.

'Can I come in?' he asks. A tousled brown head with loose long hair and bright eyes peers around the door. I have to remember my manners - but right at this moment, he looks exactly as tousled as my brothers.

'Yes. Come in, Sir. Please … do.'

As the young Mage slides around the lintel like a silly boy, I stifle a chuckle. He pulls a stool from under the opening in the wall and sets it down near me.

'Have you risen yet?' he asks, now donning the formal manner I find so at odds with his looks, and I remember again that he is a Mage.

'Not yet, Sir.'

My hand strays to rub my throat as he contemplates the dragonet. Sleeping on my lap now, its tail is curled around my arm.

'You two seem to be getting along very well,' he says, staring. 'Has he eaten?'

'He's eaten quite a bit,' I say, pointing to the appropriate crumbs. 'I don't know all the names.'

'No cheese?' he asks, looking at the tray. 'Or meat?'

'No. He's not interested,' I say, and I'm grateful. I loathe handling dead things. In the labyrinth, I had to gut dead rats when ordered to help in the First Level kitchens. Dead flesh makes me feel sick, even cooked.

'Well, he's the first dragon anyone's seen in a very long time,' he says, 'so perhaps the stories are all wrong. It's always been said that dragons ate cattle and even people when they could get them.'

He pauses to gaze at the dragonet.

'I suppose we'll find out eventually.'

'We, Sir?'

'You don't think you'll be left alone to bring up the rarest creature in the world, do you?' he says.

I sigh, one tension easing. Thank the light! So all this is not just down to me … and then I understand the full impact of his words. They're going to take him from me. My dragon. My heart curls back into a hard ball like a stone egg.

On cue, the rarest animal snores loudly, almost lifting himself off my lap. His gleaming little belly is rotund with food, and I stroke it. He's mine!

Leaning close, with brief boyish excitement, the young Mage says, 'He's really settled down with you. I think he'll flourish, but first, we must take him to the Three Mages.'

'The Mages? Why, Sir?'

He looks at me.

'You really don't know? This, Jinny, is an incredibly momentous happening! He is the first dragon to be born for hundreds of years. You will be expected to tell them everything, every detail. This is very important.'

'I … I'm not sure what I can tell them,' I say with almost a wail, twisting my hands together. 'And I don't know how to talk to Mages!'

He looks at me as though he's stifling a giggle, and then I realise my gaffe and turn red.

Smiling, he says softly, 'My given name is Ormandel, but please call me Quaryk.'

'Yes, Sir,' I say.

'No need for 'Sir', except in company,' he says. I look at him. Surely he doesn't mean it? But he nods.

'Well, alright, Si … Um … er … Quaryk.'

A sudden humming and a snuffling in my lap announce the dragonet is awake. With a wide yawn, he stretches. His tiny black claws gleam as he lengthens each toe in turn, then his tail and each wing with an audible hiss. He looks at me, then at the light coming through the hole in the wall and rises with a soft cry. I'm pretty sure I know what this means.

'I think he probably needs to um … er … you know?' I gesture broadly at the doorway.

The Mage nods.

'You're probably right,' he says, and delving into a pocket in his tunic, brings out a long thin strip of fabric or some such, with a small buckle at one end.

'What's that for?' I ask.

'This is what the genteel ladies of the Bole use to lead their various pets around,' he adds. 'I'll show you where he can do the necessary,' he says with a wry smile, 'and where you can walk for air if you feel up to it?'

He won't like that at all, I think, looking at the fabric strip, but obediently I sit up, ready to get out of bed. Stop.

'I'll just be a moment, Sir … um, Quaryk,' I say.

I'm clad only in my shift, glad that the half-stone is concealed under it. He gets up, and puts the stool back.

'I'll wait outside,' he says, going out.

Dislodging the dragonet, I slowly get out of bed and dress as best I can in the clean clothes hanging on the peg on the wall. I'm still tired, but the meal has helped.

'Well, let's go and see, shall we, Baby?' I say, picking him up.

Now the little dragon's eyes fix me with a gimlet stare that could split granite.

<*I am not 'Baby',*> a small growly voice snaps into my head. <*And you can throw that long thing away! You're not putting that on me!*>

I stare dumbly.

<*Worm got your tongue?*>

'Um, er, what do I call you then?' I whisper, aware of the Mage waiting just outside. Am I hearing things? And can he hear my thoughts?

< *I'll tell you my name when I'm ready,*> he says. <*And yes. I can hear you.*>

When my mind has completed its initial boggle, I repeat, mentally,

'*But what do you want me to call you?*'

<*Whatever you like,*> he says, <*only make it something good?*>

Then, thinking about what he's eaten so far: lots of vegetables.

'*How about Sprout?*'

The little dragon looks up at me.

<*It'll do. Now, hurry. I really need to go!*>

'*Alright,*' I think, sending my thought to him, '*but let's not tell anyone else we can mind-talk like this, eh? Come on, then.*'

<*It is called bespeaking,*> he replies like an old dominie, <*and I'm coming!*>

I am delighted: I can think-say too! Jubilant, amazed, but mostly rubber-legged, we make for the door together.

~*~

Three days pass with next to nothing for me to do. Well, not much. Sprout is good company when he's awake, but being very young, he sleeps a great deal of the time and eats as much as he can without actually bursting. Then he has to digest and snooze some more. This is the first decent food and rest I've had in years, and time to think and remember. And amazingly, Sprout has already grown noticeably heavier and longer.

'If he carries on like this, he won't fit in here for long,' I comment to the Mage when he visits.

Quaryk smiles tautly. 'I expect he'll slow down soon. But you're right. He will need a much larger place eventually.'

'I wish this waiting were over,' I say, twitching at my new clothes. I am only admitting to myself that I'm terrified of meeting the trio of Mages now.

Quaryk smiles sympathetically: am I so utterly transparent?

'How are you finding the daylight now?' he asks. 'Getting used to it?'

'I am. I like to watch the light come and go. It changes all the time, all on its own!'

I glance at the window, which opens to the Outside. To the actual sky! It's fascinating, although the hole is quite small.

'Sunsets are good,' he says. 'But I enjoy sunrises best. The best sunrises are on the other side of the Bole. My family live that side of the

Tree way out in the Glebe.'

'I like the colours of both,' I say, still watching the sky, 'and the clouds. They look so peaceful.'

'Huh! Some clouds are anything but peaceful,' he remarks. 'Wait till you see a real storm with wind and hail and rain so thick you can hardly breathe. And snow! You've a lot to learn!'

When he is gone, I muse again. Here, inside the Tree, as in the Holtanbore, we live like grubs boring through soft rock, palely writhing in tight little burrows. Everything else is Outside.

Chapter Five

I step away from the first room I haven't had to share since Three Gems; neat, clean, and all mine - for the present, at least. The young Mage is taking us to meet some of the most important people in our Great Tree, perhaps in the entire world of Leaf. As Sprout gambols around me, I remind him to behave, but I suddenly realise he can't possibly know what I mean.

'*Stay close,*' I tell him, '*and don't run around. If you can, sit still and let the Mages look at you.*'

<Why?> he asks. <Why can't I play?>

'*The Mages want to look at you. They can't do that if you are running around.*'

Sprout shoots me a peculiar look, perhaps the equivalent of a shrug, but the message is clear: he really doesn't care. I hope he'll be good simply because I've asked him to, but who knows? Quaryk raises an eyebrow, and I wonder if he suspects that Sprout and I can communicate.

At length, we stop outside a pair of finely carved double doors. It is beautiful work: perhaps wood is easier to shape than stone.

He says, 'This is the heart of the Mage Seat in the Bole, the Great Chamber. They are waiting for us here and will determine all our fates. So please be quiet unless you are spoken to. Remember, whispers can be heard everywhere here, like the Holtanbore.'

'Who are these Mages?' I ask before we enter, rubbing at my throat.

'The Eldest Mage is called Yew, the middle is Willowind, and the youngest is Elfthorn, but you will address them as Sir or Lady. And please call me 'Sir' when we are inside. Are you ready?'

Nodding, I scoop Sprout up. 'We're ready.'

My heart is beating faster. Even Sprout seems nervous as we follow him into a strangely exciting atmosphere. The air hits me like a potent drug filled with a blue mist, apparently diffused with a radiance resembling sunlight. My heart races, and I gasp until it settles. This place is a huge, inverted bowl, a half-sphere, a wooden womb. The circular walls and undulating floor are carved in likenesses of unknown leaves and flowers, the lovely grain of the Tree-wood flowing uninterruptedly throughout. A raised dais with three ornate thrones, and four plain posts at each corner, sits in the centre. Here everything seems fine and delicate, the antithesis of the rough labyrinth of the Holtanbore.

We step closer to halt when a green-gold shimmer emanates in the air above the dais, coalescing into three hazy figures feathering gently down to fill the three thrones. The four carved wooden posts begin to twine up and over, joining together to create an airy cupola which immediately bursts into leaf. As the hazy figures solidify, I stand stock still, fascinated. Sprout, always curious, twists to and fro in my arms, trying to watch everything at once. Although I itch to caution him, I hold back both thoughts and voice. I fancy this place has ears and eyes everywhere.

The shining figures become individuals sitting on identical thrones, and around them, vines trail into flowers, and insects buzz. Quaryk bows, glancing my way. I bob my head obediently as the Mages stare down at us, and Sprout squeaks in protest as I nervously clutch him tighter.

'*Sorry. Shush,*' I tell him. '*Be good,*' then he stills.

Quaryk told me about the Triad, and I understand why. They are all so different. The Mage Willowind is a warm brown woman dressed in reddish robes, with tiny twigs and golden leaves apparently growing through her thick russet hair. Her expression is intense, her voice pleasantly deep and smooth.

She says, 'Sir Quaryk, we have not spoken to you for a while. How goes your training?'

'It goes well and is almost complete, thank you,' Quaryk says with a low bow. 'This is the girl you wished to see and her dragon!'

Three pairs of eyes bore into us.

Willowind says, 'You are Jinny Morai?'

'I am, Lady,' I say. 'And this is …' I hesitate because now it seems such a ridiculous name, 'This is, um, this is Sprout.'

Sitting at attention, the dragon cocks his head up at the Mage, his eyes flinty. Wriggling, he tries to get free, and my arms ache.

'You may release the dragonet if you will,' Willowind says kindly. I let him loose. As soon as his talons touch wood, Sprout rushes up the steps of the dais, glares at each of the Mages in turn, then climbs one of the carved pillars to watch.

'Well, he is certainly agile enough!' Willowind says with a chuckle. Fixing her eyes on him, she goes on, 'Please tell us how you found him, Jinny Morai.'

When I repeat my story, she seems most interested in the globular cave.

'And this cave is in the lowest level?' she asks again.

'Yes, Mistress, in the deepest part of the labyrinth.'

'Was it a big cave? And you found the egg buried, under what exactly?' the Mage to her left, Elfthorn, asks. This Mage is dressed in green, his brown hair sporting unfurled leaves, with bright new mosses showing in his light brown beard and on his smooth, olive skin.

'It was small, and the egg was buried under layers of dirt,' I say, 'but there were thick layers of old documents above it.'

'So, the egg was buried before the documents were put there. Why did *you* find it?' the third Mage says. A small dark figure, she is bent and crabbed, with webs dangling here and there over faded and tattered charcoal rags. Her face is fallen and lined with great age, her hands like claws. This must be Yew. She squints at me.

'I don't know,' I say, opening my hands. 'I just did.'

Now I am beginning to wonder if I'm glad to have found the dratted egg. But if I hadn't, I wouldn't have Sprout, would I? And then I look up and catch his glare. Guiltily, I wonder if he's heard me.

'And this was never known before?' she asks Quaryk.

'It seems so, Eldest,' he says.

The old woman rubs her hands together in glee.

'Ah! Then this little one must be a scion of our lost dragons!' she squawks. 'The lost is found at last! But we must be sure to keep this knowledge from …'

Suddenly something interrupts her, and she bends forward, cowering in her seat. A blaring voice, terrible and nauseating, explodes into my head, bringing me to my knees. I am blinded, deafened, and completely cowed.

{*Dragon mother,*} it caws, vilely, {*come to me. Bring the old one to me so that I have the rearing of it. Now! And you? Begone, witch!*}

A freezing charnel stench erupts from nowhere, making me vomit onto the pristine grain of the floor. I curl into a foetal position, clasping my stomach and head. Then, as quickly as they came, the stench and voice are gone. After a moment, I manage to sit up.

'What … ?' Quaryk begins. His face is a bewildered mask.

I follow his stare. The Eldest lies prone, unmoving. Her glow has vanished, leaving merely an inhabited heap of faded cloth. The Mages rush to her.

'Bring the Healer,' Willowind bellows from where she kneels.

Quaryk runs. I look up. Above, Sprout is hissing and spitting fire, back arched, wings aflutter. With a start, I realise he could set fire to the whole Tree!

'*Sprout, come down, please? Come to me?*' I cajole, but he stays put. So '*Stop!*' I order him sharply, and to my surprise, he does.

Meanwhile, Quaryk dashes in with an elderly, grey-haired man. Mounting the dais, they lean over the Eldest. I allow myself to breathe now, wondering what has happened. Yew is one of the most powerful and important Mages on Leaf.

Then the Healer sits back on his heels, his homely face distraught.

'She is gone!' he says and shuffles back as a thin lavender vapour rises from the still shape, twisting and coiling upwards past Sprout to evaporate before it reaches the shadows above: her ghost. As it vanishes, a single bell-like note fills the womb, and the silence ends in a Leaf-wide mental wail as the combined minds of all the Mages of the Order grieve as one. I clutch my head tightly against the onslaught, wondering why I am hearing it at all. But again, the vicious voice interrupts, this time with deadly, gloating laughter.

{*Grieve, pitiful weaklings. Know that I can end any of you who oppose me. Bring* me the dragon and his keeper, or my hordes will pour out of my fastness to overrun you and your precious Trees.}

With a horrifying thunderclap of pure venom, the voice is gone, leaving me gagging. Terrified, Sprout runs down from his perch to curl up in my arms. It is a long time before any of us can move, and we lie stunned until Quaryk, looking pale and drawn, rouses us.

'Jinny,' he says quietly, 'let me help you back to your room.'

He supports me, but I cannot stand. He lifts me and carries me back to my room, Sprout trailing. Once there, Quaryk leaves, but the dreadful tang of the unknown voice echoes around my head, and I am horribly afraid. With Sprout, I curl into a foetal position on the bed to wrestle with my horror and distress. Curled up in the crook of my arm, Sprout's scales are pallid, and I can feel his fear.

'I'll look after you,' I say. *'I'm here. I won't let anything hurt you till you're grown; I promise.'*

He trembles, and I hug him close, wondering what the future will hold. Nothing so dire has ever happened before. For a while, I wonder if I could take him back to Three Gems, but this seems a remote possibility now. Only sleep or death can bring forgetfulness, so we sleep.

~*~

Sprout rouses me when twilight has fallen and the wall lamps are lit. The world is still and quiet, but I'm still whole and alive, despite a pounding headache. The dragonet yawns widely, stretches, and then bounces on my bladder.

<*I really need to go,*> he says, the first time he's communicated since, since …

'So I do now!' I mutter. Yawning, I rise.

When we are both more comfortable, I ask, *'Shall we go find Quaryk? He might know what's happening … What this is all about.'*

Sprout looks dubious but says, <*Alright.*>

A young woman coming towards us plasters herself, wide-eyed, against the wall to avoid Sprout.

'Hello. Do you know where I can find Quaryk?' I ask her.

She frowns. I've forgotten to say 'Sir'.

'*Sir* Quaryk is down in the kitchens,' she says primly, and I thank her back as she scurries away. Sprout mimics her sniff and rolls his eyes, making me chuckle as we head off to find him. When we arrive, Quaryk is slumped at the big table, dark purple rings encircling his eyes.

'You look better,' he says.

'You don't,' I say cheekily, moving to the hearth to pour myself a hot drink. I wouldn't have dared to speak to him like this before the scare in the Mage Seat.

He grimaces. 'There is much to think on now that the Eldest is dead, and we are threatened. It was thought that he was gone, but it seems Charnecron has risen again. His arm has become long and strong.'

Meanwhile, Sprout is investigating one of the cook's heels. She slaps at him as you would a fly, turns, and with a pained look says, 'Please keep him from getting under my feet, Mistress?'

I nod. 'Sorry, I'll stop him,' I say. 'But can he have one of those things?'

The cook tosses a root down for my dragon and he pounces on it like a kitten. While he is chewing, I say, '*Leave the cook alone, Sprout. She's busy.*'

Sprout merely gives me a dirty look and wanders away to sit by the fire.

'Who is Charnecron?' I ask. 'I've never heard of him.'

'You shouldn't have. We call him the Necromancer, for he is a fallen Mage, turned to evil, and we do not talk about him. But now it seems he has turned into a monster out for revenge.' Quaryk says, his face dropping. 'We may never be safe here again.' He bows his head over his empty mug, shaking it.

'But ... why in Leaf does he want to hurt us?'

He stares at his drink. Eventually, he says, 'I was waiting for a better time to tell you, but now this is something you need to know. Charnecron sought more power long years ago, and it seems he has found it from somewhere. It is whispered that he tapped a different source of magic, something foul and ancient dredged up in the ruins under the southern mountains, a source of evil. He was expelled from the Order and banished from the Trees of Leaf for his unspeakable acts long ago.'

Glancing at Sprout guiltily, he raises an eyebrow and continues, 'When the Order rejected him, he grew angry and veiled himself, and we lost sight of him for centuries, but it seems that he has been mustering his strength and is out for revenge. He perhaps wants to destroy our Order and, possibly, the Trees.'

Again he pauses, rubbing a pale, stubbled face in his hands. Sprout noses under the table, hunting for scraps.

'After five hundred years, we thought him long dead, but we were wrong! If he arrives here in force, there may be a terrible reckoning. The combined magic of the entire Order has only just managed to foil his first thrust.'

I have no words of comfort while my fear holds me in a vice. The only thing I can do is tentatively place a hand over his, wondering if it is allowed. He looks surprised but leaves his hand resting under mine for a moment.

'I am so sorry for the loss of the Eldest Mage,' I say.

Slowly, he withdraws his hand to wipe away a tear and says, 'She was a good, kind spirit. A friend of the whole of Leaf and will be greatly missed.'

'What did she … er … do?' I ask. After all, this is all new to me.

Quaryk stares at me as though I am an unknown species.

'Her wisdom was the strength of the Order and the Trees. She was our touchstone, and while she thrived, all thrived. We do not know what will happen now, but we must have a Triad of Mages in the Bole. Another Mage or novice must become the youngest of the Three.'

I think for a split second. 'Will it be you, Sir?'

He shakes his head wryly. 'No, my training is not fully completed. It will be a more senior novice or one of the wandering Mages.'

He slumps in his chair, seeming to slip into utter despair, and rests his head on his arms. Unnerved that a Mage should so forget decorum to this degree, I wait for him. Minutes go by until Sprout begins to weave around his ankles like a cat. Then the Mage rouses himself enough to reach down to look at and pet the little dragon.

'Ah, it's you,' he mutters.

At this, Sprout climbs onto his lap and licks his nose with a hot blue tongue. A tentative smile lifts the Mage's face.

<*Karrk!*> Sprout spits. <*Salty! But he is back now.*>

This tiny being has managed to rouse the Mage from his awful sadness.

'He likes you,' I say. 'He must because he tries to flame everyone else.'

There's a lull while Quaryk strokes Sprout's head. Eyes blissfully closed, Sprout rolls onto his back to expose his fat, scaly stomach. He does not look much like a dragon. More like a sort of scaly puppy.

<*I'm hungry,*> Sprout says after a while.

'*You always are,*' I say, looking around. There is always hot food on this hearth, so I dole out a portion of stew for us all, thinking of Outside, where these foods are grown. I have only seen a tiny bit so far. Climbing onto the table from Quaryk's lap, Sprout almost dives headlong into the bowl I set down for him.

`Hey, careful, it's hot!' I say, and then I grin at my foolishness. This is a dragon: hot is normal.

Quaryk nods his thanks.

'Eat,' I tell him, 'it's amazing to have food there whenever you want it.'

He looks at me and frowns.

'What did you eat below?' he asks.

'Well,' I say slowly, a blush rising, feeling as though everything awful about the labyrinth is all my fault. 'We had one meal a day, usually bread fungus, and sometimes a vegetable too. And there was rat, but I didn't eat that.'

His frown deepens. 'I see,' he says, and I know what he's thinking. The First Law of the Trees is 'Do Not Kill Any Living Creature.'.

We begin to eat the stew, but before we are halfway through, Sprout has cleared his plate and is eyeing ours hungrily. You never know, we might forget a bit or drop something.

~*~

The morning passes quietly. Just before noon, we are summoned by the Mages once more.

'Welcome,' Willowind says wearily in the shadowy womb, her face scored with deep new lines. 'I fear this is a sad meeting. You may let the young one climb again if he wishes.'

Once Sprout is loose, instead of climbing the misty cupola at once, he stares intently at the two remaining Mages of the Triad. They bend their glowing heads to him as if listening, and irritably, I wonder just what is going on that I cannot hear. After a long pause, the younger of the two chuckles.

'The last shall be first,' he says as if quoting. 'It seems this little one has fooled us all. This is not a he or a she, but a thing somewhere in between; a he/she. This dragon child is capable of re-populating its entire race on its own! Think of that!'

Quaryk and I stare like buffoons.

'*Really? You might have told me,*' I complain to him/her.

Sprout chuckles, saying, <*Would you have believed me? These old ones do where you may not have.*>

It seems my Sprout is not as childish as I thought, but I am still miffed.

'This dragon-child can replenish its entire race,' Willowind repeats. 'Now do you understand? If the Necromancer manages to take it, he will use it and its progeny for his own evil purposes, melding them into a fearsome army. With such a force he could rule all Leaf.' She shudders noticeably. 'Great Tree! Now d'you see why this little one is so important?'

Appalled, I can hardly breathe. My bowels turn to jelly, and I feel weak, like an old woman. Once, when I had chance, I secretly read an account of dragons firing a Great Tree in a time long ago. Even then it made me weep, and I hope never to witness anything so horrible. My fists clench as I blurt out, 'That *must* not happen. It cannot be allowed!'

Willowind eyes me, eyebrows raised at my belligerent tone, but says softly, 'Yes, the Necromancer must never lay a hand on him. Even,' and she looks at me pointedly, 'if it means that you and he must die!'

A shiver passes through me, and my bladder complains. This whole situation is abominable.

'So we must either keep you both very close or send you right away from the Tree,' she concludes. 'We cannot know if he has deliberately searched for you or simply fished in a bigger pool.'

Before I can begin to ask what this means, she lifts a languid hand to pass it over us. Sprout seems fine, but I feel fizzy as though I've drunk too much bubbly shine. The half-stone is suddenly burning, so I grab it and thrust it away from my skin. The old thread breaks, leaving me juggling it . When I fumble and drop it, the wood of the floor begins to char, and a small thread of grey smoke spirals upwards. The Mages look down at it in amazement.

'What's this - a stone?' Willowind mutters.

Her eyes pierce me, then she peers closer and starts as if pricked.

'Ah, it cannot be - but - it is! Now I understand! This is why the egg came to you. This stone draws magic to itself. Where did you get it? You stole it?'

Dignity forgotten, she speaks hastily, and I cower as everyone stares as though I'm a new and more annoying kind of snick, but as none of this was my fault.

Disgruntled, I lift my voice to declare, 'I don't steal!' I scowl at the injustice. 'The stone was buried in the old documents I was sorting, as I told you. It was inside a pile of leaves and … and … well, it was pretty, so I kept it.'

They look at me as though awaiting further explanation, but I have none. I shrug, looking at my feet.

'It is as the Eldest predicted,' Elfthorn says quietly to Willowind. 'Yes,' she agrees, 'but—?'

She looks at me. Bespeaks me.

'Come here, child.'

I hear her, like Sprout and I have to obey, so, now trembling, I ascend the dais.

'Kneel,' she says, placing her hands on each side of my head. Her hands are warm and strong. I dare not move, although my leg pains me. Something is happening inside - something strange - and I find I am looking into myself, watching my surprise, confusion, doubt, and then certainty.

'Ah, as I thought,' she says. 'Now, Jinny Morai. Only you, holding the half-stone, could ever have found the dragon's egg.'

Catching an echo of her badly shielded thoughts obviously aimed at the other Mages, I hear, '*She ... the Mage-born. Here at last! Would that we had known earlier before the Eldest died ... Ah, no ... And there is something else here - something strange within. What is this? Yes ... the prophecy!*'

Thoughts echo, seeming to come from all directions, asking questions while something turns over inside me. I wonder muzzily what they are doing as she drops her hands to stare at the half-stone. Instantly, a hair-thin, golden chain appears to thread itself through the hole in my stone, healing itself in a continuous loop. The Mage gestures for me to pick it up, and I place it over my head. My fear is replaced by an unsuspected sense of purpose.

'Keep it safe and keep it close, child,' she says and turns to Quaryk. '*She will speak soon enough,*' she bespeaks him. '*Watch for signs.*'

'Go along with Quaryk,' she says, 'and rest, if you will, child?'

Without thinking, I bespeak her, saying, '*I will,*' and she smiles broadly. Opening her hands, she places them lightly on my head in blessing. I still feel foggy, having no idea what all this means. Although I try to understand, nothing comes, so I will wait.

Then, with a jerk, Willowind squints at us as though only just remembering we are here.

'This is something we must think on,' she says dismissively. 'You will be summoned again. Quaryk, take this girl and her young friend somewhere well away from the Bole. Allow her time to understand the world a little better and for them both to mature. It may help to keep them safe. We will summon you at need.'

She turns, dismissing us. I glance at Quaryk, a question bubbling up.

'*Can I go back home to Three Gems?*'

He pauses, looks at me, but his face stays passive. He hasn't heard me. Collecting himself, he bows to the Mages and gestures to us to leave. Sprout, without comment, trickles sinuously down from his perch to pace alongside me until we are through the great doors. Then he almost dances on his tail, leaping and gambolling around.

'*Well done,*' I say, pleased with his behaviour.

He shoots out an ebullient blue flame.

'What was all that about?' I ask Quaryk. 'Does it mean I can go home?'

He stops and shakes his head. 'I don't understand it completely myself,' he says, 'but you have to go away for a while, farther than the Holtanbore - so, no.'

My heart drops as Three Gems recedes again. I decide it is high time I find out what is really going on. I have been passive for too long.

But then, my stomach grumbles loudly, and I wonder if my long years of incessant hunger made me docile and spiritless. But not now. Now I am awake. Sprout gives me a look, and I'll swear he's laughing. Something shifts, and I can smile too.

'Lunch?' I suggest.

Sprout lifts his nose and sniffs.

<*This way,*> he says, setting off at a good pace.

Quaryk and I follow as he enthusiastically tracks down the heady fragrance of food.

Chapter Six

We are going Outside.

I, Jinny Morai of the Holtanbore, am about to do something incredible - I am actually going out into the Glebe, into the wild air of Leaf! My new treasures and the spare clothes Karel gave me are packed in a brand-new bag, and even though he is ridiculously excited, Sprout is apparently on best behaviour. We are to descend to the main gate using Quaryk's magic.

'Ready?' Quaryk asks.

I nod nervously, too tense to speak, squashing Sprout a little as I hug him to me.

<*Stoppit!*> he complains, spitting sparks until I loosen my grip.

'You'll be fine,' Quaryk says glibly. Ignoring us, he crosses his hands in his peculiar way before I can take another breath. A green glow arises, and my ears ring, but this time I am determined to stay awake. Around us, a rushing begins like a rising wind. My body feels as though it is being filled with a seething green liquid, and I see nothing except a green swirl of mist. The rushing grows to climax in a throbbing howl, and I am tossed upwards, light as a toy, leaving my stomach behind. All sense of time is lost. For an anxious instant, I need to vomit, yet seconds later, I am stumbling as we are deposited right way up in a high-ceilinged, strange, smooth-walled tunnel. This must be the entrance to the Holtanbore!

Although the green glow persists for a few seconds more, folk walk busily past, ignoring us as if this is nothing out of the ordinary. Perhaps they're right.

Unbelievably, Sprout says, <*That was fun!*>

Really? I feel as though I've been turned inside out.

Daylight streams through the great semi-circular doors at the end of the wide hallway. I try to repress a shudder. I am about to step Outside, into the unknown where all shadows are banished. Even as I am yearning towards it, I am backing away. Sprout wriggles impatiently, emoting shiny excitement.

<*Let me down!*> he says excitedly, his spines rattling. <*Please?*>

A sensation of dread hits me as his body springs out of my grasp. What will happen to him - to us - out there?

'*Stay close!*' I tell him. And then, 'I can't do this,' I mutter aloud, hands flying to clasp my throat. My muscles tense and set rigidly as all the terrifying tales of Outside I've ever heard flash through my mind. 'No …'

Quaryk turns, grabs my arms, and, stepping back a few paces, drags me into a niche in the wooden wall. Thankfully this conceals the terrible brightness of the doorway. My body feels like stone; a leaden lump.

'Breathe,' he says, and his eyes fill the whole of my vision. *Such beautiful eyes*, I think, fluctuating from blue to green with each new thought. Obediently, expelling breath in a great gust, I pause and then inhale. By now, his hands are on each side of my head, and I am drowsy. Eventually, he bespeaks me.

'Trust me, Jinny Morai. Trust in me … you will be able to face the great spaces and open air around the Tree … and you will be happy outside, I promise.'

With all tension suddenly gone, my neck and spine turn to jelly, and I flop bonelessly, a pulsating sack. Quaryk grabs me as my legs fail. Yet, seconds later, my absent bones reappear, and I struggle to stand again. He smiles, encircling me with an arm strong as an old root. I am no weakling after all that digging, but there's a lovely comfort in his muscular half-circle. I have to stop myself leaning into him, but as seconds go by, I move away. A horrified hot blush works its way to my cheeks.

Seeing my expression, Quaryk withdraws his arm. 'Better now?' he asks.

Nodding, I turn away, face afire.

'Well, come on, there's a brand-new world out there for you to explore! Come on. We'll go together.'

Sprout is anything but cowed: he is delighted by the prospect of a new adventure. I glance at Quaryk's smiling encouragement, but now Sprout won't keep still, wriggling and throwing his head about so much that I have to put him down. He looks so small down there on his own, glancing from me to the Mage. But he is a dragon.

<*Come on! Come look?*> he says, spitting tiny blue flames.

'*Stay near,*' I tell him. '*There could be anything out there.*'

'Come on then, if you're ready,' Quaryk says, eyes shining in anticipation. He strides off to the threshold, and I follow slowly, blinking. My sight is hazy - so much light! Sprout halts on the doorstep, craning his head forward to look. He takes a step and, with a bounce, is gone. Still I hesitate, peering around the massive lintel.

I swallow, breathe and lift one foot to clear the sill, and then stop. This is Outside? This vast, incredible view? All this air? I never dreamt it. This is a watery, misty sort of world, moist, dripping.

'Well done,' he says, then, 'What's wrong?'

I shake my head, turning away, a second blush rising with tears. 'It's … it's …'

'It's a long, long way from the chill and darkness of the labyrinth, isn't it?' he says, his voice gentle.

'I never knew it would be so …' I sniff and gulp as he encloses my shoulders again with a long arm: the second time he has touched me today. I feel oddly protected.

'Better?' he asks, letting me go.

I nod.

'Well, come on then, this is all new and exciting. You're lucky. Look!'

Sprout is charging ahead down the long slope from the doorway towards the flatter lands of the Glebe. Quaryk has explained what we will find out here but seeing it for the first time is breathtaking. I stand staring, fears forgotten now. The cool air moving across my exposed skin lifts it into shivery bumps, and I stare at it wonderingly.

From the vantage point just in front of the massive doors, the stone-set path meanders downwards, protected on each side by huge, buttressed roots like mountain crags. Below us, where one of the great roots return to earth, lie raised lumps or nodules as though the earth has some sort of infection.

'What's that?' I ask, astonished, having never seen anything like it before.

'That,' Quaryk says, 'is a village. Those are buildings - people live in them.'

They must be like home-caves inside.

'But,' I say, 'they are open to the air and - actual *weather!*'

'That's right,' he says. 'That they are, and a lot of people live very comfortably there.'

When we draw nearer, I see the buildings are raised above the ground on thick stone piles or massive wooden stilts, with dry, open places beneath their stone foundations. The walls are made of married wood and stone, with some sort of shaggy material used for the roofs. The resulting constructions look top-heavy and seem to lean towards each other as though trying to snatch a kiss. But they have windows and doors and stone steps for access. And above all, tall stone structures issue hearth-smoke.

People look up as we pass: a man leans on a stick, watching us: a woman throws a cloth over a string; a mother calls her children to her. When they see Quaryk, some of them smile and wave, but as one, they gasp and stare when they catch sight of Sprout. For a while, I am torn between pride because he is mine and a slight anxiety - will they turn hostile? Yet we pass by the village peacefully, and a long view opens up before us.

It is all wonderful and very strange. The expanse of the Glebe stretches away in a distant, soft blue haze, a dark line delineating the point where the earth and sky meet. That must be the Girdle, the vast hedge enclosing this beautiful place. And overall, the massive canopy of the Great Tree shifts slowly to and fro in winds we cannot feel below. The light changes momentarily as vast acres of the canopy and branches slide one over the other and then part. It makes me small and confused, like a snick in a gather cavern. All that vast, airborne weight suspended above. Cavern ceilings are usually solid and unmoving: what will happen if one of those massive branches breaks?

'The Tree ... I didn't know how huge it is. Is it ... safe?'

'Ah, now you are beginning to understand,' Quaryk says. 'Happily, our Great Tree is almost invulnerable. A great many people have lived under and in it for centuries, and it is very rare that branches or twigs break. Nothing like that has been known in the past four hundred years, to my certain knowledge. The Tree is inconceivably strong.'

I glance at him: he is obviously convinced of its safety, but I am not, peering up anxiously as if waiting for a crack to appear.

Ignoring me, he grabs me by an elbow and sets off down the path. I have to scramble to keep up, noticing bright little faces lift and sway gently at each side. Are they looking for the sun? Vivid emerald daggers sprout up between them.

'What are those?' I ask, not daring to touch or even go near.

'Those? Those are flowers, Jinny. Pretty aren't they?'

I catch my breath as he strokes them and the daggers, but he is not harmed. Relaxing a tad, I bend to look closer. The flowers are notched discs in an amazing variety of colours and forms, standing within the thick green daggers. Pretty is not the word I would use. Incredible is nearer. And *so* bright.

'They're safe? And ... what's this stuff called?'

'They're safe to touch. And that's grass. But this tall plant here is needle-weed. Mind, it's very sharp! It can pierce clothes and skin.'

Sprout snuffles unconcernedly through all this strange stuff. Anxiety prickles again, so I call, 'Sprout? Take care!' He doesn't respond, but when I touch his mind, I find he's having a great time. Quaryk follows my gaze.

'Think of it like fungus. He'll be fine,' he says, 'I doubt there's anything in the Glebe that's likely to do much harm to a dragon. He is well armoured.'

Reassured, I turn back to the path. Warm peppery scents and unidentified motes drift past on the thick air, making me sneeze. When a rare shaft of hot sunshine touches my skin it tingles, and a peculiar odour arises - my own. I rub at my skin, trying to disperse the hot feeling.

'Is that uncomfortable?' Quaryk asks. 'I forgot: you haven't been out in the sun before, have you?'

'No,' I agree. 'Is it dangerous?'

'It can be,' he says. 'It can burn if you're not used to it.'

Visions of flames running up and down my arm make me flinch. 'What can I do? How long will it take before—?'

He interrupts. 'Don't worry. Just put your jacket on, and I'll find something that will take the burning away.'

He searches the grasses as we continue down the path and, at length, picks a fat leaf or two from a low-growing plant and squeezes them.

'Here, this should help. Hold out your arms,' he says. When I shrug off my jacket, he squeezes again until a wet green jelly oozes out onto my skin.

'Rub that in,' he says, 'and don't forget your face and neck. It should stop any more problems like that.'

He is right. The jelly stops the burning, and I look at the plants with calculating eyes, wondering how many other uses they may have. Now, on either side of the path, tinier versions of the Great Tree grow in clusters, much taller than us. They sport green appendages, more leaves, which clump and billow in the breeze allowing a second interplay of light and shade. Sprout noses under one of the smaller trees, pushing his nose deep into the stuff beneath it, partly disappearing in a hole.

'Sprout! Come out! You could get stuck,' I say in a panic, finally understanding Ma and her nagging now - when I was little, she was probably only trying to keep me safe. When Sprout emerges from the hole, covered in bits of earth and dead leaves, I relax, deciding that motherhood must be fraught most of the time.

It is difficult to understand most of what I see, and I feel as though I have drunk too much moon brew, like Da did occasionally. He got jolly, loud, and stupid. But enough - there's something that I really want to know.

'Where are we going?' I ask.

'Wait and see,' Quaryk says, grinning annoyingly. 'You'll like it, but we'll need to circle half around the Bole first and then go across country, and that will take time.'

Seething, I shut up and, greatly daring, walk on into the unknown.

Chapter Seven

Sprout and I are living with Quaryk's family on their farm now, far out in the Glebe. The farm is called Alder's Hollow, which lies in the village of Podbourne. This is all strange to me as there are no names for particular areas of the Holtanbore, just numbered levels above the Library. When we travelled here, I marvelled at how enormous the Great Tree and the Glebe are - and this is only a tiny part of the whole wide world.

One morning not long after we have arrived, we are watching Sprout investigating Quaryk's ma's lovely garden when my back begins to itch again. I try to scratch but can't quite reach.

Quaryk noticing my antics, says, 'What's up? Has the hayfever come back?'

'No, that's alright,' I reply, twisting like a fur-snake, 'But my back's itching like mad.'

'I'll ask my mother to look at it for you if you like,' he says, stiffening.

I look at him covertly. He is certainly handsome, but now when he talks to me, he has begun to hold himself taut as if he might fly apart. Is this my fault? I don't understand him at all, but I'll be grateful if his ma will look at my back.

~*~

Later, walking through the shady meadow behind Quaryk's farmhouse, the warming air feels good. Spring, I'm told, is progressing normally. Small bright flowers nod everywhere in the sunlight, which filters through the windy canopy in irregular shafts and pulses. Sprout is out in front and has gone deliberately deaf, so I'm following him and starting to think he does this for attention. It's high time he learned better manners, the main reason for this jaunt.

Before we left the Bole, the Mages found a very ancient, and totally ludicrous scroll from somewhere or other on dragon training and ordered Quaryk to make me follow its advice, but they obviously hadn't bothered to read it themselves. He has it now, but if I get chance, it will go straight on the back of the kitchen fire.

'What about this,' he says, thrusting it at me. 'Have you read it all? There might be something in it that will help?'

'Have you? I've read enough to know whoever wrote it had never so much as imagined a dragon. "Starve the offending beast if it not be amenable to control?" Can you imagine doing that to Sprout? What would be the point? Sprout would just eat whatever he could find outside and simply ignore us. And I won't try to starve him.'

'Jinny, you don't need to take it too literally,' he says, thrusting it at me. 'These are just supposed to be guidelines.'

I push the scroll back at him.

'It's utter rubbish!'

He looks concerned, even angry, but by now, I don't care. 'Sprout isn't a beast. He's a person! Don't ever show me crap like this again! That was then, and this is now, and Sprout's not starving on the say-so of some stuffy old Mage who wrote this hundreds of years ago! And I won't tie him up or hit him either!'

'Well, if that's what you think I meant …'

He glares at me, turns on his heel, and stalks away, the ridiculous document scrunched tightly in his fist. I watch his back until he is out of sight, and then feel guilty. Drat! Have I gone too far? He was only trying to help, and I shouldn't lose my temper. But Sprout is miles in front, and he is so young.

'*Sprout? Come back. Please?*' I ask, knowing he can hear me. If he comes, we might catch Quaryk up, and I can apologise. But he is ignoring me. I concentrate, eyes shut, trying to pinpoint exactly where he is. And then I know - he's concentrating on something in a newly sown field, his muzzle flat on the earth between short shoots of whatever it is that's planted. Ah - now I've caught his thought. He's watching a small brown animal busily excavating a hole just in front of his nose.

<Isn't he clever?> Sprout says. *<See how he pushes the earth back with his hind feet … that's digging, isn't it? I want to dig too!>*

He rises and begins to scratch at the earth and plants.

'Hey, don't! You can't dig here!' I say. 'Not bang in the middle of a field of young growth. *You can't because these plants will be food,*' I continue silently. '*Come on, we'll go back and ask if there's a good place for you to try it.*'

Sprout looks up at me in disappointment. *<But I want to dig like him!>*

'No, those are young plants for food. You shouldn't dig them up. Come on.'

We wander back to the farm. In the meadow, his scales darkly glinting rainbows, Sprout rolls and hops through the lovely, long grasses whose inhabitants melt away from our path. So many creatures, so much of everything! In the bowels of the Holtanbore there are only snicks and fur-snakes, light swarms and crawlies, and that's about it. A few rarities, like steelworms, are big and dangerous and best avoided.

'*I didn't know dragons could dig,*' I comment.

<Why not?> Sprout counters. *<My claws are strong. And my teef too!>*

I shrug. '*Teeth*, Sprout, you say tee-th. Th, th, th …'

<That's right,> he says, *<Teef!>*

He has grown to about the same height as the friendly farm dogs here, and when he hiccups, everyone backs away to avoid charred knees. A giggle erupts from me at the thought. Yet he doesn't need to be tamed as Quaryk suggests … He is exactly like a human child, simply needing to learn how to behave, with a few manners and for him, some pointers for flying. And the latter is not something I can give him.

My back begins to itch again. I have no idea why this is, nor had Quaryk's mother, Milde, when she looked at it. The nubs seem to be erupting from my back, growing fast. Milde has very kindly found an ointment for me that calms the itchiness down for a time when applied.

Finding a handy earth-tree trunk, if you can call such a weedy little thing a tree compared to the Great Tree rearing bole and canopy high enough above us to net the clouds, I back up against it to rub my sore nubs through my clothes, groaning with a sort of ecstatic pain. The fabric will wear thin and tear soon.

<*Don't break them! When they're grown, we can fly together.*> Sprout interrupts my thoughts with a wide toothy grin.

I stop and stare. 'What? What in Leaf do you mean - fly!' My eyebrows shoot canopy-wards.

<*Well, no point in having wings if you don't use 'em, is there?*> he says, stretching his own wings in turn.

'You are joking? You are, aren't you?'

Sprout grins again. <*Didn't you know? Those are wings!*>

I flop down into the damp grasses, dislodging a myriad of small angry creatures, completely stunned. Me ... with wings? This is such a bizarre prospect that I experience a sudden shaft of homesickness, wanting Three Gems, wanting Ma, and wanting everything to be normal again. She'd know what to say and how to feel about all this. I want to be small and unknowing, innocent of half-stones and Mages. As if all this isn't weird enough, I'm growing wings!

'You're sure?' I ask, hands massaging my throat. Irritatingly, Sprout doesn't answer but listening to his inner chuckles at my expense, he's positive he's right. There seems nothing to do, so eventually, I calm down enough to say, '*Come on, Let's go find somewhere for you to dig holes.*'

<*What's this? Aren't you well?*> Sprout asks, nuzzling my wet face before I can get up. <*What is this water? Why is it here?*>

'*I'm crying. These are tears, Sprout,*' I murmur, wiping them away, '*because I'm sad and confused. I want Ma, but she's too far away in the Holtanbore, where you were born. She probably doesn't even remember me now.*'

The heat of the fire, and the way the wax bubbled; the men who dragged me away; and her screams. How she fell as my leg was trapped and broken. I never saw her wake - was she dead?

Sprout puts a prickly claw on my hand and leans into me until my snuffling returns to a mere snivelling.

The whole family has gravitated to the warm farm kitchen, a long room with two big ovens in one wall. At a vast stone sink, Quaryk is scrubbing roots. He glances round briefly, but his task is apparently preferable to dealing with me. Pots, pans and implements are ranged along shelves on the walls, and a large copper pan heats water in one corner. I stand in the doorway, taking everything in. Here, he's merely one of the family and not a noble Tree Mage.

Quaryk's mother, Milde, is mixing something in a bowl on the big central table while his father, Hollis, is sitting watching her, peeling the bark from long sticks with a knife. Both Quaryk's brothers, one younger, one older, are sitting by the fire, working pieces of leather in their hands, chatting away. Lind, his sister, hovers over a big pair of scales, weighing out a dusty white powder. It all makes a lovely family tableau, and my homesickness threatens to choke me again. But as I turn to go, for this is not my family, Milde, glancing up, says kindly,

'Come along in, Jinny. Come and sit down.'

Making room for me at the table, she pushes some objects aside: a bolt of cloth, tied threads, a new packet of pins, and a roll of astonishingly bright red ribbon.

'See. A new peddler woman brought them by just this morning, a pleasant person to talk to,' she says, glancing from me to Sprout. Then, wrinkling her nose, goes on, 'She had the strangest hair and smelled odd, but her goods were fine. Aren't they lovely? Come and sit yourself down.'

We enter. I sit down at the table, feeling completely unnecessary, eyeing the redness of the ribbon. Sprout nudges my hand under the table.

<*What about digging? Ask where?*>

'Um,' I begin, 'er, is there anywhere that Sprout can have a go at digging? He's been watching a little animal digging a hole and wants to do the same, but I thought you wouldn't want holes all over the meadows ...'

Perhaps they won't understand. They seem to treat Sprout like one of their dogs - just another (if weird) animal to pet once and then ignore. As they all look up, I fancy I am curling into myself like the ancient curly shells we used to find in the rocks at home. Surprisingly, Quaryk's mother laughs, and the rest of the family look up and smile. Only Quaryk keeps his back turned.

'Bless you, girl!' she says, and I breathe out. 'It's good of you to think of it. Now, where can a small dragon practice digging, our Da? Where's the best place?'

There's a rapid, good-natured family argument before they come to a consensus. Then Hollis looks round at me and rumbles, 'Best you take him down to the water meadows, girl - they could do with draining and what with one thing and another, we haven't got around to it. Get him to dig lines of holes running down to the stream, eh?'

'Yes, that would be a great help,' Milde adds, 'and if you take some lunch with you, you can enjoy the fresh air as long as you want!'

I thank them as she bustles around, gathering food that she ties in a cloth for me, and then I slip out with Sprout. It's hard being under so many eyes, even such friendly ones.

~*~

The water meadow is a long, hot walk away. Our path winds its way through a small wood and various fields of tall stuff, a bit like the grass that grows everywhere else. The trees are full of birds and bloons, some of the strangest creatures I've ever seen. Quaryk explained them to me as we travelled here: the birds are more like us and, he said, like the with beautiful feathers, but the bloons! They are very odd - tiny mouse-like creatures almost completely enclosed in spotted and vari-coloured transparent bags that blow here and there with the wind. We were watching them sipping nectar from a flowering tree.

'Do they eat anything else? I asked him.

'No, they only take their nourishment from flowers. Winter is very hard for them, so they sleep through to spring, holding to the roofs of caves by a fine filament they extend.'

'And how do they ... you know?' I wondered if I'd get an answer.

'You mean excrete?'

'That, and ... um ... make babies?'

'Ah, they're clever. To let the gas out of their membrane would mean instant death, so they are equipped with little flaps that act like valves in their ... ah ... nether regions. All that sort of thing has to happen very fast so they don't leak too much!'

I raised my eyebrows at that. So romance is *really* rapid for bloons.

Now other creatures take my eye. Here are things with long spindly legs attached to great sacs of gas, very like bloons, but bobbing up and down along the tops of the grasses, remaining earthbound. Fast, half-feathered, half-furred, and half-glimpsed animals run and chortle underneath the trees and bushes. The bloons and birds grunt and chirrup above, and hordes of little furry things scamper and run or bravely sit upright, glaring at us, squeakily, as if we have no business here. And then, Great Leaf! The insects! Quaryk pointed out vast amounts of the many varieties when we walked the Glebe, but I like the flutterbys best. They're so colourful, clean blue and silver, rich lavender and gold, and warm, knock-your-eyes-out red in a myriad of patterns.

I love the sheer fecundity of this place! Colours, sounds, smells in unimaginable abundance, and vegetation which springs up overnight given a chance. Clean, wild water flows freely over the ground in contrast to the water in the Holtanbore, which glides silently by in unseen stone channels. It is breathtaking. The labyrinth is a far poorer place.

The little river loops around the flat fields in mirrored meanderings, a silver snake paralysed in mid-wiggle. Drooping, delicate trees root-clasp the riverbanks bright with swathes of little flowers. Occasional beams of sunlight break through the Tree's canopy overhead, dappling the land. So bright, so warm!

We flop down to eat before we contemplate anything as energetic as digging, yet Sprout is so keen to get on with it he can hardly keep still, giving himself flaming hiccups and endangering my clothes, the vegetation, and a host of innocent creatures.

'Hey, careful,' I say, ducking as he hics, spurting flame again.

<*Sorry,*> he says. <*Can I go dig now?*>

'Yes. Remember to dig ditches if you can? Long holes?'

Before I have finished speaking, Sprout is already tearing at the grass, intent on scooping out earth and thrusting it back with strong clawed feet. He's doing well, but if he carries on, he will end up shoving a mound of soil bang into the water.

'How about starting again near the water and working your way back to me?'

He looks around at me, stepping back from the hole he's dug, and looking at the river.

<*Down there?*>

'Yes.'

He scampers away, looks back, then begins to dig furiously, but too near the water, and claws up the thin strip of soil he's left beside the water.

'Watch out!' I say as the soft wet bank gives way filling in the hole he's just dug and drenching him.

My heart misses a beat. This wild water is an unknown quantity. Gasping, I rush to help him. A picture of a pale, floppy baby dragon being fished from the river fills my head, but as I near, he shoots upwards in a rosette of water straight onto the bank, and scales standing proud from his body, shakes water all over me.

'Oy! Stoppit!' I cry.

<I was all wet,> he tells me guiltily, steam rising.

'Damnit, Sprout! I am now!'

He looks abashed for a half-second, then grins, teeth flashing.

'Come on then, better see some more action! It'll dry you,' I say, wringing out my tunic. 'Dig some more, but not so deep, eh?'

Obediently he digs another hole further away from the last, which is now a tiny pool. And then another, and another. At length, there's a row of small, shallow holes stretching away from the water's edge, seeping water. Once connected, the field water will drain away easily.

'That's good,' I say. *'Come and have a rest before you finish it.'*

Sprout looks like a mud dragon and is getting very weary: his cleaner head scales are showing grey patches now. He flops into a patch of warm grass next to me, and we doze happily, replenishing our energies. Somewhere, half-dreaming, I suddenly feel as if I am being watched, a sense honed by the horrid Mabe, but when I look around, there is no one near to see.

Contemplating the canopy swaying high above, I wonder about the possibility of wings: can it be true? The hard little nubs are lengthening. Aware of them, I twist onto my side for comfort. A beetle crawls slowly up a blade of grass - up and up. Behind it, a hazy figure appears, standing at the far edge of the field, yet in a blink, it is gone. Must be imagination, I decide, and wonder lazily again that if I actually could, *where* would I fly? The wind above looks fast and scary, but the winds down here are …

{*You! Dragon girl!*}

It burns into my consciousness like acid, like a fire spitting toxic sparks. A smell of corruption floats by on the spring breeze. Then the voice is gone, the birds are singing, and a bother of bloons floats by, bobbing up and down. Did I imagine it? Was I dreaming? I'm hoping so.

'*Did you just hear something, Sprout?*' I ask, sitting up. He is agitated, flicking his tail around and rattling his spines.

<*What?*> he says, a tinge of orange panic in his thoughts. <*What was that? What's wrong?*>

No dream then.

'*I don't know,*' I say. But I do, and dread hovers me above like a black cloud, yet the day seems perfectly normal. Did we both imagine it? Now he is watching a flutterby corkscrewing its way from flower to flower. So, trying to relax, I lie back. The sky is a delicate blue between the vast foliage of the Great Tree and sunbeams spot the earth. A larger patch of brightness moves our way, and we bask in its brief heat. Drowsily, my eyelids flutter and close …

{*You! You! Dragon bitch! You will come. You must bring the dragon's brood to me!*}

My head bursts into searing pain as he pulls at me with mental talons of steel.

{*Come to me,*} he snarls, tugging harder. Abruptly, a tunnel, ringed with grey fire, appears in my mind, tempting me with its glimpse of a huge and shining place. Yet … somehow, I know that if I give in, there is no way back. I will be trapped. From somewhere, a glimmer of remembered knowledge comes - in the aether! I resist as hard as I can, writhing, clutching my head and throat tight, but he grips me harder, and I cannot move more.

{*Come,*} he says, {*come NOW!*}

I scream with every ounce of energy I have, '*Never!*' and fighting, gasping for breath, I try to twist free of him, but he is too strong. Sprout is trying to resist, but he must be too young and too weak. Charnecron, the terrible Necromancer, simply throws off our feeble attempts with despicable glee and horrid laughter. I feel Sprout being forced away from me, drawn in.

'*Don't go, Sprout,*' I say, hoping he can still hear me. '*Stay with me. Please?*'

Please?'

Oh, Tree! Is he alright? The sky, the dappled grasses and the bright river are almost gone under the shadow of Charnecron's colossal claws. A vile enveloping smell arises from the earth, a miasma of horrid decay and death. Somehow, he twists my bad leg, and my muscles scream in agony.

{*Slut! Listen well. Bring me the dragon, or I will send my hordes against you, against all your precious Trees, and all you paltry Mages! I will wreak havoc on your pitiful existence, and you will be gone, finished, as wood falls to ashes. You WILL come to me!*}

I hold my breath until, as fast as he came, he is gone.

Chapter Eight

Sprout is moaning softly, shaking and great-eyed with fright. Was this only a sending, a bespeaking? But we can be harmed as my tortured leg testifies, and he killed the Eldest, so I am glad we are somehow necessary to him. I crawl over to Sprout to share what comfort I can find, and we lie until it feels as if the land is emerging from his gross shadow.

'*Sprout? Did he hurt you? Can you hear me?*' I ask, wondering if the Necromancer has harmed the little dragon.

There is a pause in which my heartbeat rises until I can feel the pounding in my throat and ears. What if he is hurt? What if he can't speak? What if the Necromancer has gained some kind of control over him?

Relief floods through me when I hear him say, feebly, <*I'm alright, Jin. Tired …*>

Another voice breaks into my thoughts, '*Jinny? Jinny? Are you alright? Is it Sprout?*'

Quaryk is bespeaking me, his thoughts riddled with anxiety, with an odd pounding attached to his mental voice, an external thudding like a heartbeat.

'*We're alright,*' I say. '*But weak - and very scared.*'

'*Stay there. We're coming,*' he says.

We huddle together until the earth thunders and jolts under us. Four big farm horses slither from a full gallop to a halt.

Quaryk leaps down to stare at us, his jaw working with unspoken emotion. Quaryk's elder brother, Kettil, has arrived with young Deru and a farmhand I haven't met before. They dismount, concern written on their faces. I note they are all armed with useful-looking swords.

'Was it him?' Quaryk asks.

I can't speak. My hands are tight on my throat. I nod and bespeak him, *'Yes.'*

'He threatened you?' Quaryk asks aloud. 'I had no idea he was attacking until I tried to bespeak you.'

Coughing, I try to force my hands down.

'I'm afraid,' I croak, 'he tried to lure Sprout away … and he twisted my leg …'

My limb is still agonising.

'Root and twig,' he replies despairingly, then looks from Sprout to me. 'That could have been the end for us all!'

'It nearly was.'

I cough and splutter, trying to get his vile taste out of my mouth.

'How did he find you?'

I swallow to try to get the word out and shake my head.

'Dunno.'

'We must keep Sprout safe until he is grown,' Quaryk says. 'Once he's an adult, he'll be more than a match for the Dark. He'll be a fearsome creature, capable of much devastation … and our best hope!'

I nod.

'This is why your time with him is so important now. You see?'

I nod again. Quaryk has forgotten that Sprout is listening and may take umbrage at being called a 'he'.

<*I don't mind,*> Sprout says, <*you can call me a 'he' or 'she', it doesn't matter. I'm both. As long as you love me.*>

'Course I love you,' I say, wondering how long the little dragon has been listening to our thoughts. And what he's making of all this.

<*Your thoughts are pretty,*> he says. <*Patterns, all patterns, lacy and white.*>

We are interrupted by Quaryk, impatient for an answer.

'Do you understand me? Jinny? Jinny Morai?' he asks again, loudly as though I am stupid or deaf.

'I do,' I croak wearily. 'But I'm so tired - and what if he comes back?'

'We'll talk about that later. Come on, let's get them both home,' he says, turning to his brothers and the stranger.

'Please ask Sprout to let Kettil carry him home?' Quaryk says.

'Sprout? This tall man is Quaryk's brother. He will carry you back, and then we can rest together.'

<Alright,> Sprout says, <but please ask him not to squash me.>

I relay this to Kettil, who takes Sprout onto his saddle. After a squirm or two, he settles, and Quaryk lifts me up and onto the saddle of his tall horse, mounting behind me. It's high, and I wobble until his arm clasps me firmly to him.

And now, despite my pain, I secretly savour the feel of his encircling arm. Despite everything, I am acutely sensible of his masculine strength, his smell. His torso pressed against me is warm and hard, comforting and causing unexpected bodily urges.

'You all right?' he asks.

'I've never ridden before,' I say, flustered and flushing scarlet, glad he can't see my face.

'This isn't riding. I'll teach you to ride properly soon,' he answers. 'Now grip hard, or we'll both fall.'

I try to grip with everything I possess that works: if my eyelashes could grip, they would.

We bounce up and down, up and down. But, by the time we're back, my bum is sore, I feel sick, and everything has turned to rubber. Quaryk's horse is massive, so when he helps me slide down, my knees buckle, and I stagger and fall, bad leg on fire. Quaryk grabs and holds me, carrying me into the farmhouse where his ma takes over, plonking me by the kitchen fire with a hot drink. Sprout, who seems to have coped better, joins me. I wonder why my odd inner voice hasn't bothered me at all as the Mage performs a healing on my leg.

A little while later, I hear the family discussing us in the next room. Most of their voices are soft except Quaryk's father.

'What's wrong with the girl?' Hollis asks.

His voice can usually be heard two fields away, and he doesn't bother to speak quietly. I can just make out Milde's voice as she tries to shush him.

'Peace, husband; she'll hear you. No need to shout!' she says.

Quaryk replies at length, speaking in an undertone so I can't hear properly. There's a pause while they take in his words. Then Hollis says, 'Well! How dangerous is this, son? Should we be worried? I have the family and the farm to think about!'

There are more shushing noises from Lind, then Quaryk speaks again, explaining something, and Hollis grunts. Other voices join in as the whole family has its say before coming to a consensus. I understand their concern. They're fearful, and it is wrong to put them in danger, so I'll suggest we leave.

Later, when I try to tackle Quaryk quietly in the porch, he quickly disregards this idea.

'We've decided you'll both stay here with us,' he says. 'It is possible that I will be able to place a block in your mind with the combined help of the Order and the Tree, so the Necromancer cannot physically hurt you, even if he attacks again. I think it's unlikely he'll bother the rest of us - he seems to have some sort of link or connection to you that I can't fathom.'

I realise that his family have been party to our conversation when Milde appears with the others.

She nods, glancing from me to Quaryk. His father smiles reassuringly.

'It's true,' Milde says. 'You can stay with us for as long as you want to.'

'Charnecron is very strong now,' Quaryk goes on, 'but I didn't hear him at all today until he hurt you. No other Mage did, it seems. So, he's found a way to get to you alone. You must tell me if he tries again - yes? It's very important. Was it very bad?'

'Yes,' I say. 'If I could I'd find a dark hole and never leave it. It is the worst thing that has ever happened to me. Sprout was terrified.'

How does the Necromancer find me, I wonder? Yet a lovely thing has resulted from his attack. Because I am a stray with no real home, with nothing but memories and an evil attacker, I'm incredibly thrilled that this kind family has taken me in twice. I don't know how to thank them yet, but I swear I'll find a way one day.

~*~

With my head between his hands, the Mage-light's green glow makes Milde's familiar garden eerie. With the help of the Order, Quaryk is trying to protect me from Charnecron, the Necromancer, or as some say, the Dark Mage, and, through me, Sprout. He shifts position minutely on the bench, shutting his eyes. Still handsome but unfamiliar, looking like a hearth when the fire has gone out.

Sprout watches as Quaryk's mouth moves soundlessly, and a force mounts in my head. It feels exactly as though he's building a wall in there, adding stone on stone, with a strange, inner clunking sound. The noise and glow increase until I wonder what he's doing and how much longer it will take. Just as I absolutely must scratch an itch, he stops, withdrawing his hands. After staying silent for a while, he shakes himself and, leaning back, takes a deep breath as if satisfied.

'Now,' he says, 'the Order, and the Trees, combining their magic, have allowed me to stop Charnecron from assaulting you physically, as he did the Eldest. When I have caught my breath, I'll show you how to cast Wards of Protection and perform a Cycle of Exclusion yourself to help you manage any more of his attacks.'

'Will it stop them?'

Shaking his head, he says, 'He's found his way in now, Jinny, and he'll certainly try it again, so you must be prepared.'

My heart sinks to my boots. He will be able to frighten us even if he doesn't actually harm us.

'The charms will help you,' he says, 'and let you exclude him from you for a time, or at least weaken the effects.'

Following his hands and voice, I concentrate, learning the words until I can recite them back to him perfectly. He teaches me the hidden keys to unlock their power, which I memorise.

'There,' he says, satisfied. 'You have Mind-blocks and Wards to use now. I hope they'll help. But I still can't understand how he finds you.'

'*Sprout? Can you still hear me?*' I bespeak quickly, ignoring Quaryk for the moment - I don't ever want to lose touch with my dragon.

<*I'm here. Calm down,*> he adds, sounding exactly like Ma did when I got upset. I have to chuckle even as a rogue tear trickles down my cheek. Quaryk sits back, perplexed, as Sprout sends me a warm red wave of

comfort.

'What's wrong, Jinny?' Quaryk asks, flummoxed.

'Sorry,' I say, not wanting to explain. 'Too complicated. Thank you, Quaryk and all the other Mages of the Order. That's marvellous.'

'He may try to get to you by other means, so you must stay vigilant,' he continues, brows still knit. 'He may try to enter your dreams or send something stranger or even send someone to watch you and Sprout. He's clever and wily. So always watch your back and be doubly wary of strangers.'

And watch front, sides, above and below, I think. Sprout agrees with a wry, bluish roil.

'Well, we'll both try to be very careful,' I say. 'Thank you.'

'Now,' he says, 'how about doing something to cheer us all up?'

~*~

The stables are housed in a long low building. The air rings with birdsong and the grunts of bloons, smelling cleanly of hay with a deep, sweet note of manure. Sprout wants to stay outside to nose around the yard and chat to the hens. The inside is dark, but my eyes adjust in seconds.

'Come and meet Myrtle,' Quaryk says. I follow him into a loosebox where a small white horse looks around at us. Myrtle is nothing like the giant he rode to help me: she is, as horses go, pretty, even delicate. Surely too small for two to ride.

'Come and stroke her,' he says.

I put out a hand to touch Myrtle's coat, which feels smooth and warm and smells good. She gazes at me with great liquid eyes rather like Sprout's and butts me with her soft nose for attention. A gentle creature.

'Hello there? You have a kind eye, good girl ...' I say as she nuzzles me.

'See, you're a natural,' Quark says. 'She likes you! Now this is her saddle.'

He lifts a heavy leather object from a peg on the wall and places it carefully on her back. *Does a horse have to like you if you want to ride it*, I wonder?

Untangling an attached wide ribbon-like affair, he says, 'This is the girth. It goes under her belly like this … and we tighten it here. See? Stops the saddle slipping.'

Myrtle stands still while this is accomplished, and then Quaryk takes something which looks like a mere tangle of leather loops from another peg.

'Now the bridle. This is how you control her - see? It slips on like … this.'

'Doesn't it hurt?' I ask. 'All this weight and straps?'

'No, she is happy to wear it,' he says. When he is done, Myrtle is saddled and bridled, and it has only taken a few minutes. 'Now take the reins - those long straps - and lead her outside. We'll go into the big meadow. That's it, she'll follow you.' He clucks at the horse, and she walks on.

Outside he shows me how to mount and hold the reins. Expecting him to mount behind me, I'm disappointed. Apparently, I have to do this alone. A shame: I was eager to feel him sitting behind me, to feel his body pressing against me.

Sprout decides to keep well out of the way.

<*In case,*> he tells me, <*the creature panics when I get near.*>

He doesn't know much about other animals yet. The hens have long gone, annoyed, and clucking noisily. Now he is chasing bloons, batting undersized wings, like a trainee flutterby.

While Myrtle stands quietly, I scramble up her side. Once in the saddle, I pat her neck.

'*Thank you,*' I think, in case she can hear me. '*Sprout is keeping his distance - don't mind him.*'

I nearly slip off in surprise as she says, *(He's alright, just a colt!)* She turns her head to fix me with a gentle eye. *(Now sit up and balance yourself properly.)*

Gathering my scattered wits, I do exactly as I'm told. '*Is this alright?*' I ask.

(Sit up a bit more,) she says, and I straighten, noting that Quaryk doesn't seem to have noticed our conversation.

I feel precarious, but at last, Myrtle says, *(There, that's right. Stay there and grip as hard as you can with your legs.)*

Unfortunately, gripping anything with my dodgy leg is never a strong point, but I do my best.

'Well,' Quaryk says, 'you look very good. Give her a prod with your heels.'

(Don't even think about it,) she cautions, so I pretend. *(He's a good sort,)* she continues, *(but he can't hear us. Now hang on.)*

Myrtle moves into a gentle walk, and Quaryk nods enthusiastically.

'That's good,' he says. 'Very good. She likes you! Now grip a bit tighter and urge her into a trot.'

We trot and then canter, with Myrtle giving me tips along the way. At some point, I stop feeling like a sack of stones and enjoy moving with her.

'*Do we need this saddle and stuff?*' I ask her.

(No, but best keep them on for appearance's sake,) she says. *(It would only upset him if you ride me without them.)*

I agree, but I am determined never to use these things again, whatever Quaryk says. When we finish, I thank her. But on dismounting, both my legs turn to jelly. Myrtle sniggers as I teeter, but Quaryk catches me with the ease of an athlete.

'Sorry,' I say, 'I'm a bit …' and hang onto him like a leech, trying not to grin.

'Wobbly? It's lack of muscle, but it'll come.' He smiles, but his expression alters as he lays a hand flat against my shoulders.

'Jinny, what's this on your back? Is this what you showed my mother? Show me!' he demands. His look brooks no argument, but I have to try.

'It's not seemly … and your ma said …' I begin, looking round for handy onlookers, but there is no one in sight. Turning me easily, he pulls up my tunic, and I hurriedly cross my arms over my chest, trying to keep decent.

'She didn't tell me. And I *am* a healer, girl,' he says, ignoring my blushes. 'I see bodies every day. Yours is no different.'

Even so, I am embarrassed and now worried: these nubs are growing long and changing shape. Are they, as Sprout says, wings, or are they some kind of disease or growth? Long seconds pass. Then he pulls my tunic down and turns me to face him. Incredibly his face is lit with an unexpected delight.

'I would never have guessed!' he says. 'Not in a thousand years!'

He stops to think, doubling a stirrup leather in his hands while I imagine all sorts of terrible things.

Myrtle is ignoring us now, happily cropping grass. Quaryk looks me straight in the eye.

'Do you know what they are?' he asks.

I hesitate. Swallow. 'No, not really, but Sprout thinks they might be - wings?' I say, looking at my toes, blushing even hotter now. Such a ludicrous suggestion.

'So you already know?'

'No! Er, yes? Really? Do you think so?'

'When were you going to tell me?' he asks, frowning again, and then his eyes widen. 'Hey! How long have you been able to bespeak Sprout? What else haven't you told me? Come on. This could be life or death one day, girl!'

Grabbing me by the shoulders he scowls and shakes me until I blurt, 'We've always been able to talk together, and I can hear Myrtle too. And sometimes you and the other Mages. And … there's another voice I hear, but that mostly comes at night.'

He lets me loose, his face surprised, flabbergasted, and irritated until a great grin splits his face, and he looks boyish again.

'This is wonderful,' he says, and lifting me, whirls me around. Drunk with his excitement, I laugh as he says, 'We'll go and visit your first home one day, but not straight away. There's so much for you both to learn.'

I am dizzy and astonished, not in trouble, and I really like him holding me. But what does he mean by 'first home'? Is that Three Gems?

'What d'you mean? And what about Sprout?'

'You really don't know?' he asks with an eyebrow raised and deposits me on the grass. 'Here, sit down and I'll tell you.'

He plonks me onto the mounting block and sits beside me. As birds congregate noisily on the thick thatch of the farmhouse roof, he looks up at the Tree and sky and begins.

'Those are wings, Jinny, wings! Sprout was right! Once they're properly grown, you will be able to fly like the birds up there so we'll need to get you some fruit. You are one of the Sky-folk so the Canopy was your first home. You must have been born there. None but Sky folk grow wings on Leaf.' He pauses, looking me up and down like an interesting new specimen. 'I should have known with your colouring and height. And if you can hear Sprout and Myrtle and all of us Mages, you are the first person I've ever heard of to have such a rare ability. It's amazing.'

He stops to think again, and I gaze outwards, brain numbed by this discovery. The wider lands beyond are dappled by the canopy far above, swaying darkly in different winds. A mystery moves above and now within me too. *Now,* I wonder, *why, if I was born up there, did I grow up as a foundling in the black bowels of the Holtanbore? And what has fruit got to do with anything?* I suddenly have a pressing need to know exactly who I am and what happened to me, and I make myself a promise - one day, I *will* find out.

Later, Milde takes me to one side and suggests she and Lind make new clothes for me to accommodate my emerging wings. And again, she gives me a salve to relieve the burning and itching. I'm grateful for both. My clothes are becoming tight and uncomfortable.

Lind is a real friend these days, although she says she wishes for wings like mine. I'd give them to her if I could. Both she and her mother are expert needlewomen and spend a deal of time sewing seams by the big kitchen window or in lamplight. I can't ever remember having any new clothes apart from the ones Karel gave to me, and they were well-used. The new garments they make are beautiful, made from some of the fine materials Milde has in store. One set, in sensible browns and greens, is for every day, with two of everything, but there is a red gown with a full skirt for special occasions. I am even given a pair of sturdy boots and red slippers to match the dress.

At first, I offer to help, but as I know nothing of sewing, I'm only allowed to fetch and carry while the experts are working. The backs of the garments are tricky because of my growing wings, but Milde cleverly adapts them to fit around my wing roots with buttons, and they are easy-ish to put on. When they are finished, they are the finest things I have ever seen, let alone owned, and I am more grateful than I can say.

And, in the fields, in a pair of borrowed breeches, Myrtle is a good teacher, helping me to understand how to ride well without hurting her. We trot, canter, gallop and jump without tack until it all becomes second nature. Now I understand why Quaryk wanted me to learn: my leg always slows me down, and riding is fun and far easier than walking everywhere. Outside is so very big.

Chapter Nine

'*Jinny?*' Quaryk calls.

Sprout and I are in the home meadow, playing silly games, rolling amid the scented grasses. I sit up and listen, sighing. He'll want to teach me something or other, I suppose, and I'm bored with learning all the time. Yet Quaryk is still my senior Mage, and I must do what I'm told.

'*Come on, Sproutie,*' I say, '*we have to go.*'

<*You go,*> Sprout says. <*I'll stay here and snooze.*>

I shrug, thinking he may as well, and amble slowly back to the farmhouse, where Quaryk is talking with his father by the gate. When he sees me, he finishes their conversation and strides over.

'Come along,' he says, 'we must continue your education.'

'What?' I say, hanging back uneasily as my suspicion is proved true. More education? He doesn't reply, so I stagger as fast as I can after him to catch up. Sprout is snoring noisily as we pass by.

Along the water meadow, we move in and out of stray patches of hot sunlight, unfiltered by the dark leaves far above. In the far corner of a bigger field, by two fine big oaks, he stops.

'This was my favourite playground when I was a boy. I tried to climb all three trees here but only managed to climb that one.'

He glances at the great fallen bole that ends in a spreading mass of spreadeagled roots like a many-legged crawly.

'That fell last winter,' he goes on, 'and I was very sorry. Now, this is your task: set it upright for me one last time.'

'Upright? Me?' I gasp, expecting him to have grown an invisible second head. 'I can't possibly do that!'

'I think you can,' he says, giving me a strange look. 'In fact, I know you can - or you will be able to, perhaps not today, but soon. Until then, I'm going to teach you how to make fire.'

I look away, embarrassed for him, scratching an ear. Surely making fires is easy?

'That's silly - I know how to do that,' I say. 'You just get kindling and the right sort of stones …'

'Not that way,' he says and bespeaks me.

'Watch what I do …'

Incredibly, he is inviting me to peer into his mind. It's very different from mine, straight-edged and masculine, somehow, with oddly ordered thoughts that dance like captive flames across his consciousness. Yet, in some ways, we are quite similar. Flicking his eyes closed to concentrate, he contacts the Great Tree, politely asking permission to use some of its magic. When this is granted, he forms new shapes in his mind. Then, opening his eyes, he takes a fallen stick and holds it at arm's length. The Tree sends him odd thought patterns with which he forms new ones. Abruptly the end of the dead stick bursts into green flames, which turn quickly to an ordinary yellow. I jerk back, then snigger inwardly at myself. What a coward!

'Did you follow what I did?' he asks, blowing out the flame.

'I did,' I reply, *'but doesn't the Tree mind us burning a piece of its relative? And will the Tree know me?'*

This is not the familiar Tree root behind my bed in the labyrinth. Quaryk laughs.

'You are of the Sky-folk and Mage-born! You are a part of the Tree, and you can ask it anything while you are within the Glebe. It will never ignore you. Now, give it a try.'

So, that was why the Tree spoke to me back in the labyrinth? I thought it spoke to everyone! Glancing around, I find a fallen branch and holding it at arm's length, as though it might explode, I try to make the same shapes.

'Talk to the Tree first!' he says, frowning.

Stupid, I think, and blushing, I ask the Great Tree for permission to use its magic, and it sends a wave of soft green warmth into me. To me!

Now, jubilantly, I feel a real part of the vast company that is the Trees of Leaf.

'*Welcome again, daughter,*' it says, sending me the mind shapes, and after a moment of dithering, I make my stick blossom into beautiful green flames! My first real magic! I watch the flames turn yellow proudly. Who would have thought that a scruff from the lowest levels could achieve anything so fine? Choking with emotion, I suddenly wish Ma and Pa could see me brandishing this unnatural conflagration aloft until it flickers and dies. Then, just as suddenly, I'm deflated.

'*You might need to make fire fast one day,*' Quaryk says, '*so get used to bespeaking the Tree and making the right shapes. Practice until you can do it instantly.*'

Turning away, I pull a disgusted face. He sounds exactly like Ma did when I was feeling lazy. It seems that I had no choice, then or now. I sigh, but again asking the Tree for help, I ignite the stick. This time, the flame lasts longer, but just as I begin to feel clever and smug, Quaryk bespeaks me again.

'*Always remember that this magic we use isn't ours - we are only allowed to borrow it for a while. Once used, it will flow back through the aether to disperse throughout Leaf. Know, and remember, the Trees can withdraw their magic, but they are kindly and will not refuse you unless something is very wrong. Now, you must concentrate. Practice makes perfect! You are Mage-born, so you* can *do this. Come on - again!*'

As he stretches comfortably against a trunk, the fire in my stick gutters and goes out. *I could have kept it going if he hadn't interrupted*, I think, grimacing in exasperation.

'Keep going,' he says aloud. 'I'll tell you when to stop. Use your hands if it helps.'

'Are you sure this is really necessary? I can't imagine having to do this often,' I say, tossing the charred stick away.

Quaryk stares into the oak leaves above with a gusty sigh for my stupidity.

'This is the first part of your education in which the Three asked me to instruct you. So firstly, you will conquer the easy spells, and then, when you have mastered these, you will learn more difficult conjurations.' At last, an explanation of sorts. Now I am intrigued, but I still need answers to a host of questions and begin with, 'Won't the Tree mind if I keep on pestering it?'

'The Tree has been informed that you are learning the higher arts now,' he says, staring into the distance. 'I will make sure you know everything suitable for a novice to know, so don't ask anything more.'

Sometimes I swear he can tune into my thoughts without me noticing. Since it doesn't look as though I'm going to get out of this, I sigh again and retrieve my poor abused stick. With an extravagant gesture, I make smoke, sparks and fire over and over again until the whole thing seems to come naturally.

Grinning, he watches my antics until, at last, he is satisfied and nods, saying, 'Well done, but you must understand that you will need to repeat exactly the same gesture each time you want to make fire.'

So, the unsuspected downside is that the extravagant sweeping motion I am using is now the only one which will work whenever I want to make fire. I decide my gestures for future spells will be modest; barely noticeable.

Over the next weeks, he leads me through all the other elemental spells, and then we go on to more complicated enchantments, and I realise he has a point: one day, I may actually be capable of shifting that oak tree. But there is another side to learning these elemental charms: he must allow me access to his mind, and I am beginning to understand his inner world. By the time the simple enchantments are completed, a month or three have sped by. I am bound to Quaryk by invisible threads, knowing him intimately. Physically, we are still as distant as the moons.

~*~

Sprout is becoming insatiable because he is growing so fast. On a cool, windless morning of crunching leaves underfoot, we three saunter back to Quaryk's favourite spot in the meadow. I notice Quaryk giving Sprout a long hard look as the dragon rolls in the shrivelled autumn grasses.

'What is it?' I ask, a crease growing between my eyes. 'What's wrong?'

'Nothing at all that I can see,' he says. 'He's good and solid, with perfect scales. You've noticed how much he's grown in the last few weeks? Just look at those wings!'

'No, I haven't really …'

Sprout is a half again longer than the biggest horse I've ever seen, but his folded wings appear unchanged. *Have I missed something?*

'*Sprout? Please extend your wings,*' I ask. When he obliges, I see with a start that they have grown to double his length.

'When they are half as big again, he will be able to carry you aloft, although he'll have to train those flight muscles first.'

'What? *Carry* me?' I say. 'Why would he do that?'

'It seems that dragons often carried riders in the old days. I bespoke a very learned Mage in one of the other Trees who is interested in the history of the old race of dragons,' Quaryk says as he walks around a puzzled Sprout admiringly. 'He is certain dragons were used to carry people sometimes, mostly into battles, although there were few instances recorded. Can you imagine a dragon coming at you flaming and carrying an armed warrior?' He pauses to see what effect his words have on us both. 'You see? This is why Sprout is so important to the Necromancer.'

Quaryk's tone is dire, and the name seems to blot out the sun for a second, but now I can't help giggling as we watch the rare and important Sprout rolling happily in mud and leaves, enjoying himself immensely. He's been watching the farm dogs doing it. Flipping upright, he considers the great pile of dead branches left by the fallen oak, concentrates for a moment, and opens his mouth wide. With a series of thumps, bulges appear in his belly, then a searingly hot blue flame erupts and the whole heap is reduced in seconds to crackling ash. We rush about stamping on the burning grass around it in case the whole field ignites. I finally understand how much damage he can do, half-grown as he is. One big dragon alone could decimate a village, even an entire landscape. An army of dragons would be a terrible foe.

'You see?' Quaryk says.

I nod, rubbing my jaw as my heart thumps loudly.

'*So. You have to be more than a mere Mage,*' he says bespeaking me again. '*You have to manage him too. That is why we concentrate on your training now. With an army of dragons, the Necromancer could decimate the whole world.*'

I shiver, massaging my neck. What vast power lies in my ignorant hands! And if I get it all wrong, what then? It doesn't bear thinking about

- so I won't, or I will end up as a quivering lump.

A day or so later, after a long session practising magic in the meadow, we watch Sprout gambolling around us, charging past so close that he nudges me in passing.

My bad leg folds abruptly, and I sit down hard with a cry. Sprout stops, looks around, then comes to me at once, emoting concern and remorse.

<*Jinny! Are you alright? I'm sorry.*>

'*I'm alright,*' I say sharply. '*Just shaken up.*'

'Sorry, I slipped,' I tell Quaryk, brushing myself down, but to my dragon, I say. '*Be careful.*'

Quaryk eyes me, eyebrow cocked but says nothing as Sprout bounces away, tail and wings extended to frighten a bother of bloons into a whirling cloud around his head. They're beautiful - and very insubstantial.

'*Stop that!*' I bespeak him sharply.

<*Don't see why,*> he grunts and carries on.

I run to stop in front of him, and his claws dig up the turf as he tries not to squash me.

'*Stop! Haven't you noticed that some of those poor bloons are deflating - losing their gas?*' I say. '*If they can't fly, they can't move or feed, and they'll die.*'

He glances from them to me.

<*Really? They would die?*> he asks. Then he tries to blow them upwards, managing to make things worse.

'Leave them alone, Sprout,' I say. 'They'll recover, but it's cruel to play stupid jokes like that. What if you had torn an air-sac? Bloons die straight away if that happens.'

<*Oh, I didn't know,*> he says, deep violet guilt suffusing his thoughts. <*Sorry, bloons!*>

'*Alright. But you should think about other creatures before you play with them. You are so much bigger than they are and so much stronger now.*'

Sprout drops his head, scales paling in embarrassment.

<*But I have no one else to play with,*> he whimpers.

He's right, he doesn't, and I'm sorry about that too. But there it is. There is only one of him.

'*Play with me,*' I tell him. '*Only don't be so rough!*'

<*Why not?*> he asks, round-eyed.

'*You are big enough to hurt me now, like the bloons.*'

He thinks about it.

'*I wouldn't ever hurt you, Jinny.*'

With that, he comes up close and rubs my cheek with his scaly one, almost taking my skin off. I give him a hug as he wraps his tail around me and drapes a wing over me. I'm startled to see a steaming tear rolling down his mailed, rainbow cheek: I didn't know dragons could cry.

'*Don't,*' I tell him, but an instant later, his lovely liquid eyes glint with mischief.

<*Not sad! Wanna play!*> he says, and with a toothy grin, he bounces off across the field, almost tearing my hair out at the roots as it snags on a clawed wingtip.

'Ow!'

<*Sorry!*>

Quaryk laughs as I try to sort the tangle out. I give him a dirty look.

'He doesn't know his own strength,' he says, ignoring me.

'You're right! What he really needs is a playmate to get rid of all his energy. Then maybe he'd listen,' I say sourly. 'But for the life of me, I can't think of anything.'

Quaryk considers for a moment. 'I just might,' he says and beckons to me to follow. We leave Sprout happily rolling in a mud patch.

A few fields away, a dozen or so heavy horses are quietly cropping the grass apart from one skewbald who is thinner and younger than the rest. Even so, he is huge. As we watch, he shoulders one of the others aside and trots off, tail held high like a banner. Then he wheels and trots back to take a toothy swipe at a big male's rump. The stallion rounds on him and, whinnying furiously, kicks out, chasing him off. The youngster runs off to the far side, bucking and twisting until he tires. Then he stands alone sadly, looking exactly like Sprout, baby brain in turmoil.

'What do you think?' Quaryk asks. 'He looks as though he needs someone to play with too.'

'I think you could be right. It's a good idea.'

If Sprout and this horse could get on, it would allow me some free time and hopefully get rid of some of his incredible energy.

'We'll go see Galden,' Quaryk goes on. 'You haven't really met him properly, have you? He's in charge of the stables. See what he thinks, right?'

'Alright,' I say, and we head back to the farm, leaving Sprout to enjoy the mud.

'*Mind you wash afterwards,*' I tell him. '*No one will be pleased if you come home dripping and filthy*'.

Sprout sends me a picture of him grinning, splashing water, and is gone.

Chapter Ten

The farm stables are long, low, and made of the same rough brick and thick thatch as the farmhouse. Bloons and birds perch on the thatched ridge and gables, which are sewn into patterns with a salamander at one end and a weather bloon at the other. Everywhere, a pervading cocktail of odours rises; horse-sweat and dung, leather and hay. And it's quiet. The only sounds are chirrups from above and the slight movements of the horses resting within.

Quaryk stops before we enter.

'Let's find Galden. He's the head groom. He's one of my oldest friends,' he explains, 'and he knows all there is to know about horses.'

Except what they're thinking, I note smugly.

The horses are musing sleepily on grass, clear water and rest. In the stable, a few are listlessly pulling at their hay, standing hipshot, or lying comfortably in their straw, dreaming of galloping free. I follow him along a sweet-smelling passage with half doors opening off it. Saddles hang on the outer wall, interspersed with buckets, bales of hay and various bits of tack. At the far end, a brown man, who looks remarkably like an older version of Quaryk, sits at ease on a stool rubbing at some sort of harness. This is the unknown person when Sprout and I were attacked by the Necromancer - the fourth man I've never spoken to.

'Hey there, Galden,' Quaryk says with a warm smile. The man looks up, mirroring Quaryk's expression. Then he sees me, and his face closes.

'Good day, young Orm,' he answers politely, still eyeing me. 'What can I do for you and young miss here?'

'Galden, this is Jinny Morai, who is staying here. You helped me to find her.'

Galden nods and waits for him to speak. A man of few words.

'Would you mind if we take the heavy colt from the rest of the herd for a while? You probably know Jinny has a young dragon here - you must have seen him?'

'Aye, of course,' he answers dryly and a tad disapprovingly. 'Odd beast is that.'

'Well, this dragon is only a few weeks out of the egg. He's growing fast and …'

'And he's very lonely and could use a playmate,' I butt in with a smile to soften my rudeness.

Both Quaryk and Galden look at me severely as though I shouldn't have spoken, but then comes a flicker of interest from the groom.

'A playmate? What's to stop your dragon from hurting my colt then?' he asks.

'Me. I can stop him,' I say, 'and it would be good for them both to have a friend - if they get on, of course.'

Galden looks down at his cleaning, pauses, and glances up at me.

'Well, I suppose we could see how *they* feel about it,' he says, putting the harness aside. We follow him through to a room filled with more harnesses, rugs and odd bits of leather, polish and rags. Taking a rough rope halter down from a peg, he waves us through another door and strides away to a nearby field. Quaryk follows with me.

All the heavy draft horses are resting in the autumn warmth except the colt, who appears to be trying to push his way through a hedge and squealing loudly.

'What in Leaf is he doing?' I say in surprise.

'You may well ask,' Galden says with a grimace. 'Trying to get out, I shouldn't wonder. And he's a right bugger to catch.'

'Can I try?' I ask.

Galden looks at me quizzically, then sniffs. 'Suppose so,' he says, handing me the halter. 'You'll want to try to corner him if you can but be careful, he bites. He grins but ignoring this, I walk towards the young animal. His mind is a turmoil of innocent longing.

'*Hello,*' I say, bespeaking him. '*You want to see? Find out what else is out* there? If you let me, I'll lead you out. I have a friend who would really like to play with you.'

The huge colt stops what he's doing and looks around at me.

(A friend?) he asks. (Someone to run with?)

'Yes, but you mustn't be scared. He's different from you, but he's lonely and wants to play. Will you come with me?'

(Will I have to wear that thing? It rubs and hurts.)

'Only for a little while,' I say.

He takes a second or two to think about it, then walks calmly over to me.

'You're a size!' I tell him, looking up. 'Wow! You won't hurt my friend, will you? You're much taller than he is, and your hooves can hurt.'

The colt towers over me, beautiful and huge, his feet like steel drums.

(Hooves? What are hooves?)

'Your feet. Now, bend your neck so I can reach your head.'

He bends his head down low enough for me to put the halter on and leaving it as loose as possible, I say, 'Come on then. Hey, what's your name?'

(What is a name?) he asks as we saunter towards the gate. Galden is wearing an expression of absolute disbelief. Quaryk rushes to open the gate for us.

'A name is something we can call you when we want you. I am Jinny. What would you like to be called?'

He stops while he digests this.

(What is that little flitting thing called?) he asks. (It hops and flutters and goes round and round.)

'That's a flutterby,' I say. 'Why?'

(I want to be called that. That name.)

I have to try not to laugh. A colt this size wants to be called after a small insect? Incongruous!

'Come on then,' I tell the newly christened Flutterby. 'Let's go find your new friend.'

He leaps through the gate so that I have to scramble and hop.

(Where is he?) the colt asks, whinnying. (Show me!)

I dangle from the halter rope as he is carrying his head so high, and he trots faster, almost breaking into a canter.

(*Stop! Too fast! Slow down! I have a bad leg. Can't keep up!*)

Flutterby slides to a stop, his big feet ploughing up turf, and turns his head to peer at my legs. I stumble.

'*Sorry,*' he says. '*You go first.*'

Walking as quickly as I can manage, with Quaryk and Galden following, we go on. Two fields later, we enter the water meadow to the sound of splashing and roaring in the distance.

'*Here, bend down so I can take this off,*' I say. He dips his head.

'*My friend's down by the river. Off you go and remember to be careful!*'

The colt throws his head up and, with mane and tail flying, gallops off.

I turn to the men following me. 'I think they'll be alright,' I say, then quickly bespeak Sprout. '*There's a friend coming to play with you. Please don't burn or claw him. He's lonely too!*'

We walk quickly to a slight rise where we can see both young animals. When they see each other, they stop dead.

Then Sprout says, <*Hey! Come play with me?*>

Flutterby prances, his tail banner high, towards Sprout, where he is churning the mud up by the riverbank.

(*Coming!*) he says, then approaches more cautiously until they touch noses.

<*Can't catch me!*> Sprout bellows with a ferocious growl, leaps out of the mud, and hares off up the field. Flutterby wheels and gives chase, bucking and squealing.

Quaryk catches my eye.

<Looks like it's a hit,> he says aloud, and then, silently, <*Just how did you do that?*>

'Easy! Tell you later,' I reply as Galden, scratching his head, says, 'Well, never seen nothing like that before! You've hidden depths, lass!'

I hide a smile as Quaryk mutters, 'Oh, she certainly has. Anyway, those two seem to be getting along! Are you happy to let them play together now?'

'Can't see why not,' Galden says, 'long as he goes back into the field with his ma come night.'

As the two men turn to go, I say, 'His name is Flutterby, and he would be much happier with a leather halter.' They look at me in astonishment.

'That's a bugger of a name for a bloody great 'oss,' Galden says, 'begging your pardon, Mistress, Ormandel.'

As the men turn and stride away, hands clasped behind their backs, the two youngsters play at full volume. I stay to watch, grinning at their pleasure. Later, when the two playmates are settled for the night and we are taking the night air on the bench outside the kitchen door, I tell Quaryk how I caught Flutterby. He glares at me at first, then scratches his head and laughs.

'You can hear all the horses?' he asks. 'And what about other animals? Grif here, for instance?'

He strokes the big friendly farm dog sitting beside him. Grif is a whizz at rounding up the livestock.

'I can,' I say, 'but I can tell you why he's so good with the hens and the sheep. He's very polite to them, aren't you Grif?'

'*I am,*' Grif replies. '*A few manners get results. Tell him to keep that up, please? I like it.*'

Quaryk has stopped stroking Grif's head.

'He says, please will you keep stroking him? He likes it very much.'

Quaryk frowns but immediately reaches down to touch the dog again, who leans in happily.

'So, what else do you hear? All animals? Birds? All people?'

'I haven't really thought about it,' I say. 'I can bespeak you and some of the other Mages, but not everyone, I think. I can hear most of the animals I've met, but not the birds or bloons and smaller things - no, that's wrong. I can hear them, but I can't get them to hear me, and not the Tree unless I ask first. I don't know why.'

'I think you may be unique, Jinny,' he comments, eyes shining. 'Mages can bespeak each other, but no other folk, and definitely not animals. What an incredible gift you have! And, if I remember right, you said you hear a voice - when's that? Only at night?'

I hesitate for a moment as this is intensely private, but it seems I can divulge my unwanted visitor to him.

'Yes, usually, but sometimes in the daytime when it's quiet and there is time to think. It seems to come from a long, long way away, and it's someone who pleads for me to do something, but I've never found out what or why.'

I shake my head. It's unquestionably a feminine voice. Although I may never find out who she is, I wish I could help her.

'The only other voice I've ever heard like that has been … *him*,' I mutter. I can't bring myself to say the name aloud.

Quaryk frowns and rubs his beard, perhaps reliving the death of the Eldest. He shakes his head.

'Well, all may become clear soon enough. It's getting cold. Let's go in.'

Chapter Eleven

Grieving, I pant, weep, scream at once! A familiar voice is wailing: Sprout, on waking, has joined in. Outside, the farm dogs are howling. In the midst of this cacophony, the visiting voice in my head is weak and hoarse, as though it too has been screaming for hours, pleading and begging. For a moment, I don't know who, what, or if I am, then I feel cold air around me and I am back. In the black of night, that strange phenomenon, rain, is pounding on the thatch and windows. Groping my feet to the floor, I scrabble around to find my candle, but dazed and disorientated, I knock it over, and it rolls away.

A moment later, hearing an inhaled breath, muttering and scrabbling, my neck hair rises. There is a silent explosion of light. The flame flickers then steadies, to reveal Quaryk, tousled and anxious. His parents gape at the door, roused from sleep, questions in their eyes. The rest of the family peer in from the landing behind them.

Now Sprout barrels in, his mind in utter turmoil, ready to flame. I remember the barn where he sleeps is used to store hay. He needs to calm down.

'Sprout! It's alright!'

'What's wrong?' Quaryk asks.

He glances around as his father asks,

'Is she ill?' scratching his beard irritably, and Quaryk mirrors the gesture.

'What is it?' he asks again, as from outside we hear Sprout growling deep in his throat, a horrible wrenching sound.

'It's alright,' I tell him. *'Quaryk is trying to help. Try to stay calm - please?'*

Sprout grunts, and I feel him settling himself on the far side of his bed, glaring into the darkness.

<*I'll try,*> he says.

'It was just a nightmare,' I say to everyone. 'But it keeps coming back. It was horrible!'

'Must have been some dream!' someone says with a snigger from the landing.

Quaryk looks daggers at his younger brother Deru, who retreats.

'Here, you're shaking. Get back into bed,' Quaryk says, and then gets up to bring my shawl from the pile of clothes on the stool. He wraps it around my shoulders, glancing back.

'Only a nightmare,' he tells the rest of his yawning family, 'you all may as well go back to bed.'

Lind looks at Milde, who shakes her head, and with a fleeting smile for me, leaves.

Milde stays until the rest of the family have gone.

'I'll make you some hot tea,' she says, nodding to Quaryk. 'It'll calm you.'

He smiles at her retreating back.

'She's a good mother,' he says quietly, 'we're lucky.'

You don't know how lucky, I think.

'*Now, tell me everything,*' he bespeaks me. '*Was this the Necromancer again?*'

At his words, the whole horrible episode comes back, and racking sobs shake me again. Quaryk finds a handkerchief, offers it.

'Have a blow and try to stop. You won't get past this while you're weeping.'

It takes me a while. Before my last sniff, his ma returns with a steaming mug and a plate of biscuits.

'Drink and eat, lass, and then try to get some more sleep,' she says, stroking my hair the way Ma used to stroke it. She is so kind I well up again and choke back more tears.

'Thanks, Ma,' Quaryk says. Once she has left, he turns to me.

'*Now. What happened? Tell me everything.*'

He settles himself on a stool close to the bed, an arm around my shoulders. And for a moment, all I can think of is how warm and comforting this is. Without volition, I lean in. Then, realising what I'm doing, I pull away, reddening. There is a sudden bang on the window.

<*I'm here. Let me in,*> Sprout says. Early winter rain is lashing down.

Quaryk gets up, opening the window wide before Sprout smashes it. Sprout snakes a wet and steaming head through so I can stroke his nose. Quaryk replaces his arm around me, and I bespeak them both.

'It was the Necromancer, wasn't it Sprout? I must have been dreaming, then he was there - a sort of tall black figure with stubs on his back almost like mine, but bigger. He stood over me as I lay there, gloating, but I don't know why. Then he spoke …'

A shudder runs up my spine as I remember his insinuating, depraved voice. Quaryk's arm tightens as if to physically shield me from my thoughts. But I need to go on - I must unload it all.

'As soon as he opened his mouth, I was terrified. He invaded me and there was no escape except madness. But I don't want to ever …!'

<*I won't let that happen,*> Sprout says, his mind wrapping me softly like a blanket.

'Didn't you feel it?' I say, wondering why he's not shaking with terror like me. *'Didn't he try to get to you?'*

<*No, I growled at him, and he left me alone.*>

Sprout's words shock me. My young friend can combat the Necromancer already? As Quaryk told me, it seems the dragon is a fearsome foe. I suppose that's why the enemy is concentrating on me: I must have the weaker mind. Sipping again, I bite into a biscuit - apple and something I can't identify, but the taste is superb - and chewing gives me time to rally. Quaryk grabs one, and after a first bite, he bespeaks me again, saying,

'Go on …?'

I put the remains of the biscuit back on the plate. They wait until I can carry on, speaking quietly this time. Somehow, this helps to distance the event.

'He tried to charm me,' I say with a shudder. 'At first, he was pleasant, even kind, and said, "I've always wanted a child of my own, someone to look after and love, and to be my heir. You are a foundling, someone who has never known a proper, loving home. You can be my beloved child.".'

Quaryk frowns and stops chewing, as though his biscuit suddenly tastes bad.

'But then, before I could reply, Sprout was there with me. The Necromancer looked at him hungrily but just as suddenly looked away. That must have been when you growled at him, Sprout?'

Sprout emits wisps of white smoke through his nostrils. <*It was, I think.*>

'Yet he was still amiable to me,' I say. 'And then he went on, "Your dragon can come to live with us too, and we can do marvellous things together. We can build an empire and live as King and Princess of all the lands. And with your young friend there," he said, deliberately not looking at Sprout, "we can begin the race of dragons once again if he wills. Shall we? Will you come to me? Will you bring your dragon and be my beloved daughter? Or if you prefer it, my wife?" And then he became as handsome as – well, really handsome … and … well … ah, well …'

Quaryk's eyebrows shoot up, but he manages to keep his face straight. The Necromancer became the image of Quaryk, only more so, somehow. I blush hotly while shivers run down my back as I remember his honeyed words, his glamour, and the incredible effect they had on me. And, although the taint of bitterness still underlays his offer, I was tempted. It would have been so easy to give in.

The Mage says nothing but looks expectant. So, stumbling over the words, I go on.

'He … he was so persuasive that for a second, I almost gave in and said 'Yes.' There was a part of me that yearned to be his daughter, like with Ma, but it was when he began to talk about being a Princess and conquering the world that I remembered what he really is. So I set my mind against him and his wishes.'

I pause to drink.

'Did he try again?' Quaryk asks.

'When he saw I wasn't going to yield there and then, he began to taunt me, calling me "foundling" and "no-man's child". He said he would come and take Sprout away from me and became so frenzied I imagined him frothing at the mouth, but he didn't project that. Instead, he grew huge, monstrous and ugly, leering over us and looking more and more terrifying until I almost gave in and said "Yes" to his demands simply to end the horror.'

Trembling, I glance at Sprout.

<*That's right, Jin,*> he says. <*I saw that too.*>

I nod.

'Then he made his real mistake. He said, "When I took you from your slut of a mother I felt the power in you and knew I was destined to raise you! You would have become a power, a stronger Mage than any other on Leaf, but her foul sprite wrested you from me. He is still paying the price. Even now, he lies beneath me, in chains, anticipating my next visit. I have kept him alive for endless years, and all the while, he pays for this interference."'

Quaryk has turned pale, but now I must keep going. The need to cast this from me is insurmountable.

'He looked at me then, knowing that he had made a mistake and that I would never go to him willingly, not after hearing all that. My mother wasn't a slut!'

<*I wouldn't go either,*> Sprout says, comfortingly.

When I look up, Quaryk meets my eyes, his white face sad and puzzled. Sprout twists his head around as if he wants to rid himself of the Necromancer's monstrous taste too.

'I am so sorry,' Quaryk says. 'I had no idea, and the Mages haven't either. So, the Necromancer must have kidnapped you? Your birth must have been very secret. There is not so much as a rumour of such a happening, yet perhaps the Eldest knew, keeping it to herself for some reason? I will try to find out. Was that the end of the dream?'

'No,' I say between sobs, 'no. When he understood I wouldn't ever go to him willingly, he began to threaten me. He promised to come in force and take Sprout and kill anyone who tried to stop him. And … he talked about Three Gems and Ma and Pa.'

'Three Gems?' Quaryk asks, puzzled. This is the first time I've spoken of it to him.

'The cavern where my foster family live – or lived.'

They are still so important. Quaryk's family are delightful people, caring and kind, and I wish I was one of them. But they are borrowed and not really mine.

'They lived in Three Gems Cavern,' I say. 'I was with them until I was six or so – I forget – and I think of them as my ma and pa. Their boys were my brothers then. I often wonder if they remember me at all …'

'So he knows about them, and perhaps he will use them to bend you to his wishes?'

'Yes. That's right. I'm afraid he'll find them. Then, after that, when he threatened me again, somehow I saw him change to what he really is, a man dwindled into an ancient, stinking, wretched creature, all loose mottled skin and bone - horrible! But I don't understand. I know he wants Sprout, but why me?'

'I don't know,' Quaryk says. 'But I will try to find out as much as I can. There must be some record or someone who knows of your birth. But now, you must rest and try to sleep. Finish your biscuits and your drink, and I'll stay here with you. Here, Sprout?'

He tosses a biscuit Sprout's way as he retreats to the chair by the wall. A snap, and it is gone.

<Tell him thank you,> Sprout says, *<and if you can't manage all those others …?>*

Glancing at Quaryk for approval, I toss Sprout the remaining biscuits. He catches them nimbly and withdraws to go back to his warm barn. Closing the window, Quaryk quietly takes the chair, and I am grateful for his continued company.

'Sprout says thank you,' I murmur as I sink down onto my pillows. Thankfully I am too weary to care about my inner voice and sleep quickly overtakes me.

Chapter Twelve

Sprout is off enjoying himself somewhere with Flutterby.

We have been here for over half a year now, very lucky that Quaryk's family took us in. We have had nothing but good from them: kindness from utter strangers. Although I still yearn for Three Gems, another question is pressing now: I need to find out who I really am.

Sprout is almost fully grown, his wings half again as wide as his body is long, the best proportions for a flying dragon if the old records are to be believed at all. He has learned to control his flame, to know and practice his manners, and has voluntarily begun to make himself powerful enough for his wings to bear him and a possible rider.

I have learned all the major and minor arcana of the first Order of Mages: the high and low spells; the healing wards of the Trees; the whispers and the callings; the conjurations and incantations; the hidden rituals; the blessings and the canticles; and the three thaumic languages. I know not to use any of these casually. By anyone's count, I have learned as much magic and lore as any Mage could in the short time I've had, and Quaryk says I have learned more than he has in almost fifteen years. Although it is all fairly easy, I don't reveal this as there is much I need to discover to find my origin. Quaryk has delved into the records of the Sky-folk, but got no further. I suppose it is possible I may never know.

My bad dreams and sad, visiting voice still trouble me, and I can't ignore either, although I can shake both off through the daylight hours. Every few days, the Necromancer projects his presence into my sleeping head, cajoling and threatening by turns, but later taking a new tack, trying to make me feel guilty and sorry for him. I wish he would go away, die, anything. When he comes, the voice which has been with me almost all my life stops as though overpowered. I don't understand it.

A question breaks into my bleak thoughts as I contemplate Milde's sleeping garden.

'Jinny? Where are you?' Quaryk asks.

'Here! In the garden,' I say, expecting to help his mother.

I charge into the farmhouse, ready to do any mucky job in gratitude, but Milde is not there. Quaryk is standing by the kitchen window. So why has he summoned me?

'I want to talk to you,' Quaryk says aloud, pointing to a steaming mug. Following his cue, I take it up. 'Come, let's look at the view,' he continues, so I follow him outside to the chilly view over the water meadows down to the river.

'Well, what is it?' I ask, bespeaking him for privacy.

He is silent for a moment.

'We have found something,' he says. *'I asked the Order to investigate further, and they have garnered a fragment of information which may have something to do with you - but then again - it may not.'*

He gazes into the distance until I have to prod, *'Well?'*

I feel as though a fire is being lit under me.

'The Mages have found a memory, but one that was not recorded properly. It's from a Mage who has been lost for years. He remembered someone stealing into a dark place, probably at night, and taking two babies away. But that is all. I would have had more hope for this remembrance, but two children?'

He shakes his head as I wonder. *Was one of those children me?* It all seems so insubstantial.

'How does this happen?' I ask. *'How can the Mages know the memories of dead men?'*

He stares at me.

Making his mind up, he says, *'This may be hard to understand, but the Order of Mages is an over-mind, a consciousness made up of the minds of all Mages. And this remembers all we do. Oh, it doesn't know little things like which cup we use each day,'* and he flourishes his aloft, *'but it remembers the most important things that happen, and we can delve into it at will. But sometimes, memories are lost or damaged, deliberately changed, or expunged.'*

He pauses again, looking out over the fields.

'*So ... there is nothing but that one memory? Nothing else?*'

'No, it is as though his mind was wiped clean after that - or he died.'

I don't know what to make of this, but then Quaryk gives himself a mental shake like a dog shaking water from its fur. He strides off, then halts and turns as if he is just remembering me.

'Drink up!' he says, 'You promised me you would lift my tree, and this is as good a time as any!'

The oak tree lies where we last saw it, slowly rotting away. Looking at its dead weight, I wonder how I can possibly achieve this task. Perhaps it is a simple question of leverage. I will have to ask the Great Tree to allow me to use its magic.

I walk around the trunk, noting the growth of fungi upon it and wondering what in Leaf I can do, aware that Quaryk is watching. At last, summoning what courage I have, I swallow and, breathing deeply, ask the Tree for its help. There is a pause in which I am aware that it has heard me and is considering my request. Then its huge, warm voice says,

'*This may not be seen as a necessary action by you, but for Quaryk, this is a healing, necessary for his continuing good.*'

The Great Tree has answered the question uppermost in my mind. Glancing at Quaryk, I know he hasn't heard our conversation.

'Thank you,' I reply, '*you are very kind.*'

As I wonder how to shift this sodden weight of rotten wood and what spells, incantations or sorcery I should use, the Tree bespeaks me again.

'*Like this,*' the great mind says, sending a set of odd mental shapes to be made and applied in a certain order. '*Do this, and you will lift the poor corpse. Then it is up to you to steady it.*'

'Thank you. I will try,' I reply, with a tad of doubt. Then I think of the number one precept Quaryk hammered home while I was learning magic: 'Confidence will take you to places you cannot imagine - doubt, and you *will* fail.'

There is no sense in waiting: it either works or it doesn't. So, shedding my jacket, I stand still and close my eyes with a silent prayer. Now, as I begin the mental manipulation, fingers touching the slimy bark, I feel a thrumming as though a cloud of bees is enveloping me. The hum grows higher, and a green glow spreads over the fallen bole until it is brighter than any sunlight. The remains of the tree rise incrementally, faltering as I pause to organise my thoughts, then springing up skyward to thud upright onto the spidery mass of its roots. I hold it there for a few seconds, then, suddenly, the great weight is too much, and it topples over to fit almost exactly into the indentation it left in the soft earth.

An expression of sheer joy fleets over Quaryk's face. Beaming, he waves his arms. 'You did it!' he cries. 'That was marvellous! Do you remember when I first suggested this, you thought it silly? I thought you might try but fail. I was wrong. Well done, indeed!'

He claps me on the back, making me reel and almost trip. I am glad he is so delighted to have seen his oak tree in place once more, if only for an instant, and I wonder why. My legs turn to parchment, and, panting, I have to sit. This magic has cost me a great deal of strength.

'Stay put,' Quaryk says as he turns towards the farm. I watch weakly. Although my task has been achieved, I simply haven't the strength to get up. Involuntarily, my head sinks, and I fall sideways onto the soft green grass. I feel as if I lie forever, waiting for the strength to move again. Then the ground beats hollowly with the sound of hooves. I squint through the grass. Quaryk is riding Myrtle.

'Come on then, lazybones,' he says jovially, dismounting. Grabbing me, he lifts me up and deposits me on Myrtle's bare back.

'Stay there,' he says. Then, with one hand to steady me, he mounts behind me, clucking Myrtle into a leisurely amble. I lean back against him bonelessly.

'Why do I feel like this?' I ask when I can muster the energy. *'I can make fire without falling over.'*

'Depends on how much mental effort you expend,' he says. 'The Tree supplies the magic - the power - but we supply the will, and that takes a vast amount of vitality sometimes. It's far harder than making fire or playing with clouds. You'll feel better when you've had a meal or three. You will get used to it.'

I understand, I think, but energy has leaked out of me faster than the water in the drains that Sprout dug.

Chapter Thirteen

The days are glacially cold, and I've never known anything like it. In summer, I became faint with heat, but as soon as I got used to it, the days shortened and turned chilly. Now winter is flinging hail, sleet, and snow at us, frost and icicles everywhere. Quaryk's family seem to enjoy it, coming puffing in from outside work with their cheeks glowing, but it's all I can do to stay warm, spending most of my time huddled against Sprout or sitting on top of the kitchen fire. At least I can be useful there. But today, in the cosy barn insulated with the stored hay and warmed by the family cows and hens, Sprout twists his neck to peer at me.

<*Are you warm enough? I want to go find Flutterby?*> he says. <*He says there's ice on the river that really needs breaking!*>

I shiver at the prospect, thinking about the absences I've noticed recently: all the insects and tiny things that bit and bothered us all through the warmer days are long gone. I can't imagine where, but daren't ask for fear of seeming stupid.

'*I'll manage,*' I say. '*Go play.*'

With a joyful heave, Sprout rises and waits for me to open the big barn doors for him. He galumphs away, his tail whipping back and forth. He is huge, much too big to come into the farmhouse, and I sometimes ride him now to save my leg. It is good to feel his hot body under me in such frigid weather. Closing the barn doors, I hurry across the white and blue world of the yard to the farmhouse. Milde is in the kitchen with Lind and An, one of the farm maids. Apron-clad, she is busy at the table with a huge bowl before her, the girls hovering anxiously, handing her jars and packets at her whim.

'Hello? What's this you're doing?' I ask, rubbing my hands, my teeth chattering.

'I'm making our First-Comer's cake for tomorrow,' Milde answers, looking up from the table. 'It's Third Year.'

Busily stirring whatever it is, she doesn't elaborate. I've heard in passing that there's some sort of gathering, although I'm still hazy on the details. Lind turns to me as I crouch over the fire, glad of its fierce heat.

'Quaryk says the Holtanbore is almost always the same temperature, never too hot and never too cold,' she says. 'Is that right? It must be very strange for you being here. How are you feeling?'

'I'm alright,' I say, 'but I'm not used to the cold, yet.'

'Well,' she says, 'we can certainly use a hand today, and this is the warmest place in the house.'

'Yes, it is. What d'you want me to do?'

'It would be a big help if you would wash and pare these vegetables for the stew,' she says, 'and then we'll see.'

She points to two mountainous piles of roots and greens, a slight smile fleeting around her mouth, evidently expecting me to duck the job.

'Everyone on the farm is eating with us tonight,' she goes on, 'so all of it will be needed!'

I know there are more people living here than Quaryk's immediate family. Cottages for the farm workers are dotted over the farmlands, a small, scattered village of folk. If they are all coming, we'll need masses of extra food.

'Alright,' I say, and, taking up a knife and bowl, I sit as near to the fire as I dare and start peeling. 'What's happening tomorrow?'

Milde frowns at me over the table, her knife hovering over the dried fruit she's chopping.

'You really don't know? Tomorrow is Firstday, Jinny, and the whole of our folk will gather to celebrate the First Families,' she says. 'The Quaryk family was a First Family here, so we always mark this day.'

'I've never heard of it before,' I say, with a shake of my head.

She smiles, her face distant, as though looking into the past, making me wish I could, too. What must it be like to know who your parents were?

'I'm surprised you don't know of this, but I'll tell you now,' she says, continuing to work. 'This tale has been handed down, mother to mother, for all the long years since we came here. All the First Families celebrate on this day, for it was in this season that we finally found our home with the Tree. So, on this day, we remember the Great Tree that provides our home. It must have been very strange then, so long ago.'

'Where did the first folk come from?'

She looks at me, her mind elsewhere for a fleeting moment, then says, 'It's uncertain, but perhaps there were not so many people in those days. However, they travelled great distances to find a place to settle. But you'll hear the whole tale tomorrow night anyway.'

Turning back to her task with a wistful smile, she rubs her nose with the back of a floury hand and gets on, mouth moving as she murmurs to herself. I do likewise, musing on this interesting new information.

~*~

A mass of candles and lamps blaze aloft in the farm's biggest barn, a warm and lovely sight as we trickle in. All the family are here, with an unsuspected host of farm workers and their broods filling the tables. Galden waves, and I smile and nod to him. I had no idea so many people lived here.

Everyone is turning to watch as we enter. Maybe they think Sprout shouldn't be here - or maybe they're nervous of him, and who wouldn't be? He's taller than Flutterby now, with a muscular grace in every movement. And they will all have heard of his incredible ability to switch stomachs and flame at will as he's been practising.

Quaryk beckons, and I sigh with relief. He has saved a seat next to him and Lind, with a good-sized space for Sprout to settle beside us. I am acutely aware of my half-grown wings and the covert stares they engender.

'There you are,' he says. *'Come and sit down.'*

Sprout settles himself, eyes riveted on the food. He is anxious as this is such a large gathering of people, and especially because of the children here, who are an unknown quantity to us both. These are not half-starved mini adults as they were in the labyrinth: these children are children, bursting with energy, laughing and bouncy, generally making their parents frown. Yet the few who I have come across already have been extremely obedient and polite.

<I don't like children,> Sprout says. <They will tease me … and they are so small. I could squash one without noticing.>

I try to reassure him. *'You know, these children are just small people, like me and Quaryk. You like us, don't you? And they all like to play, just like you. I don't think you need to worry - if anything, they will be very interested in you and want to be your friends.'*

At this, Sprout looks happier. I feel his hostility slowly changing to interest when a small boy approaches and asks, 'Please, mistress, can I touch him?' with a mixture of awe and eagerness in his round eyes.

'Can he touch your scales, Sprout?' I ask.

Sprout pauses, summoning up his courage. Imagine a dragon his size having to decide nervously whether a little lad can feel one scale! Eventually, he gives a huff and tautly nods, saying, <*I suppose so, but mind, once only. Tell him!*>

I tell the lad. He comes closer and, carefully extending a hand, touches a scale gently. Sprout shivers and winces but stays put. Nearby, all the adults are watching closely.

'He's warm,' the boy breathes, 'and he's really beautiful!'

At this, Sprout cautiously extends his neck, sniffing at the boy's hand. Then he butts him very gently with his nose and the lad giggles. He strokes Sprout's face, and when nothing terrible happens, the adults visibly relax.

<*He's nice!*> Sprout says, <*Why didn't you tell me, Jin?*>

Sometimes I could flatten him!

'I did! See? Everyone else wants to make friends,' I say through gritted teeth.

A group of children slowly gather around Sprout and stay to pet him until, reluctantly, they are called back to their seats by their parents. Sprout is beginning to enjoy himself.

And I? I still nervously clasp my throat while we wait for the meal to begin. Stopping myself, I fold my hands on my lap, knuckles showing white. This is all new, and I watch everyone else for clues.

When everyone is waiting, seated and quiet, Quaryk's father, Hollis, stands up. An expectant hush ripples along the tables, then he speaks.

'Greetings, everyone. Well, this is Third Year and Midwinter. All of us are gathered here to celebrate the season, but more than this, the First-Comers, the beginnings of our folk and our ancestors who braved the wilderness to find our Great Trees, made their homes here. All over Leaf, in every Glebe, all our First Families will celebrate tonight. And as we have all worked hard for the last three years as they did long ago, it is time for us to enjoy the fruits of our labour. Enjoy your meal that my good wife, Milde, has prepared for us! Dig in and enjoy, everyone!'

He sits down amid a wave of noisy approbation and clapping and exuberantly begins to fill his plate. A deafening clatter arises as everyone follows suit.

'*Does this take place every year?*' I ask, bespeaking Quaryk when he passes me a dish. There's no point in trying to shout above the din. Everyone is talking, eating, gossiping, or calling for more ale or plates to be passed.

'*The First-Comer celebration happens every three years,*' he says. '*It's important we remember the first of the folk who came here and found the Trees. They must have been very brave.*'

'*What happens the other two years then?*' I ask.

It's grown a tad quieter as most mouths are full by now, so Quaryk answers aloud.

'We still have a Midwinter meal, and we dance, but it's not quite as special. See those branches with berries? The ones on the walls?'

'Those with the thorns and big red and black berries?'

The fruits look menacing, almost meaty, dribbling a gelatinous, purplish juice.

'Yes, those are gore berries. We cut and bring them inside to represent the savage wilderness our First Folk braved when they travelled here. Parties of men used to go out to bring them back each third year, but now we have small plantations inside the Glebe where they are grown, as it can be dangerous to stray too far outside. They are prickly and very poisonous, so great care has to be taken in growing and handling them.'

After momentarily grappling with these new ideas, I say, 'So, the Glebe is safe, but the lands outside are not?'

'Not as safe as inside,' he says carefully. 'Enjoy your food.'

He turns to answer his sister, who is asking him something, so I fill one plate for me and another for Sprout, who is watching everyone else eating and hotly drooling. It's not much of a meal for a dragon his size, but he is delighted to join in.

~*~

Replete and sitting back at ease, it is hard to imagine any gathering more agreeable than this. The children are playing in the hay around us; the only time they can get away with such licence. Some have gravitated to Sprout, who is proving amazingly good with the tinies, allowing them to climb all over him. Their parents, at first anxious, now smiling, enjoy an uninterrupted chat and a drink. As I watch, a toddler curls up between Sprout's forelegs and falls fast asleep. Considering his first reaction was dislike, Sprout seems to have a way with the children now, and they seem to trust him completely. When the bigger children try to tease him, he gently swipes them into the hay with his tail, and they scramble up again, laughing.

'*You'll be in demand as a babysitter,*' I tell him.

<*They are young and uncomplicated,*> he says. <*I like them now.*>

I laugh. Who would have thought I'd be here, far from the labyrinth, with a vegetarian dragon who loves playing with kids? Sprout's mouth curls a little as he catches my thought.

And then, as if someone has thrown a switch, the meal is over, and the children are gathered in. The youngest are bedded down on blankets in the hay, the eldest sitting quietly. Everyone becomes silent, watching as Milde rises to stand at the head of the tables on a wooden platform where she can be seen by all. How tall and slender, how dignified she is. As the head of the Quaryk family, a heavy green yarner's cloak is draped around her shoulders by her husband. I wriggle, wondering how a cloak like that would feel against my growing wings.

When she has decided we are all ready, she addresses us in a ringing voice, filling the barn to the rafters. 'Hear now the tale of our beginnings, the tale of how we came to live in our beautiful Trees, the tale passed down, daughter-mother to daughter-mother, through all time. This is the Tale of the First-Comers. Hear now "The Tale of Our Beginning".'

She pauses, looking down, and we wait breathlessly for her to look up and continue. She slowly looks up and around. Then, taking a deep breath, she begins.

'Our folk, it is said, came to Leaf from a far place, which has been lost in time and memory now. In those days, some of the first people, even before they were First-Comers, grew too many. As their families burgeoned, they grew hungry, and new land was needed to feed everyone. So, some decided to leave their homes to find fresh pastures. When they had gathered all the folk who would leave into a great host, they set out together to see what luck might bring them.

'After a long, hard journey, this great host was again starving, so it was decided it should split up to try to find new sources of food and homes. The folk divided themselves into a number of companies, each setting out in different directions to find their fortunes. Many did, although some must have perished in the search. One of these companies, our ancestors, and perhaps the luckiest, found the first of our beautiful Great Trees. Once there, our ancestors thrived, for the Tree provided safety, food and shelter. They made a good life and prospered, spreading out to other Trees and eventually becoming the "Three in One" that we know today.'

As Milde looks around again, smiling at our rapt faces, I make a mental note to ask what "Three in One" means, but I don't have long to wait. After a pause to sip her drink, she continues, her clarion voice swooping and soaring in the airy spaces of the barn, thunderous or light as a zephyr.

'Our folk first lived beside the roots, then delved caverns under them to live in safety.'

At this, my ears prick up - does she mean the Holtanbore? I give her next words my full attention.

'They lined their new homes with dressed stone, boring through the solid rock, and became used to living underground. Further caverns and tunnels were dug, and useful minerals and stones were mined. There, a few, called Librarians, became the record keepers of the Trees. All these folk were known as Underlings who lived in the labyrinths called Holtanbores, the first of the Three in One of the Great Trees.

'But when, in this greater safety, more children were born, and again more food was needed, and some folk spread further upwards into and outwards from the Bole. They became woodsmen, farmers, and gardeners, tilling the fertile soil around the Trees, which they called Glebes. They planted orchards and grew crops, farming the land as far as the Girdles. These great hedges, our great defenders, were planted around the outer edges of the Glebes to guard them. And there, by the outermost edges of the Glebes, the husbandmen and women kept animals and grew great orchards to supply the needs of our growing population. They made wine and ale, and all was good. Forever after, they (and we) are the Middlings, the Glebe dwellers, the second of the Three in One.'

At this, a cheer goes up. I look around. These folk must have heard this so often, but they don't seem in the least bit bored. I'm fascinated, but then it is the first time I've heard the tale, and some of my questions are being answered.

'*Is all this true?*' I ask Quaryk when Milde pauses again.

'*Yes,*' he says shortly, gesturing sharply for me to listen. It's so out of character I want to kick him again, but I don't. This is far too interesting to interrupt.

'Some of the folk moved upwards,' she continues, 'and found their living high in the great boughs and branches of the Canopy, becoming known as the Sky-Folk or Overlings. There they kept flocks of birds, bees, and bloons, and befriended the salamanders and dragons who lived there.'

<*Dragons?*> Sprout says. <*There were dragons who lived in Trees?*>

'*I don't know,*' I say. '*I'll ask later. Shush!*' He stops bespeaking but remains alert. It is, after all, the first time anyone has mentioned dragons.

Milde continues: 'They made honey, preserves and mead from the Trees' fruits in season. These fruits they also made into wine. The Sky-Folk gathered petals and leaves and the rare and precious Tree seeds.

Precious because only a few are allowed to mature by the Trees each year. Some Sky-folk became messengers, riding far on the great winged dragons. The creatures nested, in those days, in the deep knotholes and cracks in the bark.'

<*Did you hear that, Jin? Sky-Folk riding dragons! Like us!*> Sprout says, emitting joyous sunshine colours.

I nod, not wanting this tale interrupted, but now the entire gathering is staring at Sprout with interest. He is sitting up on his haunches like a great hound, listening avidly as Milde smiles and continues.

'The messengers took news and goods from Tree to Tree and to all the folk outside. And then, strangely, perhaps because they lived aloft, some of these folk changed, growing the most beautiful, feathered wings like the birds, and became the third folk of the Three in One, the winged Overlings.

Here Milde pauses to sip her drink. The barn is silent, a tribute to her rendering of the tale, although some folks are staring at my ugly wings. At length, she begins again.

'However, some of the other groups wandered far afield to find homes in the low forests and plains. Some, who called themselves the Elets, stayed in the forests, weaving beautiful living lattices with the smaller earth-trees to make their homes, existing on the bounty the forests provided. Another group, the Eltars, roamed over the long grasslands growing between the forests and the seas, living in rough tents on foods they garnered, and keeping herds of animals. When they reached the seashores, some of the Eltars, weary of journeying, stopped to become fisher folk, while others lazed by the winding rivers.

'It was one of these first watermen who, far away and long ago, found a piece of stone from a Great Tree washed up on a seashore. In a strange trance, he carved it and sold it to a passing enchanter for a few pieces of wheaten bread. It was made of a rare magical resin, a solid sap called amberla, which only one in ten thousand Trees can produce. It is literally solid magic, and the ancient stone was known ever after as the Talisman, the Ancient, or The Heart of Gold. It was the most powerful amulet ever known on Leaf. Now, sadly, it is riven, and the pieces are long lost.'

At this, I finger the half-stone on my breast in awe. Could this really be a part of that amulet? It doesn't seem possible, yet I am smiling inside: if only they knew! Something makes me glance at Quaryk, who looks at me with an unreadable expression on his face.

Milde goes on, 'The last of these folk turned to the mountains where they built towers of stone and delved deep. These were the Dwelves, a goodly folk, who, like the Sky-Folk, changed, gradually reducing in stature as time went on to live more easily in their underground homes.'

Now she shivers beneath the green cloak. Her voice changes, becoming low and menacing. 'But then, some of these turned away from the light, turning to the darknesses and evils in the world, coveting what others had, and desirous of taking more. These folk became known as the Darkkaans and were shunned by all the other peoples for their low ways. In time, they changed too: their teeth and nails grew into fangs, their nails to claws, and they were ever ready to maim and kill. Then, the Necromancer, the Dark Mage and Dragon-Killer made them his minions - but that is another tale for a different season.'

At Milde's last words, Sprout snorts and stamps. The whole barn looks around at him again. Embarrassed, he subsides, emitting small, white smoke rings. Milde nods to him before she continues.

'So, out of all the great company of folk that set out so long ago, it is us, our folk, the friends of the Great Trees, that flourished and spread the most. And because the Great Trees welcomed us, it is meet that we now raise a toast to them in health and long life! They have allowed us to live and to tap their knowledge and magical power, and we are forever grateful.'

She raises her glass, the liquor glowing like liquid rubies in the warm light of the lamps as she flourishes it aloft.

'To our friends, the Great Trees!'

We stand, raise our glasses and repeat, 'To our friends, the Great Trees!'

We sip in silence until Milde puts down her glass and draws her cloak close about her, a sign that her tale is almost at an end.

'Now, we remain the "Three in One" of our Great Trees. We have honoured them and celebrated the First-Comers by remembering their great journey on this Midwinter Day.'

Milde clasps her shoulders, dropping her head in the universal sign that her tale is done, standing tall and motionless. A momentary silence reigns, and then there is a great burst of clapping and catcalls of admiration.

'My mother has made me proud again tonight,' Quaryk says, his eyes shining with delight.

'Yes!' I agree. 'She is magnificent!'

Nothing in Milde's usual demeanour would make anyone imagine she could tell such a tale. But when Quaryk goes over to congratulate her, I can suddenly see the resemblance between them. I wonder what other talents Quaryk conceals as his mother does? Apparently, I have a great deal to learn about people - about everything. I wouldn't have missed this night for all the Trees on Leaf.

As the evening draws on, Sprout and I are included in the golden circle of the Quaryks, Galden and one or two of the other senior farm hands. We drink different kinds of wine, one almost the colour of firelight, one pale as the half-stone, which tastes of summer. Sprout dozes nearby, his tail coiled around the end of the table.

'Well, Jinny, how did you like the tale tonight?' Quaryk's father asks.

'I thought it was wonderful,' I say. 'I've never heard it before, and Milde, you told it beautifully.'

Milde smiles and nods. 'Thank you.'

'What? Never?' asks Lind. She looks concerned. She has never had to imagine a life other than her own. And she has listened to this story all her life, knowing she will continue the family tradition one day when she takes her place as head of the household.

'We didn't have any tales in the Library labyrinth,' I explain, 'but I can just about remember something - a gathering of some sort - in Three Gems.'

Galden clears his throat as the Quaryks glance at each other.

'Three Gems?' he says, his brows knitted.

'The cavern where my foster parents lived. I lived with them until I was about six or so, I think. I don't know if they're still there …'

'And before that?' he asks gently.

'I don't know.'

'It doesn't matter,' Milde says kindly. 'You're here with us now, and your wings are growing beautifully. I expect they'll develop feathers soon. It's marvellous to think you will be able to fly one day!'

Lind smiles in accord as her mother finishes.

This idea stops me again as I look at Milde. Somehow I've never managed to equate my growing wings with actual flying. They are just bony growths at present, quite ugly and merely a nuisance up to now. My face must be mirroring the feelings that are cascading through me, a sequence of surprise, interest, comprehension and anxiety. Galden watches me with a quizzical expression on his leathery face.

'You've never really thought it would happen?' he asks. He always seems to know what I'm thinking: behind those piercing blue eyes is a mind as sharp as a steel stalactite.

<*You're daft,*> Sprout says with an internal frisson which is his laughter. <*I told you! It'll be great! We'll be able to fly together!*>

'Really?' I gasp, my thoughts reeling. A scary yet fabulous thought. I notice that everyone is looking at me questioningly.

'Sprout thinks we'll be able to fly together,' I say.

Galden harrumphs and swigs the last of his wine.

'Could be useful, that,' he says flatly, putting his glass down carefully. 'I'm off to check the stables. Goodeve.'

As he gets up, he gives me a knowing glance with a wry half-smile.

'A good sort is Galden,' Quaryk's father says. 'Dependable.'

Quaryk, sitting back, looks up. 'He is that. Well, I think it's time I turned in.' He looks at me. 'What about you and Sprout?'

<*I'm comfy, so I'll stay put,*> Sprout says with a vast, toothy yawn. <*Goodeve.*>

'Sprout's happy to stay here, but I'm coming. Too much good wine.' I sway as I stand up.

Quaryk escorts me back to my bedroom, where I'm glad to roll myself in the covers and let the world loose.

<*Please don't forget to ask about the dragons,*> Sprout whispers as I fall asleep. I place my fingers comfortably around my throat as my voice steps up its eerie babbling again.

'*I'll try,*' I reply.

Chapter Fourteen

We are summoned to the Bole. Sprout, for obvious reasons, has stayed behind on the farm where Galden is looking after him. I miss his physical presence, but at least he can share this with me, seeing through my eyes.

Quaryk, a mere shifting of the shadows beside me in the strange blue light, takes my hand and escorts me to the dais. The Three who summoned us are already waiting. In Yew's place is a young Mage, a girl dressed in sunshine yellow. As we near, they rise and come down the steps. The Brown Mage, Willowind, greets us warmly, taking my hand.

'We have been summoned to bring you before the Sky-Kings. But before this, we must conclude certain aspects of your training.'

'Training?' I am surprised. 'I've learned a few spells and things, but I'm not really ...'

And then I turn to glare through slitted eyes at Quaryk. '*Wasn't all that simply something to pass the time and keep us safe while Sprout grew?*'

He grins fleetingly as though a trifle ashamed.

'I didn't realise I had undertaken serious training,' I growl. 'I never thought to be a Mage.'

'We instructed Quaryk to teach you the basics,' the Brown Mage says, 'and he assures us that you are more than proficient in these and may be admitted into the Order at the first level. When that is accomplished, you will go with him to meet the Sky-Kings, who wish an audience with you. Once in the palace, you will be taught to fly and to use weaponry to ready you.'

To ready me for what? I immediately wonder and feel like kicking Quaryk yet again. What else didn't he mention, and why? But there is nothing I can do now unless I make a scene, and I cannot bring myself to do that. These three of the most powerful Mages of our Royal Tree have decreed what my future will be, and I apparently have no say in the matter. My time in the labyrinth of the Holtanbore has left me obedient and easily subdued to a fault, yet now I am angry, and it's just as well I am speechless as the filthiest curses I know come to mind. Then, like a flash of light, I understand what else my training has achieved. This little snick is turning. Only a year ago, being ordered about was my norm: I would never dare to challenge an edict. I am beginning to want freedom of thought.

Willowind blanks for a split second as I feel her mind touch mine. She looks at me with an ironic smile but resolutely says,

'We will admit you to the Order tomorrow. Be aware that this is a serious covenant, a chance never given thoughtlessly, and so one not to be taken lightly. So now, take the rest of the day to rest and prepare yourself,' she says, and with a curt nod to Quaryk, she turns away.

We leave the wooden womb to go back to the same rooms we occupied nearly a full year ago.

Mine hasn't changed at all, apart from being far too small for Sprout now, but here I can breathe again when I open my little window on the world.

'You'll be alright here again?' Quaryk asks carefully. He must understand my turmoil.

I nod, wishing that Sprout was here with me, but at least we are always in mental contact.

<*I'm right here, Jin,*> he says comfortingly.

'*Thanks, Sproutie,*' and to Quaryk, 'Yes, thank you, but I need to know …'

'About your ordination? Come down to the kitchen when you're rested, and we'll talk.'

'But I'm …' I begin until I realise how very weary I feel. 'Yes, you're right,' I say unhappily. Because I am at the mercy of these Mages, I am nervous and worried, and it is not a good feeling. Yet I have come to trust Quaryk, despite his annoying silences, but what in all Leaf am I getting into? It seems that I have no choice, afraid that either I submit or - and this is a horrifying possibility - I will be sent back down into the Library labyrinth. So, no contest, really.

~*~

The wooden womb is Stygian now. Only three of the candle lamps are lit in this misty, blue space, mere pinpoints of light in an otherwise empty firmament. The three figures enthroned are clad entirely in the pure white of Ordination as I am. They glimmer like spectres in the crepuscular gloom. Further pale figures, hazily glowing, stand around the circular wall. I quickly check that Sprout is seeing this through my eyes, cautioning him to stay quiet. Now there is a silent pause, then the figure on the left speaks into the breathing hush: the Brown Mage, Willowind, who sits in the Eldest's place.

'Who comes?'

Quaryk, his clear voice retreating into muffled echoes, says, 'I am Ormandel Quaryk, Mage of the First Degree, and I bring the postulant Jinny Morai, who has attained the first standard set by the sublime Order of Mages in the Extramundane Arts and is accepted by the Great Trees as a practitioner of the Aether.'

Each face turns to me. I shrink a little.

'Come forward, Jinny Morai,' the Brown Mage commands. I step forward, trembling, hoping my stomach will stop churning so loudly, and thrust both hands down at my sides so that I cannot touch my throat.

Willowind smiles as she rises.

'Come,' she says, 'kneel.'

Slowly ascending the steps of the dais, I am painfully aware of my bad leg, kneeling as best I can, head bowed. A pale wraith in a circle of spectres, I am aware of their scrutiny, and my heart tries to sledgehammer up through my throat, my stomach twisting anew. But Willowind calmly lays her hands on my head and gently turns her sight inward.

She intones, 'I, Grand Mage of the Order of Mages of the Bole, desire to admit this postulant into our sublime Order.'

She communes with the Order and all the great Trees, asking them to take me into their cognisance, then she takes one of my hands, the other still placed on my head.

'Jinny Morai, before the Trees raise you, tell me your heart. Will you be a servant to them and their folk? Will you serve as other Mages serve? Will you be true to our precepts, accepting all: not to kill unless you must protect life; to be loyal to the Order and to the Trees, and to obey any order within reason?'

Do I really want to promise all this? I wonder. And then, as the Trees touch my mind, there is no contest.

'I will, for as long as the Trees want me,' I say.

'Then, Jinny Morai, we welcome you into our great gathering.'

My inner voice, usually quiet in the daytime, instantly babbles loudly. With a huge effort, I manage to suppress it as the Mage takes my face in her hands and presses her forehead to mine. The womb recedes in a flash of utter beauty, and I see the whole world as a giant web, a great network of souls, all the Trees and the Mages nurturing and aiding the whole of the folk and creatures of Leaf.

'Now! Open your eyes as the Vessel of Light,' the Mage says, as a vast warmth from the Tree flows into me, cherishing and sustaining me as nothing ever could before. A throbbing yellow-green glow like the sunlight through spring leaves fills the womb, within me, charging, changing and filling me! Suddenly the pressure becomes too great and flows of luminous aether spurt out from my body to touch each of the Mages gathered around me, revitalising and rejuvenating all. This is the gift of Leaf, and I am its channel. My initiation brings renewed life.

The Mages sing without words as the spirit flows into them. The many voices raised in song together make beautiful chords, rising and falling like bee song, or a dawn chorus. Then, suddenly, the song falters, and I open my eyes. Willowind and the rest of the Mages stare in astonishment, blatant adoration on their faces. I turn.

A separate globular glow in a deep, vibrant viridian is manifesting in the space beyond the dais. It coalesces, becoming a nebulous, luminous figure which moves up to and slowly ascends the steps. From this shifting, fluid form, a figure is further defined, but whether male or female, I cannot say. It reaches out an ethereal arm and, extending one digit, touches me in the exact centre of my forehead. A sudden feeling of incredible vigour floods through me. I am effervescent! I feel I could hop from star to star as someone cries out,

'The Woodspirit!'

'It is Galian!' another awed voice whispers. 'It is the spirit of the Great Trees - here!'

Other urgent whispers break the silence, and a concerted deep exhalation breathes around the womb.

'*Be at peace, children,*' the spirit says internally, '*be calm.*'

The figure looks about and, gesturing around the womb to the other Mages, bespeaks to all, '*This is the Chosen. This young being of light may be able to heal the world. Nurture her, younglings, and we will perhaps prevail.*'

It smiles almost sadly at me, then bespeaks me personally, '*You have two tasks, Jinny Morai: first, you must heal the Talisman. Only when two are one will your second task begin: to avert the evil that threatens our world. Now you are come, perhaps all will end well.*'

The figure smiles, bends forwards, and plants a blissful cloud-like kiss on my forehead, saying, '*We are with you - always.*'

Shaking in ecstasy, I sink to my knees as the beautiful spirit twists away, and, fading swiftly, returns too soon to nothingness. The bluish, stuffy darkness returns. After a reverent pause, the Brown Mage extends her hand, helping me to my feet as the other Mages look on silently.

'You have been blessed,' she says. 'You alone have been visited by the spirit of all the Great Trees on Leaf, the Woodspirit, which has only been seen once before.'

The Mages around the walls murmur to each other in excitement, even daring to move.

For me, life has taken on a new radiance. I am dazzled, and my lonely inner voice recedes unheeded as I try to make sense of the whole occurrence. Everything is changed. I cannot speak yet, wondering about the two tasks I have been given.

'Let us finish your initiation,' Willowind says, and gesturing around the womb, 'Peace, friends.'

The Mages quiet as she takes my hands into hers now and gives me her blessing. Then we all pour forth to the lighted hall, where food and drink is served.

<Is it over?> Sprout asks. <I wish I'd been there.>

'Me too,' I say, floating in a haze of delight, my terrible tasks forgotten for the moment.

The initiation was breathtaking, a rite of passage that has changed me again. The memory of the lovely Woodspirit will stay with me always. And now, the whole of the combined knowledge of Leaf is at my disposal. I have become part of a huge sylvan net. At need, I may call on the Trees for help or on any Mage within the Order. However, I must obey any summons, holding myself ready to give succour to any who need it, be they Mages or common folk. I am not a private person any longer, having obligations to obey the Order - but I am exchanging an old servitude for one doubly precious and for the love of the Trees. Sprout merely laughs at my fancies. He is amazingly pragmatic for such a rare being, always calling a claw a claw.

~*~

Sitting on the balcony outside my room, I am lazily watching the world turning. The weather is fine, so I can escape from the atmosphere of veneration my appearance inside the Bole brings now.

<So, what's next?> Sprout asks, bringing me down to earth with a bump. <What about these tasks of yours?>

'I don't know,' I say, a frisson of fear colouring my thoughts. 'Ask Quaryk?'

He grunts in disapproval. He never bespeaks anyone but me.

'I suppose I'll have to talk to him eventually,' I say, 'but I don't really want to - not yet anyway.'

<You'll have to,> Sprout agrees, <and soon!>

I sigh. He's right, but being this stupid chosen one is a right pain in the arse. I simply can't move without being congratulated, asked silly questions, or followed by adoring looks. Fame, it seems, isn't all that much fun. The wind teases my hair as a drift of bloons sails by. Strange creatures, floating from place to place at the mercy of the winds, like me.

'Hey. Daydreaming again?'

Quaryk appears to break my reverie. I sigh: I have to be civil.
'Hey yourself.'
'How are you feeling?' he asks, and I suppress a growl.
Does he realise how much he irritates me? His almost complete lack of communication drives me mad - it's hard being left in the dark. Then his slight movement takes my eye. He is twisting his sleeve with the other hand, and I almost jump with glee. Ah yes! The Mage is nervous - actually nervous of me!

'You could have warned me,' I say mildly, although I want to bawl him out. 'You might have told me what would happen.'

'I told you as much as I could about the ceremony, but there is a limit to what the Order will allow being imparted to outsiders. Of course, now you may know anything you wish. The appearance of the Woodspirit is unheard of. But I could not tell a postulant that anyway.'

Ah. This is truth. So, I will forgive him now.

'Alright, forget it,' I say. 'What else do I need to know?'

He bespeaks me - so these are sensitive topics.

'The Grand Mage will talk to you herself,' he says, *'but I already know what she wants to say. The Sky-Kings have asked to meet you as they have important questions for you - and before you ask, even if I knew, I would not be at liberty to say. Possibly she wants to take your measure.'*

'What, with a rule?' I ask, mystified.

He looks at me, frowns, then laughs aloud as he realises I really don't understand. A blush runs up my neck. I am still so stupid.

'No. She just wants to find out about you. You're important now. The Woodspirit has only appeared once before that we know of. Yesterday, it told us that you will bring healing, changing the world we know. I can hardly believe it has happened. It is incredible!'

'So - that doesn't always happen at initiations?'

He shakes his head, looking out unseeingly at the Glebe. 'It has never appeared before save once, centuries ago, to my knowledge.'

A frisson of a mixture of fear and amazement runs down my spine at his words, subdued by a pressing new need.

'When do I meet Willowind then?'

'I don't know,' he says. 'She will summon you.'

There's a pause while we both muse.

'What is the Woodspirit?' I ask aloud. Again, a shiver runs down my spine as I say the word.

'Ah, the Woodspirit is the manifestation of the elemental life force of all Trees. It is a thing that has only been encountered in ancient times: the Trees like their privacy. So, seeing it now is incredible.'

'Oh? Why now then? And why did it call me 'Chosen'?'

'We don't know,' he says, 'but no doubt all will become clear, eventually. But the Trees have chosen you, and that's a marvellous thing.'

Quaryk smiles happily as though I have been awarded the ultimate accolade. I'm not sure about that, and an accolade for what? Yet again, as I have done many times since I left Three Gems, I wonder *why me?*

Chapter Fifteen

The Brown Mage seems diminished as she sits on my small bedroom stool instead of the throne in the womb. She looks like anyone's mother, aunty or wife, with a subtle hint of underlying power. I sit on the edge of my bed, trying not to slouch, rogue hands clasped firmly in my lap. Willowind has asked to speak to me privately. I wait politely for her to begin speaking as she arranges the folds of her robe. She looks up.

'Thank you for allowing me to visit you here,' she begins, her hands still smoothing the brown material. 'I think Sir Quaryk has told you that the Sky-Kings wish to have an audience with you?'

'Yes.'

My throat is as dry as summer mud.

'Well, that is true. Our Order requires you to visit the Canopy soon, where you will meet with the Kings. They will want to hear how you found your dragon friend. And you will also need to learn to fly properly, so once there, you will be instructed in that and in the use of the usual weapons; I mentioned this before.'

I frown at the last, although she seems unmoved. The very thought of fighting horrifies me. No one I have ever known or heard about has ever needed to use such things.

'Why would I need weapons?' I ask.

'Proficiency with weapons is a basic requirement of our Order. All Mages need to know how to defend themselves, even though we may never need to use such knowledge. So, this is arranged for you. You are now a Mage of the First Degree, and you will have the privileges associated with it. Quaryk will tell you about them. And, as he has been your guide for so long already, we propose that he should accompany you there.'

She pauses while I take all this in. Even as a feeling of relief courses through me at Quaryk's inclusion, a burning question rises to the top of my mind.

'But what about Sprout? We've been apart far too long already.'

Her hands are smoothing her robe again.

'You and the dragon are close?'

'Yes, we've not been separated until now. We want to stay together.'

Sprout constantly asks when I am coming back. We miss each other in a way that is bonedeep. Living in the labyrinth, I never had a friend: no one does down there. So Sprout is the first and only being I have ever loved, apart from Ma and the rest at Three Gems, and I am both mother and friend to him. It hurts us to be apart.

'That is good,' she replies. 'Your friend will be as welcome in the Sky-Kings' court as you are. They wish to see him too.'

'In the Kings' court?' I blurt. 'But he is on the Quaryks' farm! He's known nothing else. How will he get here? He's too young to travel alone.'

Successive visions of unfortunate accidents that Sprout might not avoid flash through my mind, and my hands rise to clasp at my throat.

The Brown Mage smiles, a party to my thoughts.

'Do not concern yourself,' she says. 'Someone from the farm will accompany him to the Canopy; it has already been arranged, and it will work well. With you, he will be instructed in flight and wing-fighting too. It is time you both experienced life in the Canopy, which is very different from here.'

Fingers kneading the brown robe now, she continues, 'You will enjoy your time there, and … it will prepare you.'

I squirm, unsure that I want to be prepared for something she won't disclose.

After a pause, she looks up and divulges, 'Jinny, we have looked for your coming over the ages, the one being who can find the lost halves of the Talisman. But we did not suspect that you would find a dragon's egg too.'

'But I didn't do anything! The stone was simply there, and then I … and then I found the egg …'

'I doubt you would have found the egg without the stone,' she says, still smoothing her robe. 'You see, child, your coming was predicted. And it seems the time has finally come. No one else would have done this: no one else could. They are both your gifts, it seems.'

There is a pause while I fit this in with what I already know. It seems quite ludicrous.

'But, Mistress, I am a nobody, just a foundling! It cannot be me!'

'Of course it can. Take your half-stone now and hold it in your hand.'

I obey, the fine chain glinting as I lift its elegant loop from my neck. We watch the stone for some moments. Nothing happens.

'Now, please give it to me.'

I drop the half-stone into her palm. She winces as it touches her skin, and a moment later, smoke rises from her hand, and she is shaking. Sweat springs out on her face, squeezed into a network of creases like a hulnut. Gasping with effort, she turns her hand so that the stone falls. I retrieve it quickly, tucking it away, then look up to see the Brown Mage, one of the chief Mages of our entire Order, cradling her hand as if in terrible pain. Tears flow down her cheeks as she nods.

'You see? No one but you may hold or keep it.'

She extends her hand, showing me a blackened, smoking hole in the middle of her palm, the exact size and shape of the half-stone. A charred black outline of the carving, which is oozing blood, is visible. As an odour of charred flesh arises, I stare as she returns it to the shelter of its twin.

'If I had kept it, it would have burned its way up through my arm to my heart,' she grates. 'Only you can touch and use it. You are the one we have waited for, the one the Trees predicted long centuries ago. You will either defeat the Necromancer or a terrible fate will fall upon our world. As the ultimate Wielder of the Talisman, to fulfil the prophecy, you must find a way to locate its lost half. But I must stop this pain.'

Her gaze locks as she communes with the Tree. A green mist flows into her hand from nowhere, and the skin immediately draws together, healing as I watch, wide-eyed. Healing is a skill I do not have as yet. After a few seconds, her palm is as clean and healthy as it was before. She bespeaks a *'Thank you'* to the Tree.

Now multiple questions burn in me, but there is no time to ask as she rises, raising her healed hand in salute.

'Go in peace, child,' she says. 'Quaryk will arrange your travel.'

Her mouth clamps shut on the last syllable. She stares at me for a moment, and I have no choice but to thank her as gracefully as Ma's upbringing allows. With that, she goes, leaving me trying to make sense of her revelations. I wonder why I am chosen and why I must go up into the Canopy. Right up there? It will be far too high! My hand clamps over my throat in the old gesture as shuddering, I struggle to gain control. But at least Sprout and Quaryk will be up there with me, a far happier thought.

It is then I understand that I expect to be with Quaryk all the time. I have become used to him, and he's been with me ever since Sprout's egg hatched. That he could be withdrawn by the Order at any time is frightening, but what must he think of it all? Outside in the corridor where he has been waiting, I hear the Brown Mage talking and taking leave of him. There is a silence, only broken by her retreating footsteps, and then he comes to the door, knocks once and enters, his face alive with questions. I look away, snuffling. Don't want him to see me crying again. Anyway, if I am really the 'chosen', I can't afford to be so feeble. It is time I grew a thicker hide.

'Well?' he asks, plonking himself in the chair the Brown Mage occupied.

I pause, wondering how much he knows.

'It was … alright,' I say.

'And?'

'And?' I echo innocently.

Quaryk gives me a hard look. Frowns. Taps his fingers on his thigh.

'I expected you to be ready to ask lots of questions or at least tell me what you think of the Mage's plan? Was I wrong?'

'So you knew what she was going to say to me?'

'Of course I did. Willowind is part of the Overmind of the Order. She only reveals her decisions when there is something she needs us to know. But I forget … you are not completely part of it yet. She has decreed I am to accompany you, so this is my business, don't you think?'

Suitably quashed, I am relieved. The Mages must have ordered him to stay with me in the first place, yet I have a horrible thought. All this time, I took it completely for granted that Quaryk actually wanted to stay with me. What if I am wrong? What if this is an ordained task he cannot escape? I never questioned *why* he stayed with me and Sprout, even taking us into his family. I am so stupid. I thought … well, I thought it was simply because he liked me, us.

Now, somewhere deep within me, my protective wall, which has been gradually breached, rises again keeping me safe. No one will get through again or get so close.

'I'm sorry, Sir Mage, I was wrong,' I say shortly.

Quaryk rises, his face set now after possibly hearing an echo of my thoughts.

'Please make sure you have everything ready after breakfast tomorrow,' he growls. 'We will travel by physical means into the Canopy to save Tree magic which may be necessary for our defence all too soon.'

He turns on his heel and stalks out. I know that I am being childish, but I feel like one of the small figures in the game that Pa used to play with the boys in Three Gems. Serfs, I think they were called. Definitely not chosen.

~*~

The void is filled with fear, dark and still, the air thick with the stench of death. A snarl of noise comes in like a vile hurricane, screaming and whistling over a low stentorian growl. The cacophony climbs to a climax, and then, above all, a vast voice reverberates, and a gigantic hand shakes me, rattling bones and teeth.

{*Dragon mother, hear me!*} Charnecron thunders. {*This is your last chance to bring the First and Last to me to bring forth the new race. Hear me now! If you do not heed me, I will take all the folk you love and crush them like snicks under my heel.*}

A horrible vision of a snick bursting under pressure, its innards spewing out; a cavern falling to crush occupants who look very like my foster family; and his dark, vicious minions like ants overrunning, killing and maiming who or whatever they find.

He says, {*I will bring such ruin down on you so that not even a memory is left. I will ready my forces to fall upon your precious Trees and accept no surrender, giving no quarter. Heed me or I* will *devastate your world.*}

When he stops, I am filled with such unimaginable dread that my heart misses beat after beat, faltering, weakening. Am I dying? Then Sprout is calling.

<*Jinny? Jinny! Wake up! Fight! Now!*>

In the last tiny space in my mind that is still wholly mine, I remember the spells, my weapons! Heartened, I manage to utter the first word of the Ward of Protection that Quaryk taught me. As I continue in a voice little more than a hoarse whisper, a familiar green glow lights up the wicked darkness, appearing under my chin where my hands clasp my throat. As it pulses, the dread lessens, my heartbeats steady, and I manage to summon help from the Tree. By the end of the spell, I can chant the Cycle of Exclusion, banishing the dream and the one who sends it. Somewhere I feel Sprout cheering me on as, with ferocious fury, the Necromancer throws enchantment after enchantment trying to overwhelm me. But mine are stronger by the most minute margin. At length, he stops, frustrated, and the void caves in on itself. He is gone.

Waking, the dream leaves a bitter mental taste and a mouth as dry as new wood ash. Trembling and weak, I fumble the cup of water beside my bed, creating a puddle on the wooden floor. This is his purpose, I tell myself, to weaken me again and again so that one day I will simply give in. The memory of each foul nightmare never fades. Like the others, this one is profound, and I know that if I manage to go back to sleep, he will try again.

I light my candle and, pouring another cup, drink it down thirstily, then busy myself packing the few things I possess.

<*How do you feel now?*> Sprout asks. He is feeling fine as the Necromancer has ignored him, and Tree knows, I'm glad of it.

'Better now, thanks to you. If you hadn't … I wouldn't be here now.'

He stays silent, knowing how close I came to giving in. Instead, he wraps me in memories of his happy day, showing me where he has been playing and how he helped to haul heavy carts on the farm with Flutterby. When he says goodnight at last, my mind is clearer, almost calm, and dawn is breaking, so when I'm done, I wander down to the kitchen to eat as I feel somewhat safer there. The cook and her maids are familiar now, and their company takes some of the sting of the night away.

Quaryk comes in as I finish breakfast, says a civil 'Goodmorn and eyes me as I drink the last of my tea, trying to stop my hands trembling. He refrains from asking the obvious, glancing at my purple-shadowed eyes. We eat in silence, and then he rises.

'Are you ready?' he asks. 'It has been decided that we will travel on the cargo lifts to the Divide, and from there, we will ride to the Spring Palace.'

'Why don't you just - you know?' I say, yawning and making the same gesture Quaryk does when he begins his magic, 'straight up to the Canopy?'

He gives me an old-fashioned look.

'Travelling would leech a great deal of magic from the Tree. We will use quite enough just to get to the lifts.'

This sounds reasonable, so I nod and, grabbing my bag, follow him out onto a much wider balcony than I've seen before. This gives us an entirely different view over the Glebe, which is blotched and shadowed by the varying thickness of the foliage overhead. I hug the bole, staring up, starting to feel sick. Perhaps we will have to step from leaf-cluster to leaf-cluster, perhaps seeing the vastness of the airy spaces beneath us, the ground lying far below like coloured patchwork, and the terrible distances. I am terrified that I will fall and be lost, or, worse, Sprout will fall, and I will leap too in a wasted effort to save him.

Dizzy, I cling to the bark, deciding my imaginings won't help. I wish I hadn't angered the Mage and pushed him away as I did. Only fools do that to friends, and I want, no, I need, to tell him about my latest dream. But already he has begun the chant to transport us upwards. The Tree's magical glow is here in his cupped palms, so I bite down on my emotions, trying to stop my thoughts.

Already the wind of the change we must endure is whining and shrieking around us, building until every cell in my body is vibrating. With a gut-wrenching jerk, we are standing on something solid and, for an instant, apparently rock steady. I wait as the confusing effects of the journey begin to recede and, after a while, feel better. Opening my eyes cautiously, I look around.

We are in a great wooden box or tray full of roped bundles, which is swaying slightly. Looking up, great metal chains stretch upwards from anchor points on the corners, diminishing into blue heights. In all my life, I have never seen so much precious metal, let alone so much used on one object, although I have often seen it used and dug in the labyrinth.

The crust of the Bole lies a distance away because the box we're in is dangling freely over empty space and mere planks of wood stand between me, the horizon and a long fall to death. There is no ground, no Canopy, just open nothingness.

I peer through a big knot-hole in the side of a plank. The ground seems dreadfully far below us, the Canopy equally horribly far above. A dusty blue horizon lies off to the east, the sky above it dotted with small clouds like the sheep on Quaryk's farm. A vast patchwork of fields and woods stretches out to a dark green line: behind us is the rough bark of the Great Tree, too far away to reach. The vast nothingness of empty air around us wobbles with the motion of the wooden box.

This is worse than anything I have ever known!

My stomach churns. Trying not to spew, I stand and step back, thrusting out an arm for balance, my other hand clutching my throat. And then I am falling.

'Hey! What are you …?' Quaryk says. 'Don't get so close to the side! No!'

My head spins as Quaryk grabs me and pulls me to safety.

'Dizzy!' I gasp, staggering, feeling as if I am toppling over and over.

'By the Leaf! Not again,' he grunts, 'I thought you were over this? Well, if it has to be, I suppose …'

He chants briefly until the lovely warmth of Tree magic relaxes me. In an instant, I feel fine: better, but torpid.

'Sit down. Be calm.'

He pushes my head down, and I sprawl on the lovely solid boards, wedged against the beams of the side, hands so tight on my throat they are threatening to choke me. I don't want any of this, not the lifts, not Quaryk, not the thrice-blasted Sky-Kings. Who wants to live in the top of a Tree? Not me. All leaves and bugs. Ugh.

'She a Mage too?' someone with a low voice growls nearby. I expect to feel a curious prodding in my ribs, but it doesn't come.

'Yes,' Quaryk says briefly. The other man gives a low chuckle.

I don't understand why this has happened again. After Quaryk spelled me when we first travelled, I felt fine, even climbing up onto the stable roof on my own. Why has his spell failed now?

When I glean a measure of control, I ask, 'Did it wear off?'

I don't want to bespeak him: that is too personal right now.

Quaryk grasps one of the vast chains, looking out over the Glebe. He turns to me.

'Feeling any better yet?' he asks briefly.

'A little,' I say, and repeat, 'Did the first spell wear off?'

'Yes,' he says, looking down at me. 'But you know, the only real way to get over any fear is to face it. You have to confront it head-on. Then you can begin to let it flow through and away from you, little by little, until it is gone. That is the only way I know.'

There's a particular nuance in his tone.

'You've had to do the same? Get over a fear?' I ask.

He nods but doesn't say more, and I don't ask. Instead, I think about it, and it occurs to me that I have wings, and what possible good will they ever be if I am always going to be afraid of heights and open spaces? I must conquer this. If I can.

So, timidly, hanging onto the side for dear life, I look out, then down. A wave of vertigo rises with my gorge, but Quaryk's spell mutes it, and I swallow it down, growing a little bolder.

'What is this thing we're in called?' I ask. 'It's big.'

'These are cargo lifts,' Quaryk says. 'Without them, life in the Tree would be a great deal harder. We use metal chains, not rope, because they last much longer. Rope would be much more dangerous.'

'More dangerous!' My heart leaps up to my throat again.

'These lifts are checked every day to make sure they are completely safe. A novice Mage on each ledge is stationed to help in an emergency. No one ever wants them to fail, you know? Think of what they carry. Stone and ores from the Holtanbore up to the Collar, which are made into metal objects or powdered. You know of the great shaft in the middle of the Holtanbore? There are cargo lifts like this there - didn't you hear them?'

I shake my head. It's news to me. The noise must somehow have been there in the background, but I didn't understand it. So many odd noises in the caverns echoed from one side of the Holtanbore to the other, and maybe the noise of the lifts was hard to distinguish from everything else. Perhaps they were simply muted by other sounds in the labyrinth.

'So many uses!' he continues. 'They transport food from the Glebe up and down the Tree to where it is needed. And, of course, honey and fruit from the Canopy to all parts of the Tree. And messages, of course. A lot of messages. But they are tortuously slow because of the weight, you know.'

'The Collar? What's that?'

'The Root Collar is where the Bole or trunk of the Tree meets the roots,' he says. 'That's where the entrance to the Holtanbore is, remember?'

I think back a year or so ago to my first sight of the outside and the base of Great Tree. Ah. 'Yes. I remember. I remember how vast it all seemed.'

The incredible light and the vast open spaces, the colour, and the sough of wild airs against my cheek. Half of me felt like a snick crawling across an open floor, half feeling as though reborn in my own element. Then the platform jerks, and we rise almost imperceptibly as the counterweight cargo lift begins its descent somewhere far above. It doesn't feel quite so bad this time and will only actually last an hour or so.

'How many more lifts do we have to take?' I ask, hoping to distract myself with conversation.

'This one, today, and then we will lodge in the Bole for the night. It takes the loaders a good while to change the cargo. Then a short lift tomorrow will take us to the Crown, where the branches spring from the Bole. We will meet the salamanders there. You'll like them.'

With that, he turns and, squinting into the distance, says, 'You can nearly see our farm from up here,' he says. 'See?'

I gawp, white-knuckled, while Quaryk points out things of interest. If I don't look vertically up or down, I can just about cope, but I can't take in everything he is telling me in. It seems that my fear is all in my mind, as nothing terrible has happened. However, I am thrilled when the ascent is concluded in a sort of dock which is happily attached to the Bole.

Chapter Sixteen

The Canopy is completely unexpected. Everything about this tree is monstrously beautiful. Instead of the densely-packed thicket I had imagined, great airy spaces lie between the huge branches and twigs, although the smallest twigs are bigger than the trunks of the mature earth-trees down on the ground. The circular frilly leaves are huge, much longer than me, their steely stalks springing from a concave centre. And the colours! Below, all you can see is a dark silhouette, but here the leaves vary from white to yellow, green to deep azure, sometimes tinged with scarlet or orange. It is a living kaleidoscope, changing with sunlight, shadow, and weather. Great loops of pale-flowered vines hang from branch to branch, so abundant that they form vast silvery nets, scented and silkily rich. Here and there, like ruddy stars, grow upturned vermilion flowers, nodding in the breeze, each attended by a host of flutterbys, bloons, birds and insects. And, even stranger, alongside each flower, as though seasons are of no account, droops a single, heart-shaped fruit.

I sigh.

'Oh! It's beautiful!'

Quaryk turns to me, his face unreadable.

'It is. Now, come along. We still need to reach our meeting place with the salamanders, and that's a good step away.'

He turns, heading off along the huge platform to what appears to be a path. Where the Bole divides, it winds left and right between two ridges in the massive crust, wide and smooth. Quaryk chooses the left fork, but it takes me a while to understand that we are walking along the top of a branch. I can hardly believe what I am seeing.

Quaryk turns as I wonder whether to climb up the side of the path onto the crust for a better view.

'I wouldn't if I were you,' he says. 'The bark is very rough, with dangerous fissures. It's easy to fall in a hole or get a foot stuck. The path is far easier, and the best view will be further ahead.'

Of course, he's right: the bark looks like a bigger version of the skin of the oak trees in the meadow at the farm, crusty and uneven with ridges and wide crevices and here, deep holes. But I'm heartily sick of him now. He's always trying to sound so perfect and right! I wish, just for once, he would make a stupid mistake so he would appear normal. I glance around to catch his expression, wondering if he caught that thought, and I redden in shame. We need to get on, and I know nothing about this place.

We walk on and on until my bad leg is a pillar of agony. At the end of the branch, the path begins to climb, winding up and around the massive Bole in a series of staircases. I follow wearily, head down, leg dragging. Each step is a challenge.

'We're nearly there,' he calls as he vanishes upwards.

Gaining the top of the tortuous stair, he disappears, then comes back to see what's keeping me.

'Come along,' he calls, vanishing again. I clamber painfully after him, muttering ferocious curses at his back. Gaining the top step, I flop down and look around.

Up here, the path joins a flattish platform that stretches away into the far distance, made from small braided and interwoven twigs, each as big as the main branches on Quaryk's oak trees, with their surfaces levelled. Around the centre, vast branches grow up through it. I wonder if the Tree deliberately grew it this way or if someone has finished this.

Around the edge of the platform, a thick growth of shrubby stuff hides the open gulfs of air, thankfully giving an impression of enclosure. But what if I were to press through the interlaced fronds? I would fall, and fall, and fall …

A cold sweat springs up again, and my heart is jumping like a snake in a sack. The beast is back. I thought it was gone, but the world is simply too big and too empty. I am like a snick at the edge of a precipice. Rooted, I cannot move. I try to bespeak Sprout but cannot touch him. My hands are wavering between trying to claw holes in the smooth wood and strangling me. Waves of sheer desperate panic squeeze my stomach and take my breath. The awful sensation continues. Quaryk turns then hurries back.

'*What's wrong?*' he asks, bespeaking me, intimately probing to find the problem. I feel myself shrinking back. We have not bespoken each other since - well - since I was so stupid.

'C - Can't,' I say, trying to stop this horrible feeling and failing. My terror and anxiety must be flooding his mind. To top everything off, I am ashamed.

I feel him finding the memory of Necromancer's last visit and my consequent consternation and terror. Knowing how close I came to being engulfed by the evil, the hard shell within him softens.

'*So, my spells to relieve your vertigo were cancelled by Charnecron's power. No need to worry,*' he says. '*Look at me. I will repeat them. Now, look up. Look at me.*'

He forces my chin up.

'*Open your eyes.*'

I squint, still seeing myself plummeting down, crashing and banging off every branch and twig, tearing the beautiful leaves, slamming into vines for a second or two to rebound, and drop again and again until the final long descent. This scenario happens behind my lids, over and over.

'*Come on! Open your eyes properly,*' he says. Taking me by the shoulders, he turns me towards him, and the shock of his physical contact eases me. Shuddering, I stare into his face. His hands move to the sides of my head. Again! Is this going to be necessary for the foreseeable?

'*I am here,*' he says, '*look at the light.*'

A tiny point of red appears in the darkness inside my brain, and the Tree is here. A strong greenish glow permeates me, easing tension, so that my whole frame turns to water, and I slip forward into his arms, totally drunk on the sensation. Unconsciously I press my body to his.

'*Now you will cope, and soon this place will feel completely normal,*' the Tree says. '*I wish you to be happy here.*'

Quaryk raises his eyebrows, and bright-eyed, smiles. He hasn't smiled at me like this for a long while. His breath is hot on my cheek, his hands still clasping my shoulders, eyes glinting with an unexpected urgency.

Feeling our need, my lips open, my body responding in the ancient way. And now ... but no! Like a drench of cold water, we both realise what is happening, and he leans back, poker-faced, letting me loose. I really wish, I wish - but I don't know exactly what it is I want ...

Chapter Seventeen

This morning the air is awash with perfume and bathed in sunlight, the clouds small and fleecy above us. Delighted, I breathe it in until there is an abrupt call nearby. I turn to find two vast lizard-like creatures watching me and gasp. Crests and delicate filigree extrusions ripple about their necks and the sides of their powerful mailed bodies, and they have clawed limbs, long spiked tails, and in their eyes is intelligence. Blue-red tongues flicker, tasting the air, as they unfold wide wings to spread them like sails. And they sport such colours! Unimaginably bright hues ripple over their scales, glowing more vividly than the flowers in Milde's garden. My breath catches. These creatures are fascinating. One bespeaks me:

<*Good day, You are its?*>

Stunned, it takes me a second or two to understand.

'*Yes, I am,*' I say, bespeaking them. '*Good day.*'

The two come close, claws beating a tattoo on the platform to sniff me up and down like the farm dogs do. Their perfume reminds me of newly baked bread and makes my stomach rumble. They wear unusual harnesses, which, crisscrossing their bodies, have pad-like saddles with bags behind.

'*I am Jinny Morai,*' I tell them, '*and this is Quaryk. And this,*' I add, as he joins me again, '*is Sprout.*'

The same salamander says, <*Quaryk is our friend.*> And finding Sprout watching through my eyes continues, <*Greetings, Sprout. You are a dragon! How wonderful!*>

Waking, Quaryk yawns and rises. The salamanders fold their wings and step back courteously, their colours suddenly matching the wood beneath them, making them almost indistinguishable until they move.

'Good day,' he says aloud, then bespeaks them, *'We are summoned to the Spring Palace as soon as possible. Are you both here to take us there, my friends?'*

<*We are,*> the larger of the two says, <*but please allow us a brief respite to become comfortable.*>

With that, the two salamanders race off out of sight behind the leaves.

'They are modest to a fault,' Quaryk says softly with a grin. 'The model of decorum - apart from one major quirk.'

'Oh? What's that? They seem very civil and clever to me.'

'Yes, they are clever,' he says, 'and delightful in many ways, but don't get drawn into any games of chance with any of them.'

Wondering what salamanders could possibly want, I say, 'They're gamblers? What in Leaf do they gamble for?'

'Never you mind,' Quaryk replies, annoyingly, like Ma did when she thought me uppity. 'Nothing you would possibly understand, so let it go - but always be polite.'

I bridle at his assumption that I am somehow rude and stare into the foliage. In a few minutes, the two return. The biggest salamander nods to Quaryk, and he swings a leg over its back, settling into the saddle in a low crouch.

'This is how you must sit,' he says, looking up. 'It will be much harder for your mount if you are upright. Now, this is Jiss, and that is Assis, my good friends. He strokes the gleaming skin of his mount's neck, pointing to the other salamander. 'Come, she is waiting for you. We must get on.'

So, my mount is Assis.

'But I don't want to hurt her,' I say, looking at her beautiful, seemingly fragile extrusions. But before Quaryk can reply, a low rumbling comes from Assis - a rumble I later interpret as pleasure - and she says, in a grumbling hiss,

'That becomes you, youngling, but you will not hurt me. Please mount.'

Collecting myself, I bespeak her: *'Thank you,'* carefully lowering my leg over her back. Her skin is hot to the touch and smells gorgeous.

She says, *'Your courtesy does you credit. Now, the hand holds are here and here,'* and turns her head on her prehensile neck to nudge the sky-blue straps that encircle her neck and belly. *'Hold tight.'*

Her beautiful amber eyes turn to me as I make a grab for the straps, crouching low on the salamander's neck.

'Ready?' Quaryk calls.

'Yes.'

'Then we're off,' he says, glancing at our mounts in turn.

'Hold tight with your …'

Quaryk's words are lost when Jiss takes off with a hiss like a kettle coming to a boil. Assis, with a matching hiss, shoots forward to run along the path that takes us upwards. I hang on like a loose sack of roots as she undulates in fast, serpentine curves, panicking as I swing from side to side.

'*Squeeze tighter with your legs!*' Assis says.

Her words make sense when I tighten my thigh muscles. The difference is apparent straight away. Now I can ride without catching myself and feeling I'm falling off. It is a bit like riding Myrtle.

'*That's better,*' she says without stopping. '*It is much easier for me. We will be able to move faster soon. Well done.*'

I bask momentarily in this small achievement until her meaning gets through. Faster? *How much faster can a salamander go,* I wonder?

Quaryk turns his head, teeth and eyes gleaming, laughing at me. Has he been listening to my thoughts since he last entered my mind? This is such a disquieting idea that I try to keep my mind blank, but I find it impossible. When I am used to the motion and speed, my mind wanders. Eventually we leave the big platform to climb up a vast branch. Then, after what seems an age, we slow down. Thank the Trees!

Ahead, Quaryk and Jiss halt where the path widens a little. Assis follows and waits for me to dismount, but my muscles are stiff and sore, so I stumble as my bad leg folds under me.

'Well, how did you like your first ride on a salamander?' Quaryk asks me, helping me up.

'It was marvellous, but I ache everywhere,' I reply.

'That is because you use different muscles riding like this. If you hadn't learned to ride Myrtle, this would have been impossible.'

My riding lessons were another part of the plan. Glancing narrowly at Quaryk, I have to remember that he is as bound by the Order as I am now. He is delving into the packs on the salamander's tails, in turn, to bring out various parcels. When he unwraps the contents, fruits and breads are revealed.

'These were sent from the Kings' own kitchens,' he informs me, handing the food around. We eat in a companionable silence listening to the nearby birdsong, bloons' croaking, and flutterbys' thin piping. Then vast leaves flutter around us in a sudden, sharp gust of wind. Small twigs, each thicker than my body, creak as they rub together, and a sweet scent from the garlanded vine-flowers arises. The food is excellent, and we drink from clean water caught in folds of bark, or cup-shaped flowers and leaves of parasitic plants which, clinging to the branch, grow to the size of the oaks in the meadow.

I marvel at the size and apparent strength of this Tree, understanding the term 'Great'. It is unimaginable, a whole world in a Tree.

Quaryk's hand is on my shoulder.

'Time to get up, Jinny,' he says. 'We have to go now if we are to get to the Spring Palace before dark.'

Assis is here, a question behind her eyes. <*Ready to go?*>

'Yes,' I say, squirming. My leg is a rod of fire. 'Is it far?'

<*It is not far,*> she says bespeaking me again, <*and you will be able to rest soon.*>

~*~

Salamanders are amazingly strong. After running all afternoon, they show no signs of tiring as the evening sun pierces the Canopy in shafts of rose-gold and the blue shadows deepen to indigo. Roosting birds and bloons comment and discuss us as we pass, and despite my pain, I am drowsy as we swing from the path onto a flat dim expanse which stretches away before us. Lights glimmer somewhere in the distance. We speed along on parallel paths.

<*The Spring Palace!*> Assis says, jolting me from a doze.

Peering into the dusk, this is hard to make out: a vast, globular mass lit by masses of tiny flames. In the centre of the platform, huge Tree branches arch upwards, supporting an enormous edifice of living wood, woven and pleached into walls, ceilings and floors, like a vast snicks' nest. We stop suddenly and I try to dismount, but my stiff legs simply won't work. While the salamanders hiss and chatter to each other in their steam-driven language, Quaryk comes over to help again. Once I am semi-mobile, the salamanders lead the way up a long ramp to wide carved doors. Inside, all is light and warmth, and thank Leaf, a warm welcome.

Chapter Eighteen

Sprout has finally arrived, my leg has recovered, and we will see the Sky-Kings soon. I have a room overlooking the stables where the salamanders and Sprout are quartered. Next to them is the old dragon roost, where long ago, dragons lived or stayed overnight. A guide from the Kings showed us. Apparently, the scrapes and claw marks left by the big dragons are still there and made Sprout sad for a little while, but he has bounced back.

Yawning, I stretch delightfully, looking around. This room is odd, its shape conforming to the tiny twigs that form its main beams, with smaller, intricately woven shoots making up the walls, ceiling and floor. These billow and curve, and only the floor is flat. My cot is woven into the sides and floor, with a lovely carved chest for clothes at its bottom. A lamp sits on a tiny shelf, and three wonky windows peer out to the panorama of branches and leaves surrounding the palace platform.

Some of the larger beams above the bed are carved into various shapes: people, trees, animals, and dragons. The largest one depicts the story of the First-Comers. This is good to muse on while falling asleep, reminding me of Milde and the farm. But I must get up, or there'll be nothing left for breakfast. Sprout, with a belch, informs me he has already eaten.

The food here is wonderful, better than anything I've ever had, and the folk seem happy and content, chattering incessantly to each other like a roost of birds. When I reach the dining room, Quaryk is sitting with Galden and Lind, who travelled here with Sprout. The Three transported them from the Collar up here yesterday, despite the huge drain on Tree magic. Much easier than my journey, but I suspect the Mages wanted me to see something of the workings of the Tree. And, as there is only so much precious magic the Trees can release at any one time, I am very grateful for their kindness to my friends. I slip onto the bench beside Lind.

'We thought you were going to sleep for the whole day,' she says teasingly as the others give me a 'Goodmorn'.

'Goodmorn, all. I was really tired,' I say, 'and I was so comfortable I don't think I stirred all night. How was your journey?'

'Ugh! Horrible!' Galden groans, pulling a droll face and making Lind laugh.

'Getting to the Bole was easy,' she says, 'but the magic to get us up here was, well, different!'

'Not something I want to repeat,' Galden says sparingly, yet he must know he will probably have to.

I touch Sprout, *'Morn, love. You didn't mind the travelling, did you?'*

<*No, it was exciting, and the Mages made my ears buzz and tickle. It was fun!*>

I smile. He's always happy, lifting my mood. I'm so glad he's here with me now.

'Sprout enjoyed it,' I tell them sleepily, yawning into my hand.

Quaryk glances at me, then his face quiets as he bespeaks someone I don't know, then he smiles and speaks aloud for everyone's benefit.

'Well, Jinny. I've just had a request for you to have an audience in the Sky-Kings' court tomorrow,' he says, 'so you'll have all day to catch up on your sleep and relax.'

'Oh, thank you. That's good,' I say. In all honesty, I had almost forgotten why we came.

'Riding a salamander tends to make one exhausted, and everything is new to you,' Quaryk says. 'We won't be called until midday.'

I merely nod my agreement as the smell of food is so enticing. Hungrily, I fill my bowl.

~*~

<*There you are!*> Sprout says, lazing comfortably outside the stables when I arrive. <*This stuff is warm. And smooth. Nice.*>

'What stuff?' I ask.

<*This stuff I'm lying on,*> he replies.

'This is wood. Do you remember being in the Bole when we saw the Mages that first time? That was wood, like this.'

<*Ah yes, I remember,*> he says sleepily. <*That was warm too. I am very comfy here.*>

I can't blame him for feeling lazy. Galden and Lind still look strained and tired. Although grateful they've brought Sprout, I am surprised that both chose to come. Galden was the obvious choice, being Sprout's firm friend as well as mine. But Lind?

When I ask, she says, 'You know I must be the Teller for the family one day and try to fill Ma's shoes. Then I will be stuck at home for good. Before that happens, I want to see something of the world. This is my only chance. Travelling here has been fascinating. I had no idea how wide the Glebe is, how varied, and here in the Girdle, is only one small bit of the whole world.'

'The Girdle?' I say.

'What? Don't you know?' she says. 'Surely you know that is the hedge that runs around the Glebe that keeps unwanted things out. All Trees have a Girdle.'

'Yes, of course - I forgot,' I say, remembering the dark line we saw in the distance when we looked out from the lift.

~*~

Lying with my back against Sprout's warm scales, I doze. Galden is investigating the stables, and Lind has gone back to her room.

There is so much I don't know. I long to learn everything I suspect I have missed slaving in the depths of the Holtanbore. The memory of that place makes me feel sick, and I will never go back there unless I manage to visit Three Gems. I miss the loving life I led there, and that if I had stayed, I would probably have become a chandler-wife, living with Ma, Da, and the boys. And now I remember the games I played with my friends - Hide, Go Seek, Tunnel Race, and Snick Hunt …

A familiar perfume tickles my nose. Sneezing, I open my eyes. Salamanders are approaching, their crests and delicate extrusions rippling.

<*Goodmorn,*> one bespeaks me. <*You are its? You came with our friends?*>

It takes me a while to understand, then I say, 'Yes, I am its. I came with Assis and Jiss. Goodmorn to you all.' The creatures come close enough to sniff me, claws beating a sharp tattoo on the stone flags. Their new-baked scent rolls over me.

'I am Jinny Morai, and this is Sprout.'

At this, Sprout wakes from his doze and, lifting his head, looks around. The salamanders step back a pace or two. I am not surprised: he is big.

<*Goodmorn. Thank you for letting me share your bed last night,*> Sprout thanks them politely.

<*You are most welcome, Sprout,*> one of the salamanders says. <*Will you come and eat with us?*>

<*I am not hungry at present, but I thank you. I will eat with you tomorrow.*>

The salamanders ripple their extrusions in farewell, hissing as they turn to leave. I notice Sprout is looking well, his armour shining, eyes bright. Usually, he's always famished.

'Why aren't you hungry?'

<*I ate a great deal when we came here. There are a lot of good things to eat!*>

'Really?' A vision of Sprout decimating whole fields arises. I wince, changing the subject.

'How was the journey?'

<*Easy! Everyone is friendly. They are glad to see me.*>

'That's because no one has ever met a dragon before. You know we are going to see the Sky-Kings tomorrow?'

<*I do,*> he says, eyeing me as he stretches. <*But I don't know what they want.*>

'Nor me. We'll find out, I suppose.'

We settle comfortably, and I doze for a while, enjoying our physical contact. Sprout dreams of his journey here and the huge meals he has eaten, but my mind wanders to these winged Sky-folk. The children are amazing. It is hard not to compare them to my dim memories of

Holtanbore children. They are so free. The underway brought me only one concrete benefit - my ability to see in near darkness.

Here the children are fearless, happily flying in and out, swooping and stalling, landing and leaping in their games. I am beginning to wish I could fly like them, but nervous about making the attempt. Everyone would see. The adults, with their magnificent multi-coloured wings, seem so much *more* than me - confident and vital. This is probably why they are held in awe by the lower of the inhabitants of the Tree. The salamanders, like the children, run or flit like huge butterflies on vast patterned wings, floating and gliding from one branch to the next. Along with the fruits, flowers and leaves, this is an unexpectedly beautiful place, in constant and colourful motion.

My reverie is interrupted by a thunderous clapping and a flurry of feathers, revealing a tall woman who lands before us and settles her fine blue feathers into place. She wears beautiful garments displaying a prominent device, and holds a heavy, leaf-covered tray.

'Goodmorn,' she says. 'I am Silvca, messenger for the Sky-Kings.'

She places one hand over her heart and bows, then continues in a slightly surprised tone, 'They have sent a gift to you both: a small token of their appreciation before you meet tomorrow. This is a royal gift given only to those in great favour. Please - eat and enjoy!'

'Goodmorn,' I manage to answer, taken completely by surprise. 'Thank you.'

She deposits the tray beside us, steps back and launches straight upwards with a deafening down-beat of her wings while I watch, open-mouthed.

'Did you see that, Sprout?' I say. 'Wow!'

Unfazed, he asks, <*Yes. What has she brought?*>

'Dunno, let's have a look.'

Uncovering the tray, we are confronted with chunks of what must be lumps of some sort of huge fruit. The thick rind is pink and silver-streaked, with coral-pink flesh inside. The seeds seem to have been removed, if there were any.

'Here.' After examining it, I hand a heavy segment to Sprout and take one for myself. The taste explodes like sunrise on my tongue! Better than the crispest ripe applers, or the delectable pericots from Quaryk's farm, at once piquant and succulent.

'By the Light! This is amazing!' I say, turning to glare as Sprout grabs a second segment.

'Hey, leave some for me!'

<*You'll have to be quicker than that,*> he says, with a mental chuckle.

I snatch another as his tongue whips out for more. It is so good that I overeat, and after the second chunk, I feel as if my stomach will burst, but it doesn't last long. Rather than nausea, a healthy, vigorous feeling sweeps through me, and my deep-seated weariness is banished. I rise at the same time as Sprout, who is feeling as though he's just out of the egg.

Before we ate the fruit, all we wanted to do was sleep. I shouldn't wonder if all the folk here eat this. I need to move. '*Let's go explore,*' I say.

We skip and jog around the palace, a fair distance. It is amazing; old, and intricately crafted, a castle woven of withies. The Tree has agreed to all this. Here and there, extra rooms are being grown, spreading organically, with bulges and concavities, instead of regular lines. Pierced by passages and open courts, it reminds me most of our cavern, which Pa always said was originally the inside of a huge geode, knobbly and uneven. But there, the walls and ceilings were red crystal, reflecting light. Here they are alive.

<*This reminds me of home,*> Sprout says, thinking of the farm, which is always full of life and bustle. Around us, winged Sky-Folk flit and swoop on errands while a few wingless move unhurriedly about their business, and everyone notices and greets everyone else. It's quite noisy, nothing like the Holtanbore or the Bole, where absolute quiet and privacy are the norm. I imagine privacy is at a premium here, but it is a cheery, busy sort of place.

Rounding a bulge in the outer wall, we almost fall over a group of youngsters sitting in a circle, their wings folded neatly. A winged adult is explaining something. He breaks off when he sees us.

'Goodmorn,' he says. 'You must be the young mistress who has come to see the Kings? You're welcome to watch and listen to our lesson. And goodmorn to you, Sir Dragon!' He looks at Sprout, who is eyeing everyone calmly. The children stare at him, big-eyed.

'Goodmorn to you, Sir, and to you all,' I say, looking at all the faces turned to us. 'What are you doing here?'

'These children are learning the basic Rules of Flight,' he says, 'and I am Haran, their teacher. Please join us. It's not every day we meet a Lady Mage and a dragon!'

I smile as Sprout says, <*This could be interesting - and I like all these small ones! Let's stay and listen awhile.*>

'We would be happy to listen,' I say.

'Then please do,' he says, gesturing to the children, and they shuffle around on their bottoms to make room for us. We sit down, Sprout being very careful where he places his spines and tail.

'Hrumph! We had just started,' he tells Sprout and I, 'so I will begin again for your benefit.'

At once, the children cease their shuffling and quiet comments to sit respectfully again.

'Now the Ten Rules of flying once more … Bregan, the first please?'

A boy of about seven years sits up and says, 'The first rule is "Protect your wings".'

He goes on to explain the rule, of which Sprout and I had no inkling. All this feels strange as children don't gather in groups to be taught in the Holtanbore: they take whatever education their parents can or see fit to give them, and usually, that is very little. I am beginning to realise how lucky I was with Ma and Pa.

When the session comes to an end and the rules have been explained in detail, I briefly wish I had been brought up here. The children launch themselves, flitting away in groups of two or three, playing chase in and out of the vines or racing, happy and free. I am jealous for a split second and, although surprised, shake it off. But not fast enough as Sprout looks at me.

<*You should not be unhappy,*> he says. <*We will learn to fly like that soon. Quaryk told me. Wait a little and all will be well. Come on, mount me, and we'll run!*>

I scramble up on his back, and we sprint along the wooden plain until we are looking into the dense foliage at the far edge. The Tree leaves have a peppery smell and make me want to run or dance. Thick vines loop and dangle from every branch and twig. Insects whine and buzz and the air is full of chirrups and cries. A spotted bloon floats past Sprout's nose, croaking in alarm as he sniffs at it, and then he floats it onwards on a gently expelled breath. The place booms with life.

And then I spot something strange hiding behind the swaying leaves.

'*Sprout! Look! What's that?*' I bespeak him. If I speak aloud, it might spook the odd creature that is hanging by one hand - and it is a hand - on a vine, watching us. It has fur of a most gorgeous shade of that odd middling hue, turquoise. Again - all this colour! I never imagined the world might look like this.

Sprout stretches his neck to see.

<*It looks like you! A small people!*> he says.

For a moment, I am worried in case it is dangerous. Then, aware of the great bulk of what was once a tiny dragonet beside me, I shake my head at my own folly and watch the agile little creature. Chittering, it swings away, hand over hand, uttering a single high-pitched cry. It doesn't appear to have hind legs but uses a long prehensile tail to steady itself, reminding me of a boy in the labyrinth who was always climbing and dangling from one hand until overwork and starvation leached his energy. Now a dozen, no - more - small blue heads appear, and as quickly disappear as a gust sways the great leaves so that they flap and billow like washing day on the farm.

Then on one side, I catch a flash of light. For a second, I am alarmed, and then I see Sprout's scales shining as brilliantly as sunlit water. His dark oily colours have suddenly somehow grown bright and intense, and he looks like a living rainbow.

'*Do you feel alright?*' I ask, squinting at him.

A rope of half-chewed Tree-leaf is dangling from his mouth. He sucks it in and burps.

<*Course. Why? Shouldn't I?*>

'*I don't know - you look different, shinier.*'

<*Hey, you're right!*> he says, extending his neck to look at his flanks. <*What's happened?*>

I shake my head, bewildered.

'*I don't know. I think we should go ask Quaryk.*'

Silently, he complies, so I scramble aboard, closing my eyes against his brilliance. As we run swiftly back to the palace, I bespeak the Mage.

'*Hey? Quaryk? We need to talk to you? Now? Please?*'

There is a pause, and then he replies. '*Sorry, I was busy. What do you want?*'

'*Please come and look at Sprout? Now, if you can?*'

'*Is he ill?*'

'*No not ill, just ... different!*'

'*Where?*' he says politely, although he could take our general location directly from my mind.

'*Stables,*' I tell him.

As I finish bespeaking, I find I am slowly slithering down the curve of Sprout's rainbow back and I grab hold of a spine.

'*Hey, slow down! I'm falling off!*'

He flips up his tail, and I shoot forward like a snick to a crumb, but he slows a little.

<*Sorry, you will have to hang on!*>

'*There's nothing to hang on to! You are really slippery,*' I complain, gripping like a worm on wet ice. It's then I remember the nifty harnesses of the salamanders.

'*Hey, how do you feel about wearing straps like Assis and Jiss?*' I ask.

He turns the idea over and brightens.

<*That's an idea. D'you think I'd look good in them?*> he says, envisioning himself resplendent.

I smile. My baby is growing up!

'*I think you would,*' I say, straight-faced. '*I'll ask Galden. He'll know how to make you some.*'

<*That would be fine.*>

Back in the stable yard, Quaryk is chatting to Galden. They both look up as we arrive, and then their eyes widen. They are silent as I slither off onto the worn wood.

Then, 'By the Light!' Quaryk says. 'I never expected ...' He doesn't finish but turns to Galden, who, eyes narrowed, looks us both up and down.

'What in Leaf have you two been doing?' he says.

'Nothing. We just dozed a bit, then went out to look at the Canopy.'

'That's all? Quaryk asks a trifle breathlessly.

'That's all - oh, and a messenger from the Kings brought us some fruit. Big chunks, with some sort of silvery rind. It was delicious!'

'That's all!' Galden says. 'Light and Leaf!' He shakes his grey-streaked mane. 'Do you know how rare that is? Hardly anyone is given that!'

Quaryk is stifling a laugh but looking at me with oddly hungry eyes.

'What is it?' I ask.

'It is Tree fruit. As rare as worm's legs,' he says. 'It's something only Mages are allowed to taste, and then only after achieving the third level!'

'Oh!' I shuffle back, a tad concerned, awaiting further enlightenment.

<*Ask about my scales?*> Sprout says.

'Um, is that why Sprout is so shiny?'

We all look at him, shielding our eyes. His scales are brilliant, edged with gold.

'It is,' Quaryk says.

The men are staring at me again. This is getting uncomfortable.

'What?' I ask.

Quaryk waves a negligent hand in an unknown gesture, and Tree magic suddenly runs through me like a stream of fire.

'Mirror spell.'

Instantly someone is standing before me, staring intently. It's some seconds before I recognise myself!

'How …?' I cry and step back in alarm. The figure before me does the same, reaching for its throat. This is not a fleeting reflection, and it is me, but a better, more beautiful me. I look vibrant and alive, with clear dark-copper skin, bright eyes and dark red curls, which, like Sprout's scales, glint with gold. So different from the stinking creature with matted hair or even the clean, dull, usual me. I stretch, the image stretches; I smile, and my smile is like sunrise; I wave, and it waves back. I find myself fascinating, yet Sprout is more beautiful than I.

'How long will this last?' I ask, aware that eyes are following my every move.

'These obvious effects will wear off gradually,' Quaryk says, 'but while the glamour remains, everyone will see that you have been honoured.'

'Amazing,' Galden says, looking us up and down. 'I had never thought to see this.'

Now Lind appears through the gate, takes one look and steps back in alarm. Then visibly collecting herself, stands tall and throws her long braids back.

'The Fruit of Life,' she says. 'You've eaten it?'

'If you mean Tree fruit, yes, we have,' I reply. 'Why is it called that - because it's so delicious?'

Quaryk, suddenly serious, says, 'That name is given to this fruit because it can, for some individuals, prolong life indefinitely. Some Mages can live as long as they desire, although they have to consume more fruit whenever they show signs of ageing. You remember the Eldest that the Dark Mage killed? She was thought to be over five hundred years old! The fruit has healing powers we do not understand, so living such a span while retaining all the wisdom that she had gathered, Yew was a great resource for the Order. So, you see, this fruit is a gift of great honour and not given lightly.'

'Surely everyone would be glad to have a chance of extended life if they could?'

'The Trees decide that: only three fruits are allowed to ripen from each Tree every year,' Lind says, glancing at her brother. 'Each ripe fruit is allocated very carefully and given where it is thought it will do the most good.'

There is a short silence as I take this in.

Now Galden clears his throat, speaking slowly, 'But you know, some folk will never want to live so long. Some have known too much grief or trouble to want to extend their time, and some have lost too much. People are all different: everyone has their own stories, and long life is not for everyone.'

'I never thought of it like that,' I say, wondering if Galden has lost something or someone. I must ask Quaryk later as this is a lot to take in. Sprout breaks into my musings.

<*Ask about the other dragons! Please?*>

'Sprout wants to know more about the first dragons - the race that was lost?' I ask.

As if glad to change the subject, both Quaryk and Galden start to speak, but Galden stops. Quaryk nods to him and continues.

'The first dragons were here before our folk came to live in the Trees. Like the salamanders, they dwelled in the cracks and folds of the Great Trees' bark. Then, when the First-Comers arrived, before the Order of Mages was initiated, they became friends and allies, and we all lived in harmony for an age or more.'

Sprout and I are rapt - this is all new. But what has this to do with the evil growing here on Leaf and my two tasks?

Quaryk looks around as if to gauge the effect of his words, clears his throat and goes on.

'But then, over time, a young Mage named Charnecron turned to evil even as he became enamoured of the dragons and their strength. Why he changed is not important, but he is now known as Wyrmbane too. He saw the dragons as a way to gain power. So, concealing his plans from the Order, he secretly began to experiment upon some of the youngest and most easily led of the dragons. Eventually, his experiments led to the ultimate disaster. Whatever he did created a plague which spread through all the dragons of Leaf and killed them all.'

Ah, *this* is the evil the Woodspirit warned me about, burgeoning upon our lovely Leaf, and bringing my two tasks. Even though I witnessed the death of the Eldest, I can't really bring myself to completely believe it - it seems far-fetched.

But Sprout is upset. When he stamps a hind foot, I give Quaryk a mental nudge, hoping to halt him, but ignoring me, he goes blithely on.

'Our folk were not affected, although some of the salamanders succumbed. The remaining dragons, angered, began to fight the Order, killing whole Trees in their rage. But eventually, all of them weakened and fell ill. Although we had looked urgently, we found no cure and could only watch them die one by one. Yet it seems that, at the last, a desperate young mother concealed her egg in the bowels of the Holtanbore, the last place anyone would think to look.'

I turn to Sprout, whose hurt and rage are building. Although he will not bespeak anyone except me, he hears well enough. He jerks around and swipes his tail angrily from side to side, emitting red clouds of emotion.

'Hey, watch out!' Galden cries. He and Lind are flung back against the stable wall. Loose thatch and leaves cascade onto our heads.

<Is it true, Jin? >Sprout asks, twisting and writhing. <Did a Mage kill all my folk?>

'I don't know, Sprout,' I say. 'But it was a long, long time ago now …'

<What does time matter?> he bellows into my head. Filled with pain, his rage is building to a towering crescendo within him. <What does time matter? The fact is plain: I have no family now because of a Mage - because of one of your precious Order!>

He is furious. Up to now, I've only known him to be a little petulant or irritable, never like this. I rush to hold his head, stroke his scales - in this rage, he could fire in the whole Canopy if he wanted to.

'I am so sorry, so sorry. We are both orphans. I know exactly how you feel.'

His body is shaking with pent-up emotion. I try to caress his head and neck again, but he shakes me off and stamps around in a maelstrom of howling until the platform beneath us is shaking. We skip aside as his movements get wilder. Quaryk alone stands still, knowing all this is his fault.

<How can you know?> Sprout says to me in a blaze of vermilion and crimson. <You don't know who your parents are or what has happened to them! But I know now! Mine were murdered by a Mage!>

He turns on Quaryk, who has paled. A wisp of smoke escapes his mouth, and I can hear his other stomach working with great belchings and pops. For a second, I believe Sprout will flame Quaryk, but then he shakes his head and writhes sinuously away.

I turn to run after him, but Quaryk, white-faced, stays me with a hand.

'Let him alone,' he bespeaks me, 'let him come to terms with it. He will come to understand that it was only one of us that was evil.'

'Why did you tell him now, like this?' I shout. 'You've hurt him! He's too young to hear it so - so baldly, just like that!'

I shrug him off and pelt after Sprout. Once I'm outside the palace, I see him, small in the distance, near the far edge of the platform. I slow to a walk, thinking. Quaryk could have told me, and I would have broken it to Sprout. Why does everyone treat my friend as if he's dumb just because he doesn't speak aloud? Even the cattle on Quaryk's farm, good friends now, have feelings and thoughts, as Sprout does. Why don't people ever try to understand them? Surely we are all animals together, scratching out a living. Sometimes I don't like or understand my own folk. Give me animals every time - at least they are always honest.

But then … Quaryk is usually honest, except when he holds things back from me, and that is because the Order stops him. But how must poor Sprout feel? None of us are really his people. How can he ever fit in with folk who are so different? My heart goes out to him.

'*Sprout?*' I bespeak him softly. '*I'm coming. Wait for me?*'

He shouldn't be angry. He shouldn't be sad. He is only a year or so old.

'*Is Sprout all right?*' Quaryk bespeaks me.

'*No,*' I say rudely, '*and that really wasn't the right way to tell him. Leave us alone.*'

Quaryk emanates embarrassment and distress, but I don't care. He has hurt Sprout, and through him, me!

Sprout is waiting for me. Going up to him, I carefully take his great head in my arms and hold him. Unexpectedly, hot tears stream down his face, and I wipe them away from his beautiful scales with my sleeves.

'*I'm here, Sprout. No one can make you do anything you don't want to, but sometimes words can hurt more than anything else.*'

A flash of memory brings me the gloom of the labyrinth and Mabe, shaking his lamp in my face and screaming vilely. His words cut deeper than knives.

<*All my race! All my family gone!*> he says, with a second flood of steaming tears, which upsets me more than anything else. I didn't know that Sprout could weep long and hard like this.

<*I will never know my mother or father,*> he continues. <*I wish I could have known her. The one who gave me life and saved me!*>

After this, he is silent, but I feel his big body shake until he eventually calms, and we slip into a fitful sleep. When I wake, darkness has descended, lit by glow-bugs and night-fliers. Luminous mosses glow faintly along every branch and twig, huge silver moonflowers are blooming, and around us, the Canopy is full of eyes, minute to worryingly large.

Then, ridiculously, my stomach rumbles loudly in the breathing silence. I will have to wake Sprout or starve. I laugh at myself as I nudge him: these days, I am so feeble. I eat more at every meal now than I would have in two or three entire days underground.

He wakes and opens his eye nearest to me.

<*Why?*>

'I'm hungry. Aren't you?'

He opens his eye wider. Within him, I feel another surge of aching grief, but its acid edge has diminished.

'You have to let it go. It felt like that when I was taken from Ma and Pa. You will feel better, eventually. But it's late now, and we must eat!'

He shakes his head in the darkness as though trying to rid himself of some annoyance, scales luminous in the failing light.

<*As you wish. You have saved me too,*> he says, with a hot lick on my cheek.

We scramble up, and I'm stiff and a little sore. It's then that I dimly notice the flowers which are cascading from his back. Someone or something here is partial to my big friend.

~*~

Sprout is quietly eating in his stable now. The dining hall is empty as the evening meal is over, so I go through to the kitchen. This is a cavernous space, lined with ovens and big tables. Kitchen workers are trudging about wearily, tidying up for the night. One turns as I enter.

'You want something?' he asks - a short lad of about my age, wearing a dirty apron.

'I missed the last meal.' I say. 'Is there anything left?'

The lad looks me up and down, his eyes wide. I've forgotten how new and shiny I look.

'You're the Lady Mage with the dragon? Yes, there's pie and bread and cheese. Will that be enough, Mistress?'

My mouth waters. 'Oh, yes, please!'

He moves around collecting food and drink. 'You may as well eat in here, Lady. No one will bother you.'

The other workers are finishing their tasks, yawning and melting away one by one. Soon there is just me and the lad. He sweeps the floor silently. As I eat, I decide that kitchens or hearths are the main things that make any place a home. Everything that happens there is essential and worth doing.

Chewing a last piece of pie, I become aware of his presence approaching. Before I can bolt, Quaryk strides through the kitchen to my table and sits down. The lad takes one look and leaves - a Mage's presence is forbidding. Then there is a silence which I don't care to fill. If this is awkward, it's not down to me.

He clears his throat.

'Jinny, are you alright?'

A glance appraises me. Then he clears his throat again and goes on.

'Erm, I'm sorry for upsetting Sprout. I simply didn't think and shouldn't have spoken as I did. I should have softened that truth. But that is what it is, truth. You will doubtless hear more tomorrow, but I am still sorry for being so thoughtless.'

'It isn't me who you need to apologise to,' I say, still angry, and getting up. 'Good eve.'

His face falls, taken aback by my reply, but I'm not sorry. He needs to talk to Sprout before I talk to him again.

'Well … goodeve. I'll let you know when we are to see the Sky-Kings tomorrow.'

He sounds deflated. As he should be. He nods once and leaves.

By now Sprout is dreaming, and I am weary. With Quaryk gone, I wash my dishes and make my way to my room to attempt sleep despite the nagging voice in my head.

Chapter Nineteen

This beautifully crafted basket of a room is dry and warm. Shafts of sunlight from the windows reveal motes dancing slowly in the air. It is as homely as Three Gems in its way, and its comfort cannot be faulted. If this is one of the smaller guest rooms, the Sky-Kings' rooms must be magnificent.

A knock on the door makes me jump.

'Come in.'

'Goodmorning.'

A liveried servant stares blankly at me, lying rumpled in my bed. 'You are invited to attend the Sky-Kings' court today. The Chancellor will be ready to receive you and the rest of your companions by the fourth bell.'

'Thank you, Sir,' I say. 'I'll get up now. How long have I got?'

'You'll just about have time to eat if you hurry up,' he says, and his official demeanour cracks into a wide grin.

When he closes the door, I notice new clothes someone has laid out for me while I slept. My old farm clothes must not be good enough for the court. I yawn, slip slowly from the cot, and dress. The new clothes are stiff and itchy, and I am almost afraid to move in case I get them dirty.

'*Sprout? Have you eaten?*' I ask. Quaryk hasn't bespoken me.

<*Morn, Jin. Yes I have.*>

'*Have you had a summons too?*'

<*Yes, Galden came to find me.*>

'Oh, good,' I say, rather taken aback.

Sprout has used the head stableman's name, so he now thinks of

Galden as a friend. My dragon child is growing up fast and has his secrets. Mulling this over, I leave to find my breakfast. When I arrive, the dining hall is empty, but Quaryk is sitting at his ease in the big kitchen, watching something outside the windows. He looks up.

'Goodmorn, Jinny,' he says neutrally.

'Hello,' I say, helping myself to the remains of the odd, yet delicious, porridge they make here. I eat quickly, but as I finish, the bell for the fourth hour rings out briefly.

'Are you ready?' Quaryk asks. 'The others are waiting.'

I nod, wishing I had talked things over with him while I was eating. I am a fool, but it is too late now.

'*Sprout? Are you coming too?*' I ask.

<*No. They say I'm too big and won't fit. Galden told me.*>

'*That's a shame but latch on and watch my impressions.*'

<*Thanks,*> he says. I can tell he's still miffed. However, his presence remains with me.

I follow Quaryk to the stairways that twist their way through and around the maze of carved and woven chambers and galleries of the palace. The entrance to the Sky-Kings' court is through a series of simple yet sumptuous chambers. After a third set of double doors, we are redirected by another richly dressed courtier. Galden, and Lind are already waiting there, and we exchange nervous smiles.

'You are the Lady Morai?' the courtier asks, looking down a long thin nose.

Lady? I am dumbfounded. I am a dumbfounded foundling! I suppress a giggle as Sprout chuckles. Quaryk digs me hard in the ribs.

'I am,' I reply.

'I'm to lead you to the Chancellor. His office is this way. Please follow me.'

To my consternation, he dips a bow my way. This seems a bit much. I look at Quaryk, but he is taking all this in his stride. My fingers want to hug my throat, but I am managing to resist the urge. Sprout is finding all this very funny.

<*Lady Jin-ny! Woo hoo!*> he chuckles, sending an image of me snootily dressed like - like I don't know what!

'*Shut up,*' I tell him rudely.

Quaryk looks around at me.

'*You're a Mage now, and that confers a certain rank,*' Quaryk says. He is solemn as he follows the courtier. '*Enjoy it!*'

I barely have time to take this in as we are ushered quickly through a series of rooms that follow each other like bloons in a breeze. We reach a final room, only a tad bigger than my bedroom, which contains three chairs, a cupboard and a desk. Behind the latter sits a tall, thin, winged man dressed somberly in charcoal grey. His midnight wings glint greasy rainbows as he stands to greet us.

'Goodmorn,' he says in a bass rumble that belies his stick-thin frame.

We chorus the greeting back.

'You are the Lady Morai?' he asks and, turning to my companions, nods to Quaryk.

'Sir Quaryk? And …'

'This is my sister, First-Comer Lady Lind Quaryk, and my uncle, Sir Galden Quaryk,' Quaryk answers.

I try to keep my eyebrows under control. I had no idea First-Comers held the rank of Knighthood.

'Please sit, Lady Morai, Sir Quaryk,' the Chancellor says, gesturing at the empty chairs. 'I am Balwin Speer, Chancellor of the Sky-Kings.'

I sit uncomfortably as Galden and Lind have to stand behind us. The Chancellor resumes his seat.

'There is a lot of information to get through today,' he says, 'and I am extremely busy as the Sky-Kings are - ah - indisposed temporarily. So, they have asked me to talk to you in their stead.'

Through narrowed eyes, I watch him rifle through a pile of papers on his desk. *Will some poor soul have to clear all those in years to come*, I ponder? Someone shifts from foot to foot behind me.

<*What are we waiting for?* > Sprout mutters.

'Dunno - but we have to.'

Sprout snorts, and I imagine wisps of smoke issuing from his nose.

'*Stoppit,*' I tell him. '*You'll get us in huge amounts of trouble if you flame here!*>

The Chancellor looks up at last.

'Of course, Lady Morai, you all will see the Kings and the Three

Mages of the Canopy later. They will also all be most gratified to meet your other companion, the good dragon. I believe you can contact him at will?'

'I can. What do you want me to say?'

'Please say, "Good Sir Dragon, may we enquire as to your name?" the Chancellor says, 'and if you will, please be his tongue for us?'

I nod acceptance and turn mentally to Sprout. I sense him stiffening as he comes to a decision.

<*Tell him my name is 'Ardracian', but I prefer my use-name - Sprout,*> he says.

I am so taken aback that it is some seconds before I can think to relay this to the Chancellor, after which I complain, '*You didn't tell me!*'

<*Does a name really matter?*> Sprout says as I am relaying his answer to the Chancellor. There is an audible intake of breaths behind me. Apparently, Ardracian was a dragon famed long ago in one of the ballads, which I've never heard.

'Ah, thank you, Sir Sprout,' the Chancellor says. 'And thank you, Lady. Now please tell me how you came to save Sir Sprout?'

I relate the story of how I came to find my friend, what has transpired since, and also what the Necromancer intends for him. When I have finished, there is a busy silence as he considers my tale.

'But you have not told me much about the bad dreams that plague you?' he says. 'Tell me of them - please, be honest and tell me all.'

I dutifully reveal all to him, finding it difficult to put the fear and loathing the dreams engender into words. I say that they come often now, and without warning, and I tell him of my voice which seems to be weakening as time goes on. And I tell him that I do not know what any of this portends: I can only say what I know. The Chancellor listens quietly until I have finished talking. Then having spewed out all my secrets, I feel like a melting jelly in the stunned silence. Galden, Lind and Quaryk don't move a muscle or speak.

'Lady Morai, the three Sky-Mages of this Tree can tell you all that is known of the Necromancer. He was once one of the Three here. Perhaps they can help to ward you further.' He looks at my companions. 'Until then, please keep this to yourselves? There's no sense in upsetting our populace further. Now, can I suggest that you give some thought to accepting our help on your, um - quest?'

'What sort of help?' I ask bluntly, rather irritated by his tone.

Behind, someone shuffles restlessly.

'I suggest that you are escorted by some of our most experienced soldiers, a crack troop of fliers. This will alleviate some of the dangers that may face you, and they can help guide you on the first part of your journey. Of course, when you venture into unknown territory, they will be invaluable as scouts too. Just the four of you will hardly be sufficient, will you? What if you are all injured, and no one is left to hold the stone? What if the Necromancer can lay his hand on it?'

Speer looks shaken as he pauses. Quaryk looks at me.

'*What do you think?*' he bespeaks me. '*He has a point. How do you want to do this?*'

This isn't fair. A decision this huge shouldn't be thrust on me without any warning, and besides, I haven't actually agreed to anything, have I? The whole of my life was decided for me in the labyrinth, and it is hard to make my mind up at the best of times. Besides, I simply don't want to. I need time, tons of it. I glance around. The outer door is too far away to make a run for it, and Quaryk, sensing my feeling, looks around. Without thinking, I begin to stroke the half-stone nervously. Somehow, as I touch its texture, I suddenly understand what I do want.

'*If* I go,' I say, making the point, 'I will take only folk I choose - people who I can get on with and who will bring something to the task.'

Inwardly, I cross my fingers and pull on each ear for luck: I must remember I am the chosen of the Woodspirit who watches all I do. It would be hard to ignore what is expected of me.

The Chancellor looks indignant, but the whole stupid thing would be hard enough without being bossed around by some puffed-up soldier or other. Galden butts in with a question.

'Sir? A troop is how big? Fifty warriors?' he says, 'How can we hope to travel unimpeded with a company of that size? Surely we need speed and stealth. We don't want to advertise our passage.'

I cheer him on silently as Quaryk joins in.

'Goodman Galden is right, Chancellor,' he says. 'We need speed. A company that size will hardly be inconspicuous, and it would only slow us down. It would be sensible to try to avoid notice.'

The Chancellor looks surprised and more than a little indignant.

'But the Kings themselves have ratified this idea! You shouldn't be too hasty! You don't know what you may have to face.'

'Exactly,' Lind says, breaking her silence. 'We can't know what's coming, but a small party can hide, where sixty or so are an obvious target. We'll need to travel fast and light.'

'Well,' the Chancellor says, completely taken aback. 'It is Lady Morai who must decide, as it is her task to accomplish. Will you take the Kings' offer or no, Lady?'

For a moment, I dither again betwixt and between. Then the answer is obvious, but my mouth seems dust dry, and I can't raise a squeak.

<*Jinny?*> Sprout says, but I can't respond. He turns his attention elsewhere, and Quaryk jerks, looks surprised, and steps in for me. My hero - but I'll bet Sprout prodded him.

'The Necromancer has shown how much more damage he can achieve. Remember the earthquakes and attacks on the Trees?' Quaryk says. 'Nothing can stop him unless we can find the broken half of the Talisman, so we need to find it as soon as we can. It seems to me as though a hundred troops of fliers wouldn't be enough. So please allow Lady Morai to choose her companions herself, and when she goes, she will go secretly. But we hope you and the Kings smooth her path as much as you can before this.'

'In that case, *Lady Morai*,' the Chancellor pointedly turns from Quaryk to me, and he is actually wringing his hands, 'if this is your will, I have no choice but to agree and hope you are right. I don't know what else we can do. There is nothing that can help you or our Trees unless the rest of the Talisman is found. Only that, I am informed by our three Mages, would be of any use in defeating the Necromancer. And you alone can wield this half - if it is, indeed, the Talisman.'

Finding my voice, 'It is,' I say, 'and it is clear. I seem to be the only one who can find the second half of the stone, so I'll think about it.'

Then some of his meaning registers. I cough, clearing my throat while I think.

'There is some doubt?'

The Chancellor smiles wryly as Quaryk looks aghast and says, 'The Three mages you saw in the Bole may have made a mistake,' he says, 'and their claims must be verified. To this end, I ask you to accompany me to the Hall of the Order so that your stone can be tested. If it proves genuine, they will ask the question, and you *must* give your answer. Now,' he continues, rising, 'please follow me.'

My heart thuds and I am sweating. What if this thing is not genuine? Will I be sent back to the labyrinth again? But I suddenly see I am now a Mage, and that won't happen.

The Chancellor leads us down a length of twisting corridor and then up flight after flight of swaybacked stairs to what seems to be the very top of the palace. In passing, I look out of a window, clinging to Lind as vertigo threatens again. The smooth platform's curved edge is visible from way up here. At length, we enter through a small door into a vast, airy space fluttering with leaves and broken sunlight, and I feel better. The walls are loose-woven, the whole roofed by the living Canopy. The floor is steadied by great ropes of flowering vines and is mossy and alive with strange nodding flower faces that twist around to watch us as we pass by. A place of silvan silences, hushed and hallowed. We tiptoe in.

Now three figures appear from behind the curve of a huge central Tree branch, apparently floating towards us. Dressed similarly in palest blue robes, their faces are incredibly similar despite their varied ages. None of them are winged.

We make our obeisances, eyes down, and hands crossed over our hearts.

'Welcome!' they chorus, in ethereal voices, turning to look at me.

'You are Jinny Morai,' one states, 'the one graced by the Woodspirit, Mage-Born and Chosen, the Bearer of the half-stone. If your stone is indeed a part of the Talisman, with it, you may perform incredible feats. And, if and when the stone finally is made whole, it will again be the most powerful agent of magic ever known on Leaf!'

Almost dancing in excitement, another takes my hands and pulls me forward.

'Now, show us! Show us this half-stone you bear, so we may test it to prove its worth. You others, companions of Lady Morai, stand well back but watch closely - you are witnesses. Now, Lady, see …'

A green glow appears in the air, and an instant later, two large creatures appear on the moss, with a tiny still form lying before them. Our salamander friends, Jiss and Assis.

But what of the other? I step closer to find it is an infant salamander, but it is not breathing.

'Jinny Morai,' Jiss rasps, 'please can you help our little one? She came out of the egg dead like this.'

Their little child, stillborn. What in Leaf can I do to help them? My friends exude deep sadness and grief, but I don't know what to do. Surely death is something that cannot be undone?

At this moment, shocking and unbidden, the warmth of the Tree flows into me. And in answer to my thought, it is showing me the way to revive the child.

'*Try, Jinny. It is, perhaps, possible,*' the Tree says. '*Ask the stone …*'

The tree imparts that, because I have eaten Tree fruit, I may gift this child a part of my extended life. The stone burns as I lift it from my neck and lies, alive and sentient, on my palm, its heat suffusing my whole body. It apparently already knows what I want to ask of it.

'*Please help,*' I ask. '*Please help this tiny life to be?*'

It does not need to reply: I feel its affirmation, so, kneeling crookedly, I place my free hand on the tiny mite. So perfectly formed, so small, so cold, so dead. The stone feels sad but also expectant. So, concentrating, trying to exclude everything else, I turn again to the Tree. A further gush of warmth and the small creature is outlined in a soft green light, like spring sunlight through fresh leaves. The Tree is helping! Heartened, I clutch the stone in my other hand, kneading the smoothly carved surface between finger and thumb.

'*Please, let this small one live?*' I beg my half-stone. '*Help me to give it back its life? Please?*'

Behind my words are Sprout's encouragement and love. Quaryk stays watchful. The stone on my palm seems indifferent until a first tear runs down my cheek. Then, within it, a susurration begins, and it starts to vibrate, trembling like a pellet of soft mud. The glow intensifies into rich golden rays targeting the lifeless baby salamander. As gold and green mingle, I see the small, still form behind a barrier blacker than the Chancellor's wings: this is what I must breach.

The Tree watches as I push against it, the glow brightening. I thrust again, shoving against the darkness with everything I have. My heart thuds like pounding hooves and feels ready to burst. Summoning up the last dregs of power, I thrust again until a line of blinding light splits the terrible darkness. I reach in to pull the little one through. The white glow envelops me momentarily before the barrier snaps shut and the black wall closes. Then, the stunned silence breaks as, with an audible gasp, the child sucks in its first breath and expels it. Another, and another, and now a small heart is beating. The Tree and stone withdraw from me as the salamander's child raises its tiny head and, looking up at me, cries out. A baby's birth cry, its first celebration of being. The sound echoes around the walls of the globe as the others come carefully closer. With a swish of scale and tail, Assis and Jiss step nearer to nose at their baby, uttering tiny sounds of joy. Assis looks up at me.

'How can we ever thank you, dear friend, Jinny Morai?' he rasps. 'Only ask, and I will be there whenever you need me. We had despaired, but now our little one moves and breathes. She will be named Jinny after you, who has given her a second birth. May the Light of Leaf go with you forever, Most Favoured.'

Dumbfounded and weary, my happy smile slips as my strength flows away like water. I sit down heavily, watching the salamanders licking and nudging their child onto its wobbly legs. The baby looks around. Fixing its eyes on me for a moment, I feel something pass between us, a new bond.

At length, when the child can walk, the family moves slowly away, her parents adjusting their pace to hers. My friends crowd around me offering their congratulations; a hug from Lind, smiles and kind words from the men. Sprout mentally rests his head against me, and I am suddenly immensely grateful. What if that had been Sprout or Quaryk? And will it be possible to repeat this if needs must?

The Mages, incredibly, are wreathed in smiles. I sigh, knowing this isn't over yet, but I must rest.

<You have given life, Jinny,> Sprout says wonderingly. <That is way better than special.>

'I don't think it was me,' I tell him. 'I don't think I had much to do with it really. It sort of happened *through* me. But thank you.'

Quaryk sits down beside me on the thick moss. Conversations rise around me, like waves around an island of exhausted calm. Although it is a remarkable thing that has happened, to me it felt wholly natural, a gift of the Trees and the half-stone.

A gift of Leaf …

Chapter Twenty

'Jinny! Come on, Jinny! Wake up!'
 <*Jinny, wake up - please?*>
 '*Quaryk? Sprout?*'
 'Wha ... what happened?'
 'You fainted.' Lind's voice.

I open an eye. Memory rushes back as I wake properly. The Mages and my friends stand around, watching me.

One Mage says, 'Lady Morai, are you well now?'

Quaryk shakes his head at him as he helps me to sit up. An unknown someone rushes over and gives me a drink of a faintly fruity liquid which restores me somewhat. The Mages stare eagerly.

One flutes, 'Your actions have proved the identity of the stone: it is half of the Talisman! This, above all else, gives us immense hope. The Necromancer is attacking other Trees and some of the peoples living beyond the Glebes. And already some others of our Order have been murdered from afar, like the Eldest of the Bole.'

When the first Mage stops, another immediately continues as though part of the same person.

'First, he stirs his victims to anger by suggesting that we, their neighbours, or even some of the Outer peoples, are ready to attack them. He is breaking the long peace and sowing discord between all the folks of Leaf and sending his minions to spread this conflagration of suspicion and violence abroad. They seed evil rumours, sometimes setting one Tree against its neighbour, Outland against Outland too.'

This Mage stops for breath, and the last continues, 'We have no way to stop these attacks or the rumours and ill feeling they beget. Neighbour does not trust neighbour now. That is why we have decided to ask you, as the only one who can find the missing half-stone, to try to find it to help us all. To help all Leaf.'

I am sitting on the moss, still muzzy, confused, and now aghast. I am just me, just a girl and not a warrior. Not brave nor strong enough for such a terrible task. It surely cannot be left to me, alone. There must be someone courageous, strong, someone better than me. Only one solution comes to mind.

Rising wearily, like an old woman, I take a pace forward to offer the half-stone to the nearest Mage of the Three.

'Take this, if you will?' I say. 'Or give it to the Head of the Order, whoever that is, to wield? I am not a hero.'

The Three shrink back, shielding themselves with their pale forearms as unsuspected guards shoot forward to bar my way, pikes raised.

'No! No! We cannot!' the Mages chorus, even more high-pitched with fear.

'Remember! The Talisman cannot be touched by any other!' Quaryk sends urgently. I sink down again, at a loss. The stone is death to any but its Chosen. With this realisation, a wave of panic overwhelms me, and I clutch at my throat weakly.

'Sprout? Sprout, where are you?' I call, desperately needing to feel my friend's presence. He answers immediately. He has never been gone.

<*I'm here, Jin,*> he says. <*What can I do?*>

His familiar presence steadies me and stops an attempt to curl up in a ball like a snick in danger.

'Just stay with me,' I say, but becoming aware of Quaryk's scrutiny, 'Why didn't you remind me?' I ask him, glaring as though my fault is his.

'Willowind could not hold it, could she?' he replies mildly. And he's right. If one of the Mages had touched it, it would have seriously hurt them.

'*We* cannot wield it!' one of the Three Mages pipes. 'This is the Talisman, for nothing else can pierce the barrier of death to bring back life: nothing else has magic strong enough for that. And although you want to cast it from you, you alone can use it.'

The buttery half-stone lies quietly, looking entirely innocent on my palm. Why haven't I 'lost' it long before this, I ask myself. Then I feel an instant of utter shame as the stone tries to burrow into my hand. And now I ask again - why me? I am only a useless ex-slave. Sprout retreats a little, taken aback by my upsurge of harrowing emotions.

Feeling his upset, I try to quell my fears and panic, sending a wordless apology to him. In a while, when I am calmer, and the guards have retreated, the Mages, after glancing at each other, apparently come to an agreement.

'There is a lay, ancient beyond telling, which tells of the origins of the stone found by Myrthynne, a seer,' a Mage says. 'If anyone here can chant it, it may help you to understand what you hold now, although the last verses are lost.'

There is a pause until, out of the blue, Galden speaks up.

'I will sing the lay of Myrthynne's Leaf with your permission? I learned it when a lad.'

All eyes turn to the weather-beaten farmhand, the last person anyone would expect to have such a singular knowledge. I believe Galden has hidden depths.

Quaryk glances my way, and again, I am irritated beyond reason: why in Leaf didn't he tell me anything of Galden before this? When I scowl, he grins broadly, indicating I should listen, and I turn away, fuming as Galden clears his throat and begins singing in a surprisingly pure tenor:

When world was sunlit, fair and new,
When leaves danced light and rivers ran,
And clouds were white against the blue.
Then men and maids sprang, far and few,
And Trees grew under sun.

Then magic flew, a knowing blade,
from root to Bole, bough to leaf,
In far Maland - where rivers meet.
Then Myrthynne, finding leaf-stone, made
of her a witch-queen, dark and fleet.

The Dragon's Egg

That precious stone, she kept it fair,
in casket fine, with diamond shine,
With peridots and topaz blue,
and soon it turned to match her hair,
golden, in a twice-locked shrine.

Down river then, to silver shoons
of moonlight on the darkling deep,
Where waves slapped slow against her boat,
she took the stone amidst the dunes,
rowed far and wide, its place to seek.

And soon she hid the treasure fair,
The leaf-stone, wondrous pandrest,
Under the sands, above the tide,
All shrouded in her golden hair,
Under full moon, she casket set.

For all to find, if find they may
To cure all ills, restore fair life
The strongest nostrum ever known,
Conquering time, healing time's strife,
All woes besetting man or maid.

But soon the Leaf-stone, found at last
Made magic terrible and strong
Causing ill upon the land,
With axe was cloven, quickly cast
To the two winds in an icy blast.

And in the darkest days of woe,
The Chosen comes to conquer all,
Wandering to far ends of land,
With Wyrm and Mages, steeds:
Goodman, Knave and Fool all go.

The stone and Solitary One,
Found, will be restored entire
To conquer Darkness, heal all wounds,
And cleanse the land with healing fire.

Galden's last note fades away into a speaking silence. Everyone is transfixed, as though this tale, although familiar, is memorable and moving, yet I can't make root nor branch of it.

'*What do you think?*' I ask Sprout.

<*I liked it - it was pretty.*> he says. <*Does it mean anything?*>

'*Dunno,*' I say, feeling stupid.

And now, feeling even more ignorant, I ask, 'Please. I don't understand. What does that mean?'

The Mages look at me as though I'm a small, unknown bug, but one pipes up, 'In ages past, Myrthynne, a witch, was reputed to have found a stone imbued with powerful magic of the Trees. She secreted it in a casket at the bottom of a lake, laying a powerful spell on it so that it would not be found except by a maid and a mysterious "solitary one".'

This doesn't seem to relate to us until a Mage says, 'We think the "Chosen" one is the maid, which is you, Lady Morai, and the "Solitary one" is Sprout. At least, that is how we interpret the meaning.'

My head is a barren waste.

After a long moment, the Mages stir. The eldest Mage speaks softly into the silence:

'We, and all the Mages of all the Trees, have a question to ask. Only when the hidden half-stone is found and the Talisman restored, a force may exist strong enough to repel the Necromancer's wizardry. His strange magic does not stem from the Trees but from the deepest scrapes and hollows in the earth, and it is strong and fierce. We hope desperately that you can find the one power that may defeat him, so we ask you to try to find the second half and when the Talisman is united, to challenge him using this power. If you can accomplish these things, Leaf may yet be saved. Lady, will you try?'

A vision of the Woodspirit flits through my mind. This is what it told me, but now this sounds like a death sentence.

'Will you try? Will you try? Will you try? …'

The words echo through my empty brain.

<I'm here,> Sprout says, searching through the fog in my head. <What is wrong? Jinny-Jin? Are you alright?>

'They want me to go and find the other half of this stone and then try to defeat the Necromancer. But how do I do that? I'm only me?'

Sprout is frighteningly silent, but another Mage speaks. 'Only you may touch the stone, and only you can find the other half,' he says. 'We will wait for your answer, but it can be only for a little while. The Necromancer must be stopped! So, lady, will you try?'

My head whirls. I am struggling under the burden which has fallen on me. I'm only just finding out about the world. How can I fight the greatest evil Leaf has ever known alone?

I cannot find words. How can I say no? These are powerful Mages! My head aches, and my hands are making it hard to breathe.

Quaryk, watching my inner conflict, says, 'Sirs, Lady, please give Lady Morai leave to withdraw so she may consider your request?' The Mages stare, then nod as one.

One says, 'We see she is overcome for the moment. You have our permission to withdraw.'

Sprout says something, but I don't hear him or anyone else.

'Come, Lady Morai,' Quaryk says with a bow to the Mages, and taking me firmly by an arm, he marches me out and somehow gets me down to the stable where I collapse onto Sprout's bed of hay and dry leaves, in complete confusion.

'Stay,' he orders, as if I am a recalcitrant puppy. 'I'll get you a drink.'

I sit until there is a flurry of movement. Sprout snakes his way in to push up against me, followed by Galden and Lind, looking worried.

<Jinny-Jin?> Sprout says, nuzzling me. <I'm here.>

I cling on to him like tree roots cling to the earth in a gale, and my head clears a little.

'Sprout? I don't know what to do! What can I do?'

<It's alright, Jin, we can go far away and leave all this behind. Leave the stone behind and find somewhere else to live. If you want?>

For a second, I am tempted, but my conscience overwhelms me. Who else can wield it? No one. Nauseous, caught neatly like a fly in amberla, I dry-retch.

'Jinny, be calm,' Galden says, placing his warm brown hand on my cheek. 'There's no good comes of panicking.'

Then Lind puts her hand over mine, giving me silent support, quietly and kindly.

'We're here,' she says as Quaryk comes back with a steaming mug smelling mustily of herbs.

'Drink this,' he says.

I take a sip, and then another, until my shaking stops and my mind clears a little. I wish I was brave like the First-Comers who made their home in the wilderness, but deep down, I know I am only a slave, dirt from the lowest level of the labyrinth.

<*You're not now!* > Sprout declares. <*You found me and that makes you my mother! And you are Mage! You* can *be brave! Buck up, Jinny -Jin!*>

'*I can?*' I wonder, and, flooded by his love, I begin to feel a little better.

Quaryk sees the change in me. Reaching out, he clasps my other hand and says, 'Now - think! The Kings and the Mages are asking you to find the other half of the stone, and that is reasonable: like calls to like. But then you do have a choice. You can refuse more if that's your wish.'

'But if I say "no", what then?'

He looks away. I know the answer: a refusal can never be justified. If I say no and abandon my tasks, I will be a pariah, watching the world fall into ruin at my hands.

'I'm - I'm not ready,' I say, panic rising. Will I ever find the courage to say "yes"?

Quaryk looks at me kindly. 'You don't need to answer right now,' he says. 'You'll have a little time to prepare for such an undertaking, time to learn to fly, to learn to handle weapons. But, when all that is done, you will have to give the Kings an answer.'

I think of Ma, and what she always used to say when I was feeling scared and feeble, 'Come on Jinny-jin, you can do it!' And I am scared and feeble right now. With nothing else to do except run, I will have to agree with Quaryk, but it takes a while to summon my voice.

'As you say, I'll learn to fly and handle weapons, and then I'll answer.'
Quaryk, fleetingly downcast and disappointed, manages a wry smile.
'Good, then that is what I will tell them.'

I sigh. For the moment, I am safe but scared, and moments pass all too soon. I want a peaceful life and a chance to discover the world. But what a coward I am. *Does that make me evil*, I wonder - *or are we all cowards at heart?* Is courage something that must be summoned at need, or is it part of us? While these thoughts are tumbling in my brain, I deny the world, my inner voice, and even Sprout, although I still register my friends' presence.

After a while, when I can think clearly again, I know that learning to fly properly and to defend myself can only be good things. But then? Perhaps the Necromancer will go away or die or something, and the need for the stone will diminish. Maybe the question won't be asked. Yet, deep in my very bones, I know I am only fooling myself. What will be, will be. The task will remain, and the question will be asked. And then, because all Leaf is depending on me, I can't say "no", although I desperately want to.

I am torn asunder, like my stone.

Chapter Twenty-One

Learning to fly properly means building my other muscles, but this is hard. Sprout has taken to it like a bloon to the breeze, agile and strong. Quaryk says that is because he does it instinctively, and my mind is stopping me.

'Why didn't my wings grow when I was small?' I ask. 'All the little children here grow theirs as soon as they can walk.'

Quaryk eyes me oddly as if I was a bloon that talks.

'I think it is possibly because you didn't eat properly in the labyrinth,' he replies, 'and what you did eat didn't allow them to develop. Remember? You were stick-thin when I first met you. And I don't think living permanently in the dark helped you either.'

My earlier bland, monotonous diet was different from the fabulous food here, so he could be right. It wasn't until I had been on the farm for a while that my wings began to develop. And I spent a lot of time out in the open with Sprout.

Since the Tree-fruit, they have become feathered in a rich mahogany red, barred and spotted with white and black like the birds, glossy and full. Happily, when I join my flying class, I find I'm not the only older person here.

A gangling, red-headed and freckled youth looks at me across the horde of noisy five-year-olds who are swooping, landing on each other, and fighting and bawling. He smiles tentatively as I notice his own thin, underdeveloped wings. So, a late novice like me.

I smile back as the class begins. Our teacher, Alban, asks for quiet. It's not until we have unfolded our wings that we have a chance to speak.

He holds out a long thin hand.

'Goodmorn,' he says in a surprisingly deep voice. 'I am Drell. What's your name?'

'Goodmorn, I'm Jinny.'

'You are the girl with …?' He nods at Sprout, who is drinking long and deep from a bucket someone has thoughtfully provided for him.

'I am,' I say. 'My wings didn't develop until late, so I'm learning from scratch now. How come you're here?'

He shifts uneasily, rustling his feathers.

'A bit the same,' he says, explaining nothing. He smiles as though embarrassed, but I don't care. I'm just glad I'm not alone with all these tinies.

'Now we will begin with flapping, class,' Alban says. He's a tall thin man with the most beautiful white wings with a pearly sheen. He flies better than the birds, and I am awed when later he demonstrates a particular balletic manoeuvre, landing as lightly as one of his feathers.

There's a muffled groan, and one little dear sticks out his tongue. Behind him, Sprout sits at attention, head cocked, taking it all in, a perfect pupil. I suppress a giggle - he's so intense. Drell catches my amusement and grins.

'No use moaning,' Alban continues. 'Flapping and the thrust it makes are the most important parts of flying. You have to be strong enough to flap your way out of any difficulties and to make lots of thrust to push you up, so you can glide away safely. And you must learn the use of the air currents.'

I think this is going to be anything but simple. I decide I'd better pay attention.

~*~

Over the next few weeks, we learn - at least Drell, Sprout and I do. The little ones don't really need to. Born here, everything comes to them naturally. We practice the basics of flap and thrust, angling wings, gliding and soaring; stalling and managing it safely; and landing. How to retrieve a spin, and how to tilt the wings for different effects. We learn the best way to care for our wings and their parts, our feathers, our posture, and even how to sleep without damaging our pinions. Two weeks later, we three are allowed to join in an older class, practising everything until our shoulders ache and our wings are droopy.

On alternate days, a class of people of roughly a similar age are training to use weapons with a big, burly, barrel-chested man called Perinal. Drell is here too, and of course, Sprout comes along to watch. I've resisted this as I don't like the idea of weapons, protesting that I am probably too clumsy and will spear my own foot or something, but apparently, the Kings insist I try.

All but the lightest of the long practice swords are too heavy for me, so I have a short, light sword, which I dislike intensely. I can't imagine sticking it into anyone. We also practice with dagger and axe, staff and bow. Of all of these, I enjoy the staff and the longbow best, the staff because you can stop someone without having to kill them, and the bow because I am particularly good at hitting the target. It's fun to try to compete against the others.

Drell is my partner in the weapons exercises. We are almost evenly matched, both weaker than most of the others. But in a few weeks, I can hardly recognise myself, no longer the squalid, underfed child, now winged and powerful.

The summer is here, and the palace is beginning to feel homely. One day we are sitting on the big platform after practice, and Sprout is dozing nearby. Drell begins to talk, telling me of his past.

'I was brought up Outside,' he says, shaking his head, 'and I still miss my family.'

'It was the same for me,' I say, 'but I was brought up in the Holtanbore.'

'It must have been strange to come out into the light after darkness.'

'Not as odd as it sounds. I suppose it must sound odd, but the cavern where we lived was always full of light.'

And life. Sprout, listening and watching, catches and appraises every emotion flowing over and under my words. He knows me like no one else - apart from Quaryk, these days.

'What sort of light?' Drell asks.

'There was always firelight, of course, and Ma made candles. And then there was the light of the fireworms - a sort of warm blue - and lots of fungi that glowed in the dark.'

Drell looks puzzled.

'Fireworms?'

'Tiny creatures living on cave walls and ceilings,' I explain, 'which Ma encouraged by growing a type of fungus to feed them. Fungi are plants that don't need light to glow in the darkest places. Some are really pretty …'

I remember the beautiful feathery fungi that used to sway and flow in the slightest draught. 'Useful markers for good air flow,' Ma always said.

'So it wasn't all dark and gloomy?' he says.

'No, it was all warm, and bright, and - lovely.' I can't stop the note of yearning creeping into my voice, but I can suppress the hand trying to encircle my throat. 'What about you?'

'I was brought up in a forest by a family of Elets.'

'Elets! What sort of people are they?'

I have a flash of memory - Milde has said something about this.

'They're woodsmen and family,' he says simply, and then, sadly, 'I've never known anything else, and I miss them.'

We are silent for a few moments in contemplation of a mutual bond.

'What is the forest like?' I ask at length.

'It is very beautiful. There are earth-trees for miles upon miles. When I was little, we lads used to swing from branch to branch, vine to vine, going for miles without touching the ground once.'

'Did you live in a Tree like this?' I ask, intrigued.

'No, the trees there are nothing like this size, but big enough for us …' He grins. 'We live in a woven house rather like the palace. Pa's father made it between three of the biggest trees in our part of the forest. It was much rougher than this palace but warm and dry, roofed with turf and moss. My mother ran the house and gardens, and my father hunted and tended the trees. There was a little brook that ran just below the bank our house was on, and she used to wash the clothes and us there. And we gathered cresses …'

I hear the homesickness in his voice. 'How big is your family?' I ask.

'There are three boys and two girls besides me. I used to love the great bonfires we had when a bard wandered through the wood. We'd gather in a clearing between three fires, and the bard would sing or speak tales of distant places and strange peoples. I began to make up stories and poems of my own, and then, when my wings began to grow, I was sent here to study.'

I am amazed. 'But aren't all stories true?'

He looks at me as if I am strange.

'No, most stories are made up, although many are *based* on truths.'

People actually write lies? Despite my work in the records, I had no inkling about this.

'So what about the story of Myrthynne's Leaf?'

'That one is supposed to be based on a true happening, although it must have been a very long time ago.'

He looks at me carefully. My wings are trembling.

'Would you like me to show you some stories? Um - er - um, can you read?' he asks.

'I can read,' I say, a little ruffled. 'Ma taught me to read and write really well.'

'Come on then,' he says, 'I'll show you the library here. There are many stories for you to read. But you'll need permission, so we'll go and see the Librarian first.'

Sprout, who has been dozing during our conversation, lifts his head now.

<*You are excited,*> he says. <*I wish I could come with you, but I probably wouldn't get into the library, so I will go and play with the salamanders now.*>

'Thanks, Sprout. Have a good time. I'll tell you what I find out.'

He rises, and the platform shakes as he stalks away to find the young friends he's made. Everyone loves Sprout - except Drell, who watches him warily.

'He won't hurt you,' I say. 'He's a very kind and lovable friend. Give him a chance?'

'Um, well, I will, but he's so - well, he's so big!' he replies rather shakily.

I laugh. 'He is, but what does that matter? I found him when he was this big.' I hold my hands apart a little.

He looks doubtfully at Sprout's retreating back.

'Anyway, what about these stories?' I ask.

Relieved, he leads the way to the Library, a large nest, yet smaller and far neater and tidier than the one in the Holtanbore labyrinth. I notice the scrolls are carefully placed in niches woven into the walls, and loose records must be stored in a neat array of wooden boxes. I wait until Drell has talked to the Palace Librarian, waving and gesturing like a broken windmill. He comes back.

'He wasn't too keen on your coming in until I said you were the girl who found the dragon,' he says, but he's alright about it now. I expect he'll keep a beady eye on us anyway. The tomes are very precious.'

I follow Drell to the far side of the room, aware of the Librarian's eyes. He nods to a side table. Stacked neatly, five objects lie there, which look like fat rectangles.

'We have permission to touch these,' Drell says. 'But we must be very careful not to tear or mark them.'

He opens one. The leaves are sewn together at one side like the leaves that sheltered the half-stone.

'This is a tome - or book - containing the story of a hero and his lady, deeds and romance,' he says, smiling. '*Sarendar and Elinea, a Tradgedie.*'

He hands it to me. The book is thick, all the pages full of words.

'Really? This is *all* one story?'

He grins. I am suffused with delight. One story, perhaps containing riches beyond imaginings. Gingerly opening the first leaves, I cannot help myself as I begin to read. A sentence or two in, and I'm hooked by imagined lies - I am Elinea. But my heart sinks: I can't possibly read this all in one go.

'Do you think I can come and read it again?' I ask, sliding down to sit on the stool beside the desk.

'I'll ask …' he begins, but I hear nothing more.

~*~

I blink. Drell has gone. Blink again. It's dark, and I'm stiff. The Librarian looms above me.

'It's time to go,' he says gently.

Taking the tome from me, he places a clean leaf between the pages. 'You may come back tomorrow. I'll leave the book out for you here, but please tell me when you arrive.'

'Thank you,' I say, the story whirling around my head. 'Thank you very much!'

That night my voice doesn't stand a chance. I tell Sprout the beginning of the story of the lovers and their adventures, and when I sleep, it fills my dreams. I wake wanting nothing more than to read on. Once my practice and duties are over, I head straight for the Library, knowing I can read every book there if I ever have time. A waiting feast.

~*~

Now is the last day of our flight training.

'Pay attention,' Alban told us yesterday. 'Now there is nothing more to teach you, so it's up to you - fly or fall. We will gather at the edge tomorrow for you to take the test.'

Today our salute echoes from the great branches around us as we chorus, 'Fly or die!'

This is the point of no return. We must fly over the abyss of thin air from one huge branch to another to return safely or fall. Hopefully we will not die, as there will be two flyers waiting to catch us if we fail, two brawny young men who have smiled and winked at me since I was halfway through my training. Our talented teacher, Alban, will oversee the trial. Only Sprout needs to be strong enough now: it would not be easy to catch a falling dragon, even though a safety net has been rigged beneath our flight path.

The test day has dawned beautifully, although it is quite hot and sticky, even up here.

<*Good flying weather,*> Sprout says eagerly. The sky smiles sunshine through streamers of high white cloud. The warm air resonates with the chirrups of birds and bloons, but beneath, the ground is veiled by layer

upon layer of leaf and shadow. And I? I am first to fly, shaking inside. My friends, and a good many others, are watching my attempt, increasing my nervousness twofold. My hands itch to clasp at my throat, but with an effort, I manage to resist it.

Alban turns to me and nods, calling, 'Now, Jinny!'

I swallow, flex my wings and try to think myself light, like the feather Quaryk compared me to. Not so feather-like now, I step forward to the edge of the platform and focus on the great branch before me instead of the emptiness beneath. I must fly there. To that other branch. I tell myself it is not as far as the palace from here.

Taking a deep breath, I extend my wings, and push them down hard with all my strength. Feeling lift, I fly forwards, air flowing over and under my feathers, the pressure building as I twist my wings downwards, thrusting again. I thrust again and again to gain height, then soar, wings tilted to deflect the air almost until I am stalling, then dive until I can fly fast enough to flap and climb and glide again.

This is pure pleasure! I feel the air obeying the thrust of my muscles, the precision of my primaries, secondaries and coverts as they direct the flow. The freedom this brings! A thermal rises halfway, and I wheel, soar and flap, soar and flap, then glide down until the branch looms huge. Losing height, I stall over the centre and touch down with one foot. I've done it! Down safe!

A cheer rises behind me, and I wave at my audience as Alban glides effortlessly over to me.

'That was fine,' he says. 'Now, straight back!'

Grinning, I thrust down. Rise, thrust and rise, and glide back, Alban flying beside me. Halfway, we meet the thermal again and circle until we are high enough, and then, swooping, glide back to land next to Sprout.

'Well done, Jinny!' Alban says with a big grin. 'You have mastered all that I can teach you. Practice on your own now, but don't become over-confident. Many young fliers have come to grief because of that. And always remember the rules: keep them in mind whenever you fly. Congratulations!'

With that, he runs a little way and, with a rustle and boom, is gone to start the next candidate.

I am a flier! And I didn't feel sick once! Turning to receive the congratulations of my friends and the rest of the onlookers, I notice a gap - Quaryk is missing. My heart drops.

<*He knows,*> Sprout says, <*but he's busy, and I am here and happy for you.*>

I turn to my dragon to kiss him beside his eye.

'Thank you, Sprout. Your turn soon! Good luck!'

Sprout accomplishes his flight with the ease expected of a creature born for the air. We watch Drell and the rest of the class, cheering them all when they are done, but when we are back in the stables, the question I have happily ignored returns to haunt me, hanging like a fireball in my consciousness. And an ominous dread envelops me, like a cloud covering the sun.

I have no more time left.

Now I must decide. Either I say, 'yes' and have to look for the second half of the Talisman, or 'no' and condemn my folk - no! - all the folk in every Tree - to vicious attacks by the Necromancer. My fears crash down again like granite blocks. Sprout is tired, so I don't burden him with it. I am young and want more life, more happiness, more friends, and perhaps, even love one day, but not what is facing me. To steal a little more time, I hide out for the rest of the day with Sprout, trying to find an answer for the Sky-Kings. Later, slinking back to my room, the night feels oddly warm, but I creep into bed. A single startling shaft of blue-white light fills my basket but doesn't come again. Exhausted, trying to ignore my nagging voice, I wrestle again and again to find an answer.

Chapter Twenty-Two

The bass growl echoing through my dream becomes real, its reverberations howling around me as I wake. Without volition, I scream, 'Beware!' As ever, I am trying to choke myself, the half-stone increasingly hot against my skin. My fingers sting when I snatch the stone away.

A horrid nauseating laughter arises. The Necromancer's voice, louder than the thunder that once shook the farm, is twisting my thoughts as well as my bowels.

{*So, dragon-mother, you continue to deny my will! But I* will *take the dragon - and you will pay my price for your disobedience. I will tear your precious Tree apart, root, Bole and branch - and labyrinth!*}

A charnel odour fills the withy room as it begins to leap up and shake in violent motion, throwing me up, down, everywhere. My cup of water on the windowsill tumbles, drenching my face. I splutter, trying to wipe my eyes as the motion gets wilder. Even with my labyrinthine night sight, I can see nothing. My bed is behaving like Flutterby bucking. It shakes me up and twists to one side, then plunges down diagonally. A primal fear of falling envelops me, and as I scream, 'What's happening?' Sprout dives into my mind, terror-struck. Afraid for him, '*Stay still, stay down!*' I send, screaming.

He doesn't reply.

'*Sprout? Sprout!*'

No answer. Is he all right? Is he ... oh no! Is he gone ...?

Someone howls somewhere amid a cacophony of ligneous groans, followed by a moment of calm. I try to scramble out of my bunk, but the bucking begins again, and my good leg is slammed hard down on the side. Groaning with pain, I can only just hold on. Eons later, the motion gradually weakens, fading incrementally to a shudder, and then is gone. The air is full of dust, and I choke and spit. After a while, I dare to move. Both legs are screaming in agony.

'*Sprout! Where are you?*'

Weakly, as he replies, I sigh in relief.

<*I - I hit my head,*> he says.

'*I'm coming. Stay there!*' I tell him, though Leaf knows how I will manage.

I fumble for the door and crawl painfully out towards the staircase as fast as both duff legs will carry me in dusty utter darkness. Terrified, I dare not extend my wings: all echoes are chaotic, so the palace's inner spaces are altered. I suddenly feel nothingness with a hand, back up a little and try to move to the left. The fragile surface under me gives a tortured creak and falls out from under me. I plummet into nothingness, thudding into unknown objects as I fall and smack down like a brick onto a further wobbly surface. Unnerved and breathless, a stabbing pain in my head brings tears. When I feel my temple, there's a stickiness.

'*Where am I? Sprout? Sprout!*'

'*I'm still here. I'm alright,*> he says with a whimper.

My turn to groan. With the breath knocked out of me, I hurt all over, and my good leg is incredibly sore. Then, a slight noise beside me. Lamplight appears beside me. Squeezing my eyes against the glare, I half-expect Mabe's coarse voice and kick.

'Jinny? Jinny, are you alright?'

It is Quaryk. If I could get up, I could kiss him. And then I wonder, this is a strange and intriguing thought. As he shifts the lamp, I look up. Above us is a vast hole open to the stars, a massive rift spearing up through the entire palace, dividing it in two. I fell from somewhere up there? Leaf knows why I am still alive. But now, the surface I am lying on creaks loudly with the slightest motion as if something is about to give. How far could we fall again? This is still incredibly dangerous.

'I'm hurt ... and I fell. What's happened?' I say. My breath comes in hard, fearful gasps.

'An earthquake,' he says, glancing at two winged bodies lying on the platform a little way off.

'Are they ...?'

'Yes. Both … gone,' he says, his face distraught. 'But Sprout is well, and he's being looked after.'

I try to grasp what he said.

Sprout. Then … earthquake? Strong enough to do this much damage? All Charnecron's doing? I catch my breath. What in the Light has happened to Ma and Pa? For a while, I can hardly think or breathe for weeping, feeling as though snicks are crawling all over me. Eventually, I stop, feeling Quaryk's strong arms around me, steadying and comforting. I lift my face up to his, and for an instant, he lowers his lips as if to kiss me. But, shaking his head, he withdraws silently and releases me. In the lamplight, his face is drawn.

'Can you stand?' he asks. 'This place isn't safe. We need to get down.'

In answer, I struggle up, clutching at him, and find I can stand but cannot walk: my good leg is too painful, my bad one too weak. My wings seem alright.

'I don't think I can,' I say.

Without further ado, he picks me up as though I'm still feather-light, and we negotiate the ramps and staircases until we reach the main platform level. Somewhere above the Canopy, a shaft of dawn light dimly illuminates an intact lower guardroom. He places me against a wall, shivering in my thin nightrobe, so from somewhere, he finds an abandoned cloak and covers me.

'Stay here while I get help,' he says, eyeing me until he's sure I've understood. My head is fuzzy, and I am sleepy …

'Yes.'

I'm not going anywhere. My limbs are broken twigs, and my head is throbbing. A peculiar giggle is rising in my throat, and woozy, I am slipping sideways …

~*~

Daylight streaming.

'Whu …? What?' My mouth tastes of dry sand and crawly's web.

<*Jinny? Jinny-jin? Jinny?*>

Sprout, bespeaking me.

I garner a feeling of fast movement. He must be charging about in panic. Trying to calm him, I say, '*Sprout? I'm here. Stop and listen!*'

<*You're back? You are hurt?*>

'Only my leg, and it's just a nasty bang.'

At this, he steadies and slows to a stop. Panting, he is watching a bloon floating by.

Then Quaryk is kneeling beside me.

'Here, sit up a bit,' he says.

I'm on some sort of makeshift bed. A woman sitting across the room is watching as Quaryk helps me to sit up and hands me a drink of something hot and spicy. I splutter and cough, but it's good and makes me feel warmer. Quaryk looks drained. His white face is smeared with muck as he nods to someone who moves away. A hollow feeling drops into my gut. I don't want to remember. It is too hard.

'Your face is dirty,' I tell him.

He smiles wryly, saying, 'There has been a movement in the earth, big enough to cause a great deal of damage. You fainted, so I left you with this kind lady. But the damage is much worse in the Holtanbore, and all the healers are needed. I'll get back down there if you are alright for now?'

'I must see Sprout,' I say, trying not to think about it. Not about caverns, family, asking or answering any questions.

'Can you walk?'

'Maybe.'

His arm pulls me close to him, a strange yet marvellous sensation. I want him to hold me forever, stay right where I am. Our eyes meet, mine questioning, until Quaryk clears his throat, looking away.

'Put your weight on your leg,' he says. 'There, that's right.'

I find I can hobble a few steps now, although I am very bruised and sore.

'We'll go find Sprout, and then I must go back.'

He thanks the woman before we navigate the maze of broken corridors and courtyards to the stables, which, thank all Leaf, are largely untouched. Sprout is resting on his bed, and I launch myself at him to lose myself in his aromatic warmth.

Eyeing us oddly for a second, Quaryk says, 'Stay safe. I'll come when

I can. And … I'll try to find out about your family.'

Cupping his hands, he murmurs the transit spell and disappears in a haze of green light before I can thank him. Empty and vulnerable, my fingers are at my throat until Sprout wraps his tail around and drops a wing over me.

'*I'm glad you're here with me, Sprout,*' I say. '*I don't know what I'd do without you.*'

<Shh. Sleep,> he says softly.

~*~

'Wha …?' I mutter and try to turn away, but someone shakes my shoulder again. I hurt all over. It is all too much.
Another shake, harder this time.
'What? Leggo!'
They shake me again. Why? And I remember - the earthquake! I turn my head away and close my eyes.
'*Jinny, you must wake up! You must eat now!*' Quaryk bespeaking me.
No, no. All I want is to sleep and sleep. But something is stirring.
<Jinny?> Sprout says, <Please Jinny! Wake up!>
I can't ignore him. A wash of cold air makes me shiver, and it is dark. Again? Or is it still …
'Come on,' Quaryk says aloud. 'You can't keep sleeping. You've been out all day. We've hot food now, so come and eat.'
Sprout is already eating avidly.
'*Are you alright?*' A mark is showing on the side of his head where the scales have been scraped.
<I am,> he says, <but now I'm famished. You must eat too!>
I stir, trying to rise, and wince when I put any weight on my good leg. My bad one is stone.
'Here,' Quaryk says. 'Let me.'
He takes my bruised leg between his hands and summons Tree magic. The glow is weaker now but still there, and the vast purple bruise dissipates as I watch.
'Hey, shouldn't you be using that for others who are badly hurt?'

He pauses and looks at me sadly.

'All the folk that could be helped have been helped. I healed your head while you slept.'

My head? How many dead, and what of the Holtanbore? I am afire to find out but wait until he has healed the great bruise, and I can scramble up.

'The Holtanbore? How bad?'

He is pale and weary. And he has been weeping.

'Bad,' he says slowly. 'There's a great crack down there now, but that can be repaired in time. But some caverns have gone, and others are damaged. Three Gems ... well, Three Gems is finished, but your foster parents are alive.'

I gasp with a mixture of relief and sadness, yet before he speaks again, I already know.

'I'm sorry, Jinny, but your foster brothers ...'

He doesn't finish but holds me close while my weeping rises and subsides. This is the beginning of the end of the world. What will the Necromancer do next? Who can tell where and who he will attack? It seems there is no way to stop him.

'*Come and eat. You need energy,*' Quaryk says. I rise automatically and follow him. I eat, but I do not taste, I see, but I am blind, hear, but I am deaf. My mind is numbed.

For the rest of the day, I help Quaryk heal the Sky-Folk and salamanders who have been hurt in the stable yard. This is good: I don't have to think or speak, just do. Later, when I can't move for fatigue, I hear Quaryk bespeaking to one of the courtiers.

'She is in shock, and it may take some time to get over it. Give me leave to care for her, please? She will give her answer as soon as she is well and able.'

I fall to wake in the stable, curl up again, crashing into uneasy dreams.

~*~

They have already begun to clear and repair the palace, but there is no singing, no chatter, no jokes. Quaryk bespeaks me that he is breakfasting with Galden and Lind so I rise obediently and go to the kitchens.

'You're up!' Quaryk says with a smile. He is looking a deal better today. 'Come and sit with us.'

'How do you feel?' Lind asks. Galden merely nods and makes room for me on a long bench.

'I'm alright,' I say, sitting down as they glance at each other. I eat something, but at length, I have to ask, 'Quaryk? Can I go and see my parents? Will you help me?'

It's too far and too complicated to go alone because of my leg, but with his help, I could go straight down to the Holtanbore using Tree magic. Seeing my pressing need, he nods.

'Yes. I'll bespeak the Mages to allow us a day or two longer. But that is all: they require an answer from you.'

I nod numbly. This is poisoning my life. I must find out about Ma and Da, and how can I possibly find the other half of the stone and stop the Necromancer? My heart says "yes", but my head says "no".

He glances at me sharply, now sensing my inner conflict. He can bespeak me easily enough, but I don't think he senses my under-thoughts as I do his. He has become an open book to me, but as yet, I haven't revealed this: I might never. Apart from that one, deep, inner space, a hidden, secret place. His gaze blanks as he bespeaks the time and extra help for our journey.

'They have agreed,' he says at last, 'but they're not happy for you to stay away long.'

Then he bespeaks me, *'So, now we'll go and see how your foster parents are for a short while.'*

Stupidly I ask, *'Why? Why the rush? I have been training for weeks.'*

His face pales and tautens as he replies.

'News came yesterday that a huge army is camped, readying itself on our borders. And although it would take some time for them to reach us, the whole court is frantic. The Necromancer has never gone as far as this. His threat is growing fast. We have had many reports of incursions by his army of Darkaans in our lands. But now he has struck at the very heart of our Tree-lands.'

He rubs at his eyes and face as though trying to wash his words away before he bespeaks me again, desperation and dread flooding his mind.

'We have also had reports of a far Tree toppled by the same sort of earthquake we've had here, with most of its folk killed. It is incredibly dangerous to delay flooding for the other half of the Talisman any longer. It could take months to achieve. The Order needs all the help it can possibly get as soon as possible, or our lands, and the Trees, will be overrun and he will enslave us all.'

He looks away, trying to get his emotions under control.

'Now, please tell Sprout to wait for you, and we will go down to the Holtanbore. You understand this may be dangerous?'

I look at my feet, almost overcome, swinging between elation and terror. A tree toppled! And what will I find below? And what will I answer the Kings?

Now he turns to my friends, 'Young Sprout will have to stay here with you and Lind,' he says to Galden, 'If you don't mind?'

'We're happy to look after him,' Lind says.

Galden harrumphs, and says, 'That's right.'

He understands Sprout now and will make sure he doesn't do anything too silly. But Sprout has something to say about it, however.

<*Why can't I come? Galden and the sword girl are nice, but I can look after myself. I'd rather come with you. I'm not silly!*>

'You simply wouldn't fit in the Holtanbore,' I say. 'Remember? You would get stuck - the Holtanbore is a web of very narrow places.' I send him remembered images of the dark passages and sense his disappointment as he realises I'm right.

'I won't be away for long, and then we'll be back together. You can practice your flying and have races with the salamanders, eh? While I'm gone?'

A brief anticipation of these delights flares in his mind as he pictures himself joining in the young salamanders' games.

<*Alright, Jinny, but make sure you come back!*>

'*Of course I will,*' I say, pulling my left ear for luck. '*Of course!*'

Chapter Twenty-Three

The Holtanbore smells sour, as though the air has been reused too many times, and it has a peculiar alien chill. And the darkness is so depressing. How did I ever imagine this was the whole world? Glancing around the dim and surprisingly squalid Gathering Hall, I feel a mixture of familiarity and disgust.

'We used to come here for meetings when there was news or something to explain and for elections,' I say, 'before the new Master came. But then it was cleaner and brighter.'

Quaryk says nothing. Tight-lipped, he nods slightly. No Mayoral elections anymore … Apparently no cleanliness either.

'We should get on,' he says but stops. A deputation from the said Master in the shape of a couple of clerks is marching up. They stop and bow.

'Sir Mage? My Lady?' the first says, still bobbing.

I forgot that I wear the purple sash now: I am Mage too.

A pale-haired man, the head clerk, is a good two heads shorter than Quaryk and me. His black Holtanbore eyes seem huge: I'd forgotten that. The other cowers behind him.

'Yes?' Quaryk replies with a frown. 'What is it?'

'Sir, Lady? The Master asks you sup with him. We are immensely honoured by your presence at this difficult time …'

'I'm sorry,' Quaryk says, breaking into the start of a possible diatribe. 'We're in a hurry. Kindly tell him we will be pleased to meet with him another time.'

'But the Master says …' the man begins to argue, echoes rebounding off the stone, but Quaryk rounds on him.

'Do not trouble us or hold us back,' he says, 'or you will answer to the Order.'

The man subsides and, at a loss, bows again as we walk away. I look back. He turns, cuffing his silent underling out of his way, a scowl of fright on his face. Is he more scared of us or the Master?

Once out of the Hall, we ask directions as I don't remember the way to my aunt's cavern.

'I think we'd better bespeak each other down here,' Quaryk says warily. 'Too many ears, and we can't be sure all is solid and safe above us.'

'Yes. You're right,' I say and glance upwards. A loud or sharp noise might bring the whole lot down around our ears since the earthquake. We go on carefully, although I am itching to run and see if they are still here and whole. Everywhere debris is underfoot, and it would be easy to turn an ankle or worse. I just hope the ceilings are still solid.

'Down here,' I say, recognising the rock formations at last. 'This is the way - I remember it now.'

The narrow passage is rough-hewed, black-shadowed and twisting, with loose stone underfoot and hardly any light. Quaryk stops for a few seconds to produce a faint green glimmer in a cupped hand to see by.

'Not a good excavation here,' he comments, touching the wall. 'This rock is very loose.'

'It always was weak,' I agree, shivering. I remember Ma's hand holding mine as we trod carefully.

'The stone flakes: it needs lining,' she'd said, 'but I expect that won't happen anytime soon.'

At least it hasn't been blocked or cracked apart by the quake.

'Is this it?' Quaryk asks. A dusty curtain with a bell hanging outside gives an air of normality.

I try to breathe deeply and choke a little.

'Yes.'

This is Aunt Evia's cavern, where Ma and Pa are said to be living now. Breathlessly, as though I have run hard and long, I hesitate, rubbing my neck. My heart pounds, my mouth dust dry. Are they really alive? Are they hurt?

'Take a breath,' Quaryk says, glancing at me. 'No hurry.'

But there is. I ring the bell, its sound magnified by the hollow stone. What will greet us? What happened when Three Gems was ruined, and, most importantly, will they remember who I am? Footsteps approach, and now I wobble, hand on throat, heart bumping, knees weak. It has been so long. This is a huge mistake! Quaryk grabs me by the arm.

'Take courage!' he says. 'Come.'

At this instant, Ma's sister, neat and clean as ever, appears around the curtain. I find I am looking down at the parting in her white hair instead of her face. She peers up at us, eyes dark and huge in a pale, wrinkled face.

'Yes?' she asks, 'what can I do for you, Sir Mage, and, er, Mistress?'

Her eyes widen, her eyebrows rise, and her voice rises a notch as she takes in my folded wings. She looks flabbergasted and wary, ready to turn and vanish inside.

'It's me, Aunt Evia,' I say weakly, 'Me - Jinny.'

She peers at me for a second, then, gathering herself, a smile dawns, and transforms her scared face.

'Jinny? Our Jinny? Oh please, please come in! And you too, Sir.'

Quaryk grins at me as she bustles aside and holds the curtain open for us to enter. We go through a passage redolent of drying fungi into the main cavern. It is not as large as Three Gems but smells clean and dry and is warmed by a good fire which sends shadows quivering and dancing on the walls. There, sitting beside the hearth, are two of the people I've ached to see for so long, looking small and old, but just as dear. They look up in astonishment as we enter. Then Ma rises creakily, and as she steps forward, her eyes widen, and she flings her arms out.

'Jinny? Is that you, my little Jinny-jin? It is! I'd know you anywhere! Oh, my Jinny! It's a miracle!'

'Ma! Pa? Are you alright?' I ask, gulping, and then in a rush, 'I - I know … about the boys. I'm sorry, so sorry!'

We rush together, weeping, and hugging each other. For a while, I am overwhelmed by my emotions: sadness and grief for my brothers that are lost; gladness in finding my foster parents again; and an aching for all our lost years. By the time we separate, all our cheeks are wet, including Quaryk's. Like Da, he manfully ignores them, swiping them away with a sleeve.

Sprout touches me now, extending the comfort only he can give. He savours my emotions and learns from me. *'I wish you were here,'* I say.

<*Me too,*> he says, then he's gone.

Da reaches out, and I go to him. He grips my hand, his face working, but he doesn't rise. His left arm and leg are splinted and bound.

'My poor boys were caught in the mine when the ceiling came down. There's no finding them now, but here *you* are! Great Leaf! You're back!' He looks at my leg doubtfully. 'You're limping! Sit down, girl. And you, if you please, Sir Mage,' he says, gesturing politely. I pull up a bench and we sit. Ma nods in Da's direction.

'Your da got those saving me when the roof of Three Gems began to collapse,' Ma says, following my eyes. 'He's a hero! But he got a broken leg and arm from it.'

Pa gives me a wry look as Quaryk studies him.

'If you will, Sir, I am a healer. I might be able to help you,' Quaryk suggests.

'That would be most kind, Sir,' Ma says. 'Wouldn't it, Da?'

'I'd be very grateful, Sir Mage,' Da says, grimacing as he forgets and tries to rise. He inclines his head to Quaryk.

'Please, there's no need for this formality,' Quaryk says with a smile. 'We are all friends here, so please be comfortable. Call me Quaryk.'

With that, the atmosphere changes. The family have been on best behaviour for an unknown Mage, but we all relax now.

'So ... how is it you've got here?' Ma asks, sniffing joyfully. 'What happened to you, love, and how did you come by this?' She touches my twisted leg gingerly, then strokes it. 'And these?' she turns to stroke my feathers proprietorially. 'Beautiful,' she breathes. 'They're beautiful.'

'They grew late,' I say, but don't say why. I owe her and Da far too much.

'Alright, now tell us the story of what happened to you, everything mind, and don't you leave anything out,' she says and looks at her sister, who is still hovering. 'Come and sit down Evia, all that will wait. Our

Jinny's back!' She turns again to me. 'Your leg then?'

'You remember when they took me?' I say. 'When Da and the boys were working two levels away, and there was just us home?' She nods. 'Well, when that man hit you and knocked you down, another man pulled me from behind that big rock by the hearth where I was hiding, that big one that was too hard to shift - by the cavern's entrance, remember?'

Ma glares, frowning at the memory of the rock.

'Well, he grabbed me and tried to choke me because I was screaming and biting, and I couldn't get a breath ...'

Quaryk watches my hands creeping up to cover my throat. He nods once, finally understanding and says, *'Go on.'*

My family look at me with a mixture of rising anger and regret.

'My foot got caught between that rock and the wall. He pulled hard, and it twisted, breaking my leg. And then, after that, they took me down to the lowest level and just left me, so it wasn't splinted, and it grew twisted. I couldn't walk for a long time. If it wasn't for the girl who looked after me, I suppose I would have died then.'

'Jinny! We couldn't find you, and then we weren't even allowed to try,' she says. 'Every time, the Master blocked us, and in the end, he threatened to turn us out of Three Gems. Who helped you?'

She's twitching where she sits, wanting to act, to do something, anything, to salve her anger and frustration at our treatment. Quaryk looks grim, but then he never asked, did he?

'An older girl, Fan, shared her food and stole a little extra to give to me. She hid me as best she could so that I wouldn't be noticed and be made to work.'

'Is she still there?' Pa asks.

'No, she died ...'

There is a silence as we all think about the selfless girl who fed and cleaned me when, as a child of six or seven, I couldn't do much for myself.

Ma sniffs, her eyes wet.

'We will remember her,' she says, taking Da's hand. 'But ... tell us everything.'

We sit beside the fire as I relate my story. I tell them of the Library; the work; finding Sprout, and meeting Quaryk. I tell them of the Three Mages, but not of my initiation; of Quaryk's farm; and the friends I have now. And then of the Canopy and flying. We talk of the earthquake and how it has decimated dozens of caverns. How the people in them have died instantly as a whole formation, a quarter of the Hotanbore, crashed down, crushing them. All folk I knew, some I'd played with, and my poor brothers.

'It's been a terrible, terrible time,' Ma grieves. 'How has all this come about? It's rumoured that some rogue Mage is at the back of all this, that he triggered the quake and caused all this death and destruction. But for what? I don't know! What are things coming to? And what will happen next? We don't know whether we're up, down or sideways till tomorrow!'

Sitting hugging herself, she rocks back and forth, not knowing whether to laugh or cry. At length, she wipes her face and gets her breath. Aunty Evia quietly pats her hand.

'What's next?' she moans again as Da takes hers with his good hand. 'What does this evil man want? None of us will survive if he does it again. Half of our Holtanbore is gone! It's horrible!'

She sits shaking her head for a moment, and Da takes up her story.

'A great noise came like a million maids tearing cloth, and then the whole cavern began to shake. Me and Ma didn't know what to do at first, but then I pushed her outside into the passage - into that bit where it narrows, remember? As she got out, a lump of rock fell on me. She managed to pull me after her. The quake went on for ages, and I thought we'd be buried alive like …' He stops, his face working. 'I never want to go through that again!'

Ma, having recovered a little, looks around at us all.

'But … what of our Tree? How long can it stand if this happens again? Its roots are broken right through in some places! Surely, if there is too much damage, it will fall!'

'That's right!' Aunty Evia puts in. 'Our Tree can't take any more of this! What will we all do?'

In the ensuing silence, I bow my head. Fire shadows slip and jiggle. Knowing what the Necromancer wants, I am horrified, feeling completely guilty. I had never considered what effect an earthquake would have on the Tree itself. None of us here have: earthquakes were unheard of here. Foolishly, I have always thought of the Great Trees as I think of water and rocks - eternal.

'*Would another shift really damage something so huge and so alive?*' I ask, bespeaking Quaryk.

'*It's true,*' he says, '*if there's too much damage, our Tree may fall. In fact, we now have a report of another Tree reportedly leaning dangerously since the Necromancer caused the earth to move under it a few days ago. If he carries on like this, we could lose most of our Trees. So that's why ...*'

'*...the Kings and the Mages want me to find the other half,*' I finish for him.

This is terrible. The Necromancer can strike again at any time he wants! He can decimate the Holtanbore, even the whole Tree. And with time enough, he could bring the whole of the Trees of Leaf down around our ears!

'Is there nothing that can stop him?' Da asks plaintively. Usually taciturn, our predicament has stirred him to speak. 'Do we know why he does these things?'

Quaryk looks at me, eyebrows raised. Guiltily, I look away. Should I tell them? And then, with a dropping sensation in my stomach, I know I must.

'We know why,' I say. 'I found the dragon's egg, and he found out. Now he wants my Sprout to build an army of dragons, and - I have refused him.'

There's a stunned silence.

'You? Even down here we've heard of all this,' Ma says after some seconds. 'That was you? And you, with wings and all - and - a real dragon?'

To ease the shock, I tell them how big Sprout's grown.

'And he's up there now, waiting for you?' Aunty Evia looks up as though she can see through solid rock. 'Tree and Leaf! How amazing!'

'He is,' I say, as I listen in to Sprout's inner laughter. 'Ma, Da, Aunty, we mustn't stay too long. I need to get back because there is something I have to do.'

They all look at me.

'You're important,' Da says. 'A Mage now?'

'I am,' I say.

Quaryk looks questioningly at me. I nod, a hand to my throat.

'Jinny may be the one person in the world who can save us,' he says. 'She found the half-stone, a half of the Talisman, which was lost for ages. Now, if she can find the other half, there is a chance that she can use it to save all Leaf from the Necromancer.'

Ma, Pa and Evia goggle at me, eyes forming dark questions in white faces.

'You could save Leaf? Save us all? Oh, girl! I'm so glad I found you all those years ago,' Ma says. 'You're special! I always said so.'

She puts out her hand and, taking mine, strokes it. The action is so poignant that my eyes fill again. Ma and Da, despite the earthquake, despite the years, are hardly changed, and now they are proud. Looking back, I think of the years I spent here with them, happy and carefree, and then the darkness of slavery until, sifting through rubbish and finding the half-stone, and then Sprout. It is all meant to be, somehow. And when I think of Milde's words at the First-Comers celebration, 'Some must have perished on their search,' the hair rises on my spine. Will we perish like them?

'Will you go to find the other half?' Da asks. 'Will you do it for our boys? They shouldn't have gone for nothing …'

He turns away with an anxious but eager expression.

'Come on, Jinny-jin!' Ma says, seeing the naked terror on my face. 'You can but try, eh? You can do it! I know you can.'

Their eyes bore into mine, a desperate hope written there. I didn't understand exactly what my actions would mean until now. All hope is lost if I don't even try. I shudder, but then, as if from far off, a voice like the soughing of wind through leaves says in my mind, *'You are strong enough, Jinny Morai. Do not falter. Now is the time to summon your courage and take up your tasks.'*

It is the Woodspirit. Somehow, as its voice fades, my faltering courage rises, and thank all Leaf! My mind is made up now, doubts and fears cast aside.

'I will try,' I say, glancing at Quaryk, whose eyes are wide as he perceives the Woodspirit's presence. He smiles, and his hands slide towards me before he remembers and pulls them back.

'I will try,' I repeat, 'so we must leave soon.'

'Not until you've both had a decent meal,' Evia says stoutly, and she bustles around, fetching plates and cups.

'Your young man seems a very good sort,' Ma whispers in an aside. I blush like a shepherd's sunset.

'He's not really …'

She grins at me. As I turn my head away a little, she whispers again, 'Oh, I think he is, you know,' and then louder, 'Now, you'll come again? When all is done? One day?'

'I will, Ma,' I say. 'Nothing will keep me away. But you take care, will you? Please?'

While Evia and Ma prepare our meal, Quaryk sets to and heals Da's arm and leg as much as he can. The green glow of magic permeates the firelight, making odd shapes and colours appear. When he has done, Da can bend and use his arm and hand, but he is still lame.

'You must be careful with that arm for a week or three,' Quaryk tells him, 'but keep off your leg entirely. You'll have to let it heal on its own now. I can only do so much: the Tree is weakened.'

'Well, this is champion!' Da says. 'The pain in my leg is almost gone, and I can use my arm again! Thank you kindly for your healing, Sir Mage - um – Quaryk.' He invites us to the table with a wave. 'Come and eat.' So, sitting companionably, we talk of small happenings.

I am determined to stop anything as horrible as the earthquake from happening again. So, if I must go to find the other half of the Talisman, I will. For our lost boys - and all of Leaf.

Chapter Twenty-Four

We walk through a maze of passages and sunlit rooms, senses full of the rustling of wings and gorgeously dressed waiting courtiers. The floor is smooth and polished, and on the walls, carvings depict scenes from the life of the Great Trees and the Glebes. At one, I stop to look. Here the Woodsman splits the Talisman in two with his great axe, and I wonder why. Lind prods me, nodding at the eyes riveted on us, and we hurry on. And we begin to sneeze. From each and every person, a different scent arises.

Galden, wrinkling his nose, breaks out into a bout of coughing. Lind looks almost as pained, pinching the bridge of her nose. Alban and Perinal glance at each other, trying not to breathe too deeply, and I can't blame them, for my own nose is prickling, and my eyes are itchy. Quaryk, and my friend Drell, who I invited to come with us, show no signs that they've noticed the unpleasant mingling of robust odours.

We walk on, guided by a winged Herald, a young man in livery. Two guards, hands on hilts, eye us as we approach imposing twin doors. The Herald nods, and they throw the doors wide open for us to enter. On the threshold, as one, we stop dead, gasping in silence.

This is the most imposing space I have ever seen: a vast, airy globe woven from living branches, each bursting with leaves and flowers. The scented air is warmed by shafts of sunlight which stream through high, narrow windows. One sunbeam spears the Twin Throne on a high dais in the exact centre. There, two ancients, splendidly illuminated sacks sprouting grey threadbare wings, look up slowly.

At the Herald's prompting, we begin the long walk towards them.

Under their scrutiny, I am afraid I might trip or sneeze loudly, feeling overwhelmed and dizzy for an instant. Automatically I feel for the comfort of the half-stone.

<*What's it like, Jinny?* > Sprout asks, watching all this with excitement and curiosity.

'It's huge,' I say, awed, '*and very quiet, although it's crowded. I daren't make a noise as everyone is watching. The Kings are very old and scary.*'

<*I want to come too,*> he says, and I have a sudden vision of him battering his way through the walls! No doubt he could easily if he wanted to.

'*Please wait, Sprout,*' I say. '*You're here with me anyway. You can see what I can, can't you?*'

Sprout mutters to himself, inadvertently allowing me to see through his eyes. Two guards are stationed outside. They look terrified as he is stomping around a balcony. It's high, with a wide view of the Canopy.

<*I'm always left out,*> he mutters. <*Not fair!*>

'*Stoppit! Calm down and stop banging around! You're frightening those two men!*'

<*Me? Frightening them? Really? I didn't think...*> Feeling sheepish, he stops stamping about.

'*Shush now, this is important,*' I say. '*Watch ...*'

'*Jinny!*' Quaryk interrupts urgently, bespeaking me. '*They've asked you to step forward.*'

Flustered, I look up. The Herald is trying to catch my eye. In the ensuing hush, I fancy the Kings are glaring. I swallow, walking forward to the spot he is pointing out, and look up.

Two sunlit, ancient faces like wrinkled halnuts peer down at me myopically. Their pale eyes, long noses and wide mouths are identical. Their only difference is in the colour of their robes, one a vivid emerald and the other a lovely sky-blue. These robes, vast as sails, contrast starkly with their hunched and shrivelled owners. The King in blue to my left scrabbles down his side of the Throne to find and raise an odd thing, a piece of glass in a wooden mount. As he looks through it at me, I step back in alarm. Quark bespeaks me hastily.

'*It's alright, Jinny, it just helps him to see you!*'

A shocked murmur arises at my poor manners from the watching courtiers, so, unclenching my fists, I step forward again, heat rising in my face. An age later, the blue King raises himself slightly to speak in a querulous whisper to the Usher, who waves a hand, trying to placate him. The Green King seems unaware of the argument as they come to some sort of agreement, and the Blue King creaks around to look at me.

'She is very young,' he says loudly to the Herald. Then, addressing me, says, 'You are the Lady Morai?'

I find my voice. 'I am, Your Majesty,' I quaver.

'Come up here, girl, and let me look at you properly!' he says huskily.

I climb the seven steps until we are almost eye to beady eye. His twin is sleeping, soft snores erupting regularly from his gorgeous green pile. I daren't look behind, although I can feel eyes on the back of my neck.

'You bear the half-stone?' he asks.

'I do,' I say. 'Would you like to see it, Your Majesty?'

He doesn't answer. Instead, he is ferreting through his robes, apparently looking for something. I wait and watch until the Herald comes closer to whisper in my ear.

'His Majesty is looking for something he lost many years ago now. He will never find it, but his looking has become a sort of - well - a tic that happens now and again. You must forgive him.'

I must forgive a Sky-King? This idea is so novel it takes my breath away for a second.

'He will remember you are here soon,' the Herald breathes, then bows, addressing the Blue King.

'This is the Lady Morai, Sir. You wished to ask her a question?'

The Blue King looks round at me, and I watch his face change as he suddenly comes back to himself.

'Lady Morai,' he asks in a creaking mumble, 'you are the bearer of the half-stone? A half of the ancient Talisman?'

'I am, Your Majesty.'

Fully awake now, he stares into my eyes, and I see his hawkish intelligence.

'Then are you willing to use the stone to look for its other half? You know this may be the only way we can save the Trees and our world. Our Leaf, as we know it now.'

He glares regally, lifting himself up a tad, awaiting an answer. He gestures with a claw for me to speak. The other King is snoring as I clear my throat.

'I am willing, Your Majesty,' I say, my heart dropping into my boots. Sap and sucker! No going back now. A vision of Ma's face flutters through my head. 'I will try to find the missing half-stone.'

'Then Leaf and our Great Trees may continue to flourish with your help,' he says, 'and even if this hope fails, we will all be in your debt forever. Thank you, Lady Morai.'

Now I am astounded: a Sky-King has thanked me and is in my debt! Me, Jinny Morai, the weird foundling!

A wave of emotion chokes me, and I try not to weep, masking it ineffectually with a cough. But thankfully, no one is looking at me.

Now that he has completed his task, the King crumples, retreating into his robe. A sudden universal sigh of approbation echoes around the vast space, and a soft patter of loyal clapping rises like summer rain. It seems that no one wants to disturb these ancient Kings. The kind young Herald smiles as he hands me down the steps to my waiting companions, then draws himself up and announces to the waiting courtiers,

'The Kings are weary now and will not give any more audiences today.'

As one, the scented courtiers shuffle softly towards the doors, dispersing into the reception rooms to wait again in a heady odiferous cloud for Their Majesties to wake.

~*~

Odd emotions are running through me - surprise, pride, but eclipsing all others, a growing fearful chill.

<*You've done it!*> Sprout bespeaks me joyously. <*You talked to a King!*>

'Yes,' I say. '*Wait - we're nearly there.*'

He stretches his neck to watch over the woven wall as we head into the stable yard. Once inside, he comes to greet me, nuzzling under my arm for a hug. I oblige, thinking how marvellous he is, but a second later, we race for the shelter of the stables in a sudden heavy downpour. My wings are soon sopping. I shake them, spraying drops like a dog shaking itself, thinking *good job I don't need them*. Inside it is warm and dry.

'Hey, cut that out!' Drell complains. Lind and I snigger as he wipes his face and gives me a dirty look. He loves to play silly jokes on others, and it's not often I get to return a favour.

Sitting on Sprout's bed of dried leaves, I am turning today's events over. Everyone else is doing the same.

This fragile peace is broken by Galden, who, as usual, speaks bluntly, 'Well, we're in for it now. We're going to have to go and get this other half-stone. And where that will take us, I wonder?'

Quaryk gives him a wry smile, but Perinal, the burly weapons master who taught me to fight, seems eager.

'This will be a glorious adventure,' he says, beaming, his vast beard bouncing, 'and who knows? We may even find it?'

I frown at him, but enthralled at the prospect, he ignores me. Not much of a vote of confidence! Alban, the flying master, settles his white wings more comfortably, with a sound like damp parchment.

I asked both men if they would accompany us when we begin our quest, Perinal for his knowledge of arms, Alban because he is by far the best flyer I know and because both have become good friends. This last may be the worst reason, but I am comfortable with them. Drell also wants to tag along to return to his home but knows he may have to continue alone once we are out of the Glebe. We shall see, for who knows where that dratted lost half is? Certainly not me.

'How do you want to travel?' he asks, glancing from Quaryk to me. 'And how much baggage can we afford to carry?'

<*I can carry stuff,*> Sprout offers.

'That's good,' I say, '*but, hey, let's wait to see what we decide.*'

I look around. My companions who, against all common sense, said "yes" when I asked them to come with me. Mad fools!

'I think we should, um, choose a leader,' I say. 'We can't decide everything together all the time, or we'll do nothing but argue. One of us has to come forward - and it won't be me!'

Quaryk looks serious. 'That's actually a good idea,' he says. 'Do you want us to vote or decide yourself, Jin?'

'Well,' I answer. 'Who is most experienced in travelling outside the Glebe?'

Quaryk says, 'I've travelled Outside. I've done quite a bit for the Order, visiting other Trees as part of my training.'

Drell says, 'Me, but only from the White Wood.'

Perinal and Alban say nothing, shaking their heads slightly. They have mostly kept within the bounds of the Glebe so far. Lind, who has kept silent, looks at Quaryk, shrugging.

'Then it's settled,' I say. 'As we need someone with experience who's actually been Outside, you're it, Quaryk. I think Perinal should be our weapons master, and Alban – perhaps you would act as our scout?'

Big, blustering Perinal is visibly delighted to be put in charge of our weaponry, but Alban merely nods soberly. I turn to Drell.

'Hey, you know a lot about woodlands, don't you? Will you help with finding paths, that sort of thing, if we need it?'

Drell mutters something at his feet: he's a little shy in the company of the older men.

'What about me?' Lind asks.

'I think you and me should organise our supplies. Anything we'll need.'

For a moment, she looks rebellious, then nods. 'Alright.'

'So - how do we travel?' I ask.

The others look at each other until Galden says, 'I've made arrangements to have a number of horses brought here from our farm stables if that suits? They should be arriving down at the Bole by tomorrow or the day after. I suggest we all ride, taking packhorses. Three of us are not winged, and we'd only slow you all up if you were to fly …'

'That's marvellous! Thank you, Galden,' I say, noting his smug glance at Quaryk. They've had this planned.

Alban glances at me and Drell. 'Flying is not ideal as we would tire all too easily on a long journey anyway. Horses will be much better,' he agrees, rustling his feathers to dry them.

'I'll sort us some weapons,' Perinal says. 'We'll need a good variety outside.'

'Nothing too heavy?' Galden insists, and the two begin a spirited exchange about what is sensible to carry and what is most useful. In the end, it is decided that we will each carry a sword but will pack bows and staves.

'I'll organise enough supplies for a month or so with you and Lind,' Quaryk says now, 'but there's one other thing. You've all agreed to come with Jinny and I, although it will be dangerous. But I want to tell you all, and you too, Jinny, that the Order has decreed an extra member should join us. This is a Mage of a much higher degree than either of us to make up a Triad which, as you may know, is optimum for working with Tree magic.'

Drell looks puzzled.

'But what if there are no Trees where we are? What if we are in open grasslands or earth forest,' and he shudders, 'or desert?'

'It is known that the roots of the Great Trees stretch far under all the lands,' Quaryk says, 'and in some places even grow new shoots. You've seen how they can drop aerial roots from the great buttress roots or branches into likely ground to grow into new Trees. Possibly we will be able to find one of these or an emerging root. Then we can tap the Tree magic for whatever purpose we need. Having three Mages will magnify the intensity of our magic. The new Mage is said to be an expert in a number of things, so it should be much safer.'

'So, who is it?' Perinal asks.

'I will introduce our new companion tomorrow,' Quaryk says, with a 'that's that' air. I'm almost certain he's hiding something, but let it slide. At least we are not going to be burdened with soldiers, and there's enough to think about anyway. We'll discuss what to take and what we need to pack.

Eventually, after a break for lunch, we begin to narrow it down to the least baggage we can get away with. I am sitting with my back against Sprout's warm flank.

'Well,' Quaryk says. 'Now, all we have to decide is *where* we are going.'

I am silent. The enormity of the task I have taken on is almost paralysing.

'There are the five of us,' Lind begins, 'and then Alban and Perinal. That's seven. Drell makes eight.'

<*What about me?*> Sprout says sleepily.

'You are nine,' I say, and he subsides.

Quaryk glares at his sister now.

'Are you sure you should come?' he asks. 'You'll be head of our family one day. You shouldn't put yourself in danger, do you think?'

Lind looks daggers back at her brother.

'Why not?' she asks. 'The family will survive. Why not me? Jinny is coming.'

'She has to,' Quaryk says bluntly, 'but you don't. Perhaps it would be better to take someone stronger …' He doesn't finish.

'You think I can't defend myself, brother?' Lind hisses through clenched teeth. Her eyes are wild as she draws the short sword she carries. 'Come on then, a test of arms! *Make* me stay! And no magic!'

Quaryk looks astounded then angry but rises and grips the hilt of his own sword. I jump up as he draws his weapon, and Perinal moves closer to Lind. If I don't do something, the Leaf-rotted lot will be at each other's throats!

'Please, don't!' I cry. 'This is stupid! And it's definitely not the right time for a quarrel!'

'Lind can hold her own with almost anyone in a fight,' Galden says, pushing between the siblings. 'You should know that, young Quaryk. If she says she's coming, she's coming.'

Quaryk slams his sword back into its sheath.

It seems that Galden has had the last word. Both siblings relax, but his own hand stays on his hilt. *But why is everyone armed?* I wonder. Then the answer is obvious. They are all guarding me, us! I've been too wrapped up in my own inner troubles to notice.

<*Of course they are,*> Sprout says. <*You are the most important person in the world now, bar me, of course!*>

There's a smugness in his words, but he's right. I am taken aback for a second or two and then grudgingly have to accept this fact as I have had to accept everything else that fate has thrown at me. So, if this is true, it is time I took charge.

I glare from Quaryk to Lind, 'You two, stop this now! Lind is coming, right?' I glare at everyone. 'We don't have time for this. Now, we must decide how to find this second half. Any ideas?'

They stop bristling at each other. Quaryk's eyebrows knit together.

'We might find something in the old records of the Order in the library here,' he says, and it's all I can do not to roll my eyes. They can ferret through anything as long as no one expects me to do it! Sprout sniggers. I give him a hard look.

'I'll go and search later,' Quaryk says.

I nod. 'Anyone else?'

The stone seems to quiver as it sits on its chain on my breast as though in anticipation. As though it wants to talk …

'There's an old story which says the halves of the stone were taken east and west after it was split,' Lind says. 'We could try going in both directions?'

'That would mean splitting up, and it would take far too long,' Galden says, scratching his leg, 'and anyway, Jinny's half was found here in our Tree, so where the other half has gone is anyone's guess.'

'I think you're right,' I say. 'Would it be best to seek advice from the three Mages first?'

'That would simply mean more delay, wouldn't it?' Galden says. 'I thought the main idea was to get off as quickly as we can?'

The argument continues as various ideas are put forward only to have them shot down. Then a quiet voice intrudes on my thoughts.

<Why not ask the half we have got?>

I look at Sprout. Of course! He's right! Why didn't I think of that?

'Hang on!' I say sharply to get their attention. 'Listen! Sprout says we should ask the half-stone as it may know where its other half is. But to do that, I need to concentrate.' Surprisingly, they all shut up.

I've never asked anything of the half-stone apart from asking for the life of the salamander's child. I don't know whether it will respond or not, yet something in the way it feels gives me hope. Taking the stone in my hand, I close my eyes.

Immediately its presence flashes into my mind like a burning sun, a small point of light exuding power: yet it is a fractured power. Incomplete, it is yearning to be whole: why haven't I seen this before?

'*Stone,*' I bespeak it, '*please tell me where your other half is?*'

The stone vibrates as I finish but remains silent. It has not spoken yet, so how can I expect …? And then I gasp as it suddenly moves on my palm. It rotates, then I know it is pointing, moving towards the east, towards … Yes! A vast beach, windswept and barren. There, between the sea and the land, a great hillside or circular wall rears up, stretching far out into the waves like a breakwater. The landward side of this great construction soars upwards, but the seaward side is eroded almost to nothing. As the scene draws closer, I can make out the remains of vast buttresses that once shored up a huge living being. This is the last remains of an ancient Great Tree.

Gasping, I soar over the wooden wall and down into a cavernous hole in a morass of mud and splintered rotten wood. Within, deep down, a minuscule beacon flashes once, and the half-stone in my hand shivers, yearning towards it. Now I understand! That flash denoted its other half.

The half-stone pulls so hard I close my hand to stop it slipping from my grasp. I try to remember every detail as the stone ceases to vibrate and the vision fades. Can I remember enough? At least I have an inkling where the stone lies now.

'We need a map,' I say, opening my eyes. The others stare as though the Necromancer is behind me.

<*You're back!*> Sprout says, emoting relief.

'You faded!' Lind gasps. 'You were here, and then … you vanished!'

'I faded? How could I fade?' I say. 'That's daft! We need to find a map and know where north is. Then I can see where to go …'

<*Where* we *have to go,*> Sprout puts in pointedly.

'Alright - we!'

'You want a map?' Lind asks. 'Do you know where the other half is then?'

'I do, and then again, I don't,' I say, trying to explain my vision, pointing. 'I sort of know where it is, but I've no idea how to get there! It's over there, on a beach somewhere.'

Quaryk shuts his eyes for a moment, then grunts, pointing. 'North is this way, so the stone must be saying east.'

'How about the Library?' Drell offers, looking slightly dazed. 'For a map?'

Quaryk is silent, watching me.

'*Are there any maps there?*' I ask him. He will help, won't he? I have to count on his support and advice now.

'*There should be,*' he says, apparently giving nothing away.

He is unusually reticent, even for him.

'*What's wrong?*' I ask, anxiety building.

He turns away for a second, then looks askance as though ashamed.

'*I have no knowledge of any of this,*' he says, grimacing and looking utterly taken aback. '*It is not known in any of the annals of the Order.*' But aloud, he continues for the others, 'We must visit the Library and see what maps there are, if any.'

I wish I could dissemble like him. What I'm thinking is always plain on my face, but we are both blind in this. However surprised I am at his pretence, I have to agree. All those old records in the Holtanbore, all those decaying scrolls and leaves! I didn't understand what I was throwing away then. How many old maps were there, and how much vital knowledge did we lose?

We leave Sprout to do as he will and make our way to the Library. The Librarian seems particularly cagey about showing us anything until Quaryk pushes him.

There are maps, at least half a dozen, but most are disappointingly blank where the east should be. There is only one showing a tentatively drawn coastline where the northern sea dips down to form a great bite or bay at the edge of the landmass east of a big river. There is hardly anything else denoted apart from an area forming a wide barrier named 'Forrest' and another snaky line that must be another river.

'This seems to be the only map that shows anything useful at all,' Galden says.

'But there's nothing there!' I say. 'How much of the leaf-rotted coast will we have to travel before we find this stump? We could be looking for it forever, and we'll have to find the coast first!'

Will we ever see this place again, I wonder, as I look around at my companions. All of us are daunted by the scale of this undertaking.

Quaryk looks pensive, then says, 'If anyone doesn't want to do this, now is the time to speak up.' He looks pointedly at Lind. She glares stubbornly at her brother.

'I'm coming,' she says. 'I'm coming to look for the stone whether you like it or not.'

'Well, in that case,' Galden remarks calmly, 'I'm coming. Someone has to look after you two and stop you from brawling.'

'Thank you, Uncle,' Lind replies demurely. My eyebrows shoot up. Uncle? I didn't know that.

'You all know the odds are against us?' Drell mutters. It looks as though he is panicking beneath his brave facade. I wonder how long he will stay with us.

He subsides as he looks around us all, and now Quaryk turns to Alban, who merely nods acceptance.

With a sinking feeling in the pit of my stomach, I bespeak the Mage, *'That's it then. We start tomorrow.'*

There is no other choice now, no time for anything. I am a leaf in a whirlwind.

He sends me a green flash of approval, but Sprout, as usual, has the last word, and as usual, he's thinking of his stomach.

<*Better get a good feed then, eh Jin?*> he says, seriously.

I hope you enjoyed *The Dragon's Egg*.

Now that you have finished reading the book, it would be a big favour to me and future readers if you left your review on Amazon. Whatever kind of review you leave would make my day knowing you have read the book and shared your experience.

Please go to https://amzn.to/3FWm0WB

If you enjoyed this first book of 'The Chronicles of Leaf', look out for the second part of the story, *The Quest for the Half-Stone*, out soon.

www.facebook.com/hamayauthor
www.instagram.com/leafworlder

Thank you,

H A May

About the Author

H A May is the author of *The Dragon's Egg*, the first book in the epic fantasy series, 'The Chronicles of Leaf'. This is a feel-good, coming-of-age story for young adults and upwards set in a magical, arboreal world where some trees grow huge.

H A May was born in Staffordshire and grew up there. After school, she was an art student and then became a teacher through Keele University.

She taught fine art and English for some years and sold portraits of people and animals, winning a category in the BBC Wildlife art competition and having artwork hung in the Mall Galleries.

Now she works full time as an author, making up worlds and writing about them, and if she ever gets more time, imagining the characters in different media. She lives with her human and canine family in a quiet corner of rural England.

Follow H A May on Instagram @leafworlder
and Facebook as H A May.

Printed in Great Britain
by Amazon